$130 BILLION! WHERE IS THE CITY GOING TO GET THAT KIND OF MONEY?

The deadline is slashed to six hours and Mayor Ben Boyle must, in a race against oblivion, unravel the maze of technology and mystery surrounding the Cherokee Indian, George Mahle. Idealistic genius, or terrorist madman? Whichever, it is *his* finger poised on the doomsday button.

"A MAJOR WORK
that every city and inhabitant of the city can take a lesson from . . . a well-written, well-developed novel."
South Bend Tribune

"A FAST-PACED THRILLER,
as timely as the headlines."
John Barkham Reviews

THIS CITY IS OURS

A NOVEL BY

DENIS PITTS

AVON
PUBLISHERS OF BARD, CAMELOT AND DISCUS BOOKS

AVON BOOKS
A division of
The Hearst Corporation
959 Eighth Avenue
New York, New York 10019

Published by arrangement with
Mason/Charter Publishers, Inc.
Library of Congress Catalog Card Number: 75-5881
ISBN: 0-380-01851-9

First Avon Printing, February, 1978

To the much mugged, frequently burgled, heavily taxed, noise-ridden, sense-assaulted, much maligned, and very special people of New York whom I have come to love.

ACKNOWLEDGMENTS

There were many people in on the making of this book. (*Too* many, I'm afraid, smiled in a kindly way and said that it was impossible to bring a 500,000-ton supertanker up the Hudson. Then, after a look at the charts, they agreed that it was indeed practical. My worry is not that it could happen—but that it *will* happen, sooner or later, somewhere in this world.)

I am especially grateful to James A. Cavanagh, First Deputy Mayor of New York City (who is splendidly unlike the deputy mayor portrayed in this book); to numerous members of the City Hall staff; to Fred Schmid of the Hanover Group Inc., and Ray Foster of IBM, both of whom helped immensely with the computer aspects; John Button of the London Stock Exchange, who unraveled the mysteries of international high finance; Keith Morfett, who was especially helpful on Indian affairs; and Captain John Pitsios of the Niarchos Line who, with the Burmah Tanker Group, guided me through the world of supertankers. I am grateful also to the U.S. Coast Guard Service on Governors Island and to the New York Port Authority; to Mason/Charter Publishers, who told me a lot more about computers than I ever dreamed I could learn; and to Adrienne, who showed much forebearance.

How canst thou walk these streets, who hast trod
the green turf of the prairies?
How canst thou breathe this air, who has breathed
the sweet air of the mountains?
Ah! 'tis in vain that with lordly looks of disdain
thou dost challenge
Looks of disdain in return, and question these
walls and these pavements,
Claiming the soil for thy hunting-grounds, while
down-trodden millions
Starve in the garrets of Europe, and cry from
its caverns that they, too
Have been created heirs of the earth, and claim
its division!

Henry Wadsworth Longfellow
"To the Driving Cloud"

The weather satellite Zeus watched it happen from one hundred fifty miles in the atmosphere.

It started as a smudge of rain over Atlanta that grew larger as it moved, first at a leisurely pace over Maryland, then, with increasing speed, over New Jersey as the jet stream hurled it toward the Atlantic.

The smudge had become a large, black, rain mass by the time it crossed from land to sea. Two hundred miles off Long Island it stopped moving. Twin Atlantic gales joined and began to toy with the huge, low-pressure area; it was absorbing more and more moisture from the warm Gulf Stream below.

The satellite's camera watched the rain mass begin to turn white, then plotted with impartial dispassion the sudden and ominous move it made back toward the landmass.

The Atlantic gales had become a powerful cyclone. The rain had turned to snow; Zeus watched as the storm started to swirl around a clearly identified vortex.

The vortex was the island of Manhattan.

THIS CITY IS OURS

1

Gaunt and high above the furious seas, the biggest ship in the world hardly rolled or heaved or pitched in that gale. Her size seemed to dismiss, if not tame, it with awesome ease.

Smaller craft had long since scuttled fearfully for shelter, but this ship could ride out any weather with an easy, majestic contempt.

She was the *Jersey Lily,* all 507,000 tons of her, all 1,650 feet of her—the pride of the Kure shipyard, the flagship of the Eftyvoulos Line, a dream ship for her owners and the compilers of record books. A nightmare for conservationists, harbor masters, and the owners of holiday resorts.

An hour earlier she had been plowing her way over the crests and troughs of that wild ocean with consummate and imperious arrogance. Now, as she neared the 30th latitude 400 miles from the American coastline, she made a long sweeping turn and heaved her bulk directly into the storm.

The *Jersey Lily* slowed to a stop. She was well away from the main shipping lanes and air routes. No prying Coast Guard aircraft would witness the strange events on the red-leaded, treeless boulevard called her deck.

Leaving Houston four days earlier, the tanker had been fully laden down to her 90-foot waterline, with gasoline, crude oil, natural gas, and chemicals. For the last three days, a bank of auxiliary pumps had been slowly lowering the level of gasoline in her forward tanks; and now, as the great ship lay worrying at each of her welds and rivets, her crew, braced hard against the wind, was disconnecting the pumps.

Heavy, steel-lined hoses were being lashed back against bulkheads. The pumps were covered with bright orange tarpaulin. Even in that wind there was a foul, acrid stench of gasoline everywhere, and the crewmen wept, red-eyed, as they struggled out there on the fully exposed forecasing.

One of them, dressed like the other crew members in a white boiler suit with the blue company logo emblazoned on his back, took a small two-way radio from his hip pocket and slid the aerial from its socket. He had to shout against the anger of the wind.

"Bridge?"

A voice crackled. "Bridge here."

"All pumps secured. Ready when you are."

The voice at the other end was sharp and cold. "Get the men below. Stand by for detonators."

The men on deck unlashed a number of miniature cycles and began to ride—full pelt with the wind behind them, struggling like circus artists to keep their balance against the roll of the ship—to the shelter of the bridge. As they neared the stern they saw a large hatchway open at the foot of the towering bridge. A man in a black rubber wetsuit, goggled and wearing full breathing equipment, began driving a small electric golf buggy along the deck toward them.

He stopped at the forward hold and climbed out. The leading crew member helped the diver along the deck to where a gaping oil exit port lay open. Then, secured by a rope the crewman held, the diver climbed into the port and was lowered toward the reeking high-octane fuel. The crewman on deck felt the strain ease and stop. His next job was to lower six heavy cylindrical packages.

Below in the blackness of the cathedral-like tank, the frogman received the packs one by one. Swimming through the gasoline, he attached each of them, using the cleaning ladders at either side of the hold, to the metal sides of the ship.

When he had completed this task he swam to the dangling rope which had let him down and secured himself carefully. He gave three jerks, and the crew member above hauled him out.

The diver spoke to the bridge.

"Detonators in place."

"Bridge. Closing main exit port."

Automatically the heavy metal cover slowly lowered itself into position. The two men on the deck-casing secured the eight hand bolts that held the cover in place and climbed into the golf buggy. They drove slowly down the length of the tanker and into the hatchway.

The entire operation had been watched from the bridge of the *Jersey Lily* by a thin man with a striking face, a handsome face, but a face devoid of expression. Only an occasional glint in his otherwise empty gray eyes revealed anything of the satisfaction he felt at the way the operation had gone. He was dressed in the uniform of a first officer, and he fitted well on the bridge: binoculars slung from his neck, collar gleaming white, the peak of his officer's cap emphasizing the long face and strong, prominent nose.

"Half ahead," he ordered.

A voice from the engine room came through the desk speaker in front of him.

"Half ahead, sir."

The first officer turned to a man sitting at a console which was arrayed with navigational instruments.

"Bring her around in a slow circle to the left and steer three-zero-zero. The smoking light can go out."

The first officer opened a drawer in front of him and pulled off the red seal from a box of long, handmade Sobranie cigarettes. He unlocked another drawer and took out a gold cigarette lighter. He lit the cigarette and enjoyed his first taste of tobacco since they had begun to spill the gasoline.

"Bring in Willy Joe," he said.

A few moments later, two members of the crew came through the bridge companionway, clutching between them a third—a fattish man whose dark-skinned face had turned gray from fear.

The first officer looked at him dispassionately.

"Willy, I don't want to give you a long lecture. You know what you are guilty of?"

He held up a book of matches, opening the cover and separating the three unused matches inside.

"The worst crime you could commit on this ship," he said. "The rules were very carefully laid down before we started. No matches. No cigarettes. Every pocket empty. And you were carrying this."

He motioned contemptuously to the other two men, who began pulling Willy Joe away from the bridge. Then, from the height of the bridge, he watched as they and two others half-dragged, half-carried the fat man along the deck.

The four men dumped Willy on the deck and moved back, forming a half-circle around him. The fat man climbed to his feet with difficulty and stood facing them. He was shivering now with terror. He glanced around and saw immediately behind him a strip of copper mesh lying on a thin carpet of vinyl. He looked back and saw that the others had knives in their hands.

They toyed with him for a bit, thrusting the knives close to his face and his chest and his belly. Then one of the knives flashed close enough to make a neat score along the fat man's chin.

He jerked back almost involuntarily.

The man watching on the bridge pulled a small lever switch on the console. An auxiliary motor started to whine.

The fat man looked behind him again. Then he moved forward, this time directly onto the tip of a knife against his chest. He turned and, screaming, tried to run.

As his feet touched the copper sheeting, a thin, crackling blue spark engulfed his body. Stumbling, his whole shape outlined in the vividness of the blue, he fell forward on his hands. He had stopped screaming before they touched the copper and began to melt.

The first officer slid the lever switch back to its original position.

He wrote briefly in a logbook: "Electromatting test. Satisfactory."

He spoke into a microphone. "The matting is deactivated. Will you dispose of the body?" Then he walked across the bridge to a door which led astern. He unlocked it and went in.

A grayhaired man in the uniform of a merchant captain lay on a bunk in this cabin. He was a man of perhaps 60. His face was drawn and taut. He did not look up as the first officer entered.

"I hope you are comfortable, Captain," the first officer said. "Our organization is dedicated to the success of our cause; however, that need not make us inhumane if it can be avoided."

The captain said: "Call yourselves what you will; you are a bunch of bastards in any language."

"I'm sorry you feel that way. I have assured you of your safety. You will be put ashore when we dock and held in our custody for the duration of this exercise."

The first officer picked up a photograph of the captain's family.

"Put that down, Mahle," the captain said. "What the hell are your men doing? Christ, I told the company a hundred times what could happen when they started manning these tankers with eight-man crews. Now a bunch of crazy red Indians have hijacked my ship."

"It's been a while since I was called a red Indian. Liberals and college professors call us 'native Americans.' We prefer to be known just as Indians. This is what my people call themselves and it is in their name that this operation is being conducted."

"What is this operation?"

"The less you know of it, the better, Captain," said the first officer. "I will report, however, that we have successfully emptied 70,000 tons of the high-octane fuel from number one and number two center and wing tanks. In a few minutes we will begin blowing 59,000 tons of methane from number four tank."

The captain turned in his bunk to look at him.

"I don't know what you are doing, Mr. Mahle, but I hope *you* do. You realize that you have put this ship into a highly dangerous condition?"

"I do, indeed, Captain," Mahle said. "A bunch of crazy red Indians have taken control of what will be very shortly the equivalent of a fair-sized atom bomb."

2

It was late afternoon when he waked from his nap. He lay quietly and gazed up at the ugly hotel chandelier for a long time. Then he roused himself sufficiently to look at his watch lying on the bedside table. It was 4:30.

In seven-and-a-half hours he would be mayor of New York. The thought brought a smile of pleasure to his face.

He, Ben Boyle.

He, Ben Boyle, a master plumber operating out of Queens, would soon have charge of that great, sprawling, vibrant, siren-screaming city which pulsated in the darkening gloom outside. He, Ben Boyle, who could not even cope with his own business taxes, would be controlling a budget of $11 billion a year. He, a plumber with four employees, would be coping with 220,000 civil servants.

It was a rare thought and he savored it. He liked the idea of control and responsibility. He could make things happen. As they had not been happening in the city.

He did not completely like the idea of occupying the mayor's official residence, Gracie Mansion, with its ever-attendant flunkies, bodyguards, and deferential counselors and commissioners at his beck and call. There would even be two chauffeurs.

Two chauffeurs. That he liked. One for day and one for night. No need to worry about getting a goddamn parking ticket for four whole years.

He smiled.

No parking tickets—and seventy thousand bucks a year.

He climbed out of bed and walked across the dark

room and stood naked at the window. The whole city was alight now, and he breathed in the wonder of it.

He was a tall man with a strong, powerful frame but with gentle, easy movements. His face was strong, too. It was a handsome face, although craggy, with a nose knocked out of shape in boyhood boxing, and a jutting, aggressively Irish chin. Big green eyes were the dominant attraction of his face. They were eyes of both strength and compassion.

He looked out over the panorama of this great city and felt very frail.

There were people out there, eight million of them. Citizens of the greatest, dirtiest, most expensive piece of real estate in the world. Now that he was mayor, those citizens were going to give him living hell until the city started working again.

"Ben."

She was talking from the bed.

"Ben Boyle, if you are not careful, the mayor-elect of New York City is going to be arrested for indecent exposure."

He turned from the window and looked at her. She was lying in bed with a sheet pulled up to her shoulders.

"The Mayor-elect of New York City has never felt quite so naked," he said.

She looked at him directly and innocently. "I'd like the mayor-elect to come back to bed."

He sat beside her on the bed and held her head in his big hands, then leaned forward and kissed the tip of her nose.

"Lady Mary," he said.

"I'm no lady, as you may have gathered in bed today," she said.

He pulled the sheet from her shoulders and looked at her breasts, which were small, firm, and white; then he leaned over and gently kissed the nipples.

"Do you like big breasts? I wish mine were bigger."

"I don't," he said. He kissed them again.

"I like the way you kiss them," she said. "It means you do like them."

He pulled the sheet down and let his fingers make long lazy circles around her navel.

"I love your body, all of it," he said and lay down beside her. He held her very close.

"The Mayor-elect is a very gentle lover," she said. Her fingers played down the length of his spine and then traced his ribs, while he kissed her lightly.

She held tightly to him now, kneading the muscles on his lower back. She was breathing deeply, and he was holding her close to him, desperately aware of the slender, fragile body he was holding, afraid that he would break it with the violent passion he felt.

"The Mayor-elect is a mayor-erect," she said. "Kiss me, Ben. Kiss me very hard."

She pulled him to her, opening her thighs to him, pushing herself out to meet him, her hands grasping for him, her eyes closed, her mouth reaching for his.

Later they lay on the bed and talked.

"There's no real reason why you shouldn't live at Gracie Mansion," he said. "Hell, it's going to be *my* house."

"No, Ben," she said. "No way. It belongs to the city, and you are the mayor."

"So?"

"So, you were elected by the people to run the city properly. You are Mr. Clean to them. You've got a lot of work to do. You've got to put all those pledges into action, all those promises. You are not going to do that with me as a distraction."

"We could get married."

"No, Ben, it wouldn't work. I was never cut out—me, an earl's daughter—to be the First Lady of New York. Hell, Ben, launching freighters, opening flea markets, cutting tapes—that's not me. I've lived here a long long time, and I love the city as much as you do. I just want to be me."

"Mary, I love you."

"The other fact—and it won't help you—is that I *am* a bloody lady. I'm English aristocracy, and you know what the knockers will make of that. No, Ben, you great lovable chump. You've got a lot of work to do; you don't need me about."

"Mary, I *do* love you."

She kissed him gently on the forehead.

"Ben, I'm going to hide my eyes while you dress and go

away and get yourself sworn in. At midnight you will be Mayor Boyle. I shall be bloody Cinderella, all rags and tears on Fifth Avenue. No fuss, no nonsense, no great good-bye scenes. Good-bye, my darling."

"I won't let go," he said.

"Put on your Sunday suit and go and make the subway work," she said. "Come on, Destiny calls."

"I love you."

"Please go, Ben."

He climbed off the bed and walked across the room, then looked back. She had covered herself with the sheet and was lying very still.

He turned to the window and saw that half the pane was now opaque with snow.

"Jesus, a blizzard," he said. "And the whole damned Sanitation Department's on strike."

There was a noise from the bed. He wasn't sure whether Mary was chuckling or sobbing.

3

The blizzard hit at exactly five o'clock on New Year's Eve. It came with a force and fury that shocked and staggered and numbed and frightened, as the snow, lashed on by 70-mile-an-hour winds, blinded Brooklyn and Queens in a matter of minutes and swept over the muddy East River to Manhattan.

The crosstown streets took the initial impact; the wind—screaming, moaning, and then sometimes venomously silent—hurled the snow everywhere. The evening rush hour had begun. The streets were filled with homeward-bound commuters. It had been a mild winter. No one was dressed for the blizzard. Practically no clothing could withstand that wind; it gave each flake of snow a savage cutting edge which slashed and seared one's face.

People ran before it, some trying to hide their faces from it with newspapers, gasping for breath. They ran to any kind of shelter, to shop doorways, to bars, to the already crowded subways, and stood bewildered, almost catatonic in their helplessness. They would cope. People always did. But for these first few minutes they would know nothing but dread and fear.

For awhile the drivers and passengers of the thousands of cars, taxies, and buses jamming the streets were luckier. But no windshield wiper or heater could cope with the swift, black ferocity of the storm, and in a matter of minutes, street traffic was at a honking, roaring, complete standstill.

Some abandoned their cars and ran through the blizzard to the nearest hotel. A fraction of them had perhaps originally thought of trying to make it to the Plaza or the Hilton or the St. Regis; but beneath the onslaught of the wind, they were happy to find *any* sanctuary, anything, the closer the better, wherever they happened to be.

Some drivers sat and waited in the belief that it couldn't last long, their engines screaming to keep the heaters running. A number of them would die that night in the very heart of the city, asphyxiated by their own exhaust fumes.

Only the masochistic fringe of cab drivers were happy. Now they could sit and curse and chain smoke and truly vent their hatred of weather forecasters and anyone else they thought responsible for this latest calamity.

By the East River, on the FDR Drive, where the winds were hitting full force, a Wall Street-bound bus, its driver blinded by the snow, swerved, hit the dividing barrier, rebounded across the traffic stream, crushed a yellow cab against the opposite barrier, and overturned. Southbound traffic was blocked.

Quickly lines of vehicles formed behind, powerless to move in either direction. Realizing the danger of sitting still, some drivers formed shivering chains of men and women, strangers all of them, holding hands and coattails as they struggled away from the accident scene, heading for the relative safety of the inner city.

Night completed the confusion. Street lamps were dimmed to distant, eerie yellow glows by the coating of snow; street signs were unreadable. People who had lived and worked in the city all their lives stumbled helpless and lost.

In midtown Manhattan the wife of a New Jersey Baptist minister, distraught with fear, ran into a moviehouse for shelter and sat watching permutations of the sexual act which shocked, surprised and finally delighted her into her first orgasm. Later that night, still trapped in the city, she paid five dollars for a dirty blanket and two square yards of threadbare carpet in the lobby of a cheap hotel and lay awake all night, terrified by the snores around her, but exhilarated by the memory of the strange new sexual warmth.

On Ninth Avenue, where silent automobiles lay snow-covered, pointing generally toward the Lincoln Tunnel, a lone drunk, a bottle of whiskey in his hand, fought his way against the fierce wind for a block and then was lifted to sail down 42nd Street, the biting wind raging behind him, until he reached a snowdrift and fell. He staggered up, then fell again. He drank the fiery whiskey and said: "Goddamnit to hell," and then went to sleep. A few minutes later the only trace of him was a small hole in the snow through which snored whiskey-flavored steam.

All that night the storm ripped into the heart of the island of Manhattan. The winds, which should have eased, did not. Instead, they gained strength. Few left the safety of homes or hotels or whatever shelter they had managed to find. To go out into that night was to court death.

One man who did go out, who knew that he must, was the mayor-elect of New York.

He paced the hotel lobby which was rapidly crowding with refugees from the snow, pausing every few minutes at the hall porter's desk, his face red with frustration and anger. "Look, son, somehow I've got to get to work."

"I know that, Mr. Mayor," the porter said. "We've been trying City Hall and your party headquarters. City Hall is busy. No reply from the other number."

"Police?"

"We keep trying. Busy. It must be the blizzard."

"Damn right, it's the blizzard. Where the hell is my car?"

"We've tried the 911 calls. That number's tied up, too. Everyone in the city has an emergency."

"Oh shit," Ben said in a voice louder than he'd meant. People turned and looked at him. "Keep trying," he said. He walked away and started pacing again.

He saw himself in one of the lobby mirrors: his new suit, delivered that morning, was exactly what he had wanted for the swearing-in ceremony. Two hundred and forty dollars' worth, more than he had ever dreamed of paying for a suit.

To hell with it, he was thinking. Where in God's name is the limousine, the chauffeur, the escort? What were they up to at City Hall? Seven o'clock and the car was promised for six. Typical of that administration, that awful, crap-ridden, no-good, lousy bunch down there.

It's not me I'm mad about. It's the office. The mayor. The new mayor of New York, standing here in a hotel lobby waiting for some damn sign of service.

He walked over to the porter's desk for the tenth time, pushing his way through all the people asking about rooms.

"If you get through to City Hall or they get through to you," he said, "tell them that thanks to their incompetence, the new Mayor has to go to his swearing-in by subway."

He put on his overcoat and stormed out through the revolving doors. It was only after a few steps that he realized why no limousine had come to get him.

4

Ben Boyle had to grip hard on the metal rail as he took the full force of the blizzard at the top of the subway steps at the West 14th Street station. Below, hemmed in by hundreds of stranded passengers, he had been sweating freely; now, exposed again to the violence of the wind, the sweat froze instantly on his face, and he felt it crack as he swore for the first of many times on that journey. But despite the wind and cold, he was glad to be out of the subway.

Underground he had been part of a cruel human zoo, with people driven to near panic. He was happy to rid himself of the powerful stench of steaming wet, fearful people, of the noise of shouting at helpless subway staff, of the fistfights over a handful of telephones, of the youngsters, natural denizens of the subway, who ran in tight packs through the crowds, jostling, jeering, and occasionally causing something approaching a riot.

The Mayor-elect had been jammed for two hours in a car that stopped and started fitfully and lurched finally into the West 14th Street station.

It was crazy, just crazy. Tomorrow he would have the run of the city. Now he was as helpless as any one of those squashed up around him; and none of them were suppressing their feelings about the people at City Hall.

Most of them had known blizzards before, but by now,

they reasoned, something should have happened. Someone somewhere should have created some kind of order. The snow plows and the salt-spraying trucks surely should have been clanking their way through the streets by now.

The mood of bewilderment and fright were beginning to turn into something more ugly. Too many of those stranded in the subway had had an early start on their New Year's liquor.

Ben was sober. Now, as he grabbed onto the rail of the subway exit to steady himself against the wind, he felt a deepening sense of responsibility for those people down there; indeed, for all the beleagured of New York. In a few hours he and his new administration would be taking over; this, he thought, was a hell of a way to start.

He was not able to think like that for long.

Generalized worry about the city was instantly overtaken by a simple urge to survive as he made his way—stumbling, falling, stooping low against the power of the wind, his head hidden deep in his collar, his eyes locked half-closed by the freezing snow—slowly, agonizingly, along Broadway toward City Hall.

What he could see through the flailing snow was a wilderness of giant drifts building up against the brick of the West Side; only an occasional glass and concrete structure blocked the gale.

He moved more by instinct than by any plan. He was certain he was on Broadway when he heard the snap of a maple tree, heavily overladen with snow and ice, crashing to the ground in Washington Square. From moment to moment he stopped and sought shelter against the wind, breathing hard and furiously through cupped gloves, gathering strength to continue for a few more tortured steps.

He forced himself to go on, plodding, stumbling, falling frequently into the heaviest drifts; sometimes trying the street.

Ben Boyle was a brave man, but tonight he was frightened by the immensity of what he was up against: the whipping savagery of the storm was turning the exposed skin of his face into a raw mass of pain.

On Canal Street he fell for about the twentieth time and crashed, all the breath knocked from his aching lungs, into the gutter. He gasped hard for air and lay back to rest. He looked with difficulty at his watch. It was midnight. At that moment, he remembered, he, Ben Boyle, a plumber from Queens, Boyle, whom no one ever expected to win, became mayor of New York. His frozen face couldn't even smile at the irony of it: the mayor of New York lying in a gutter on Canal Street like any Bowery bum.

He heard a distant church bell carried on the moaning wind. The snow was already beginning to pile up against him. The pain and fatigue were being subtly replaced now by warmth and a strong desire to sleep. He could have slept. It would have been so easy to lie there on the soft mattress of snow and not get up. Why not just bed down right here and leave it to the experts? he thought. Those guys must have some kind of plan to cope with all this. That's what we pay them for. To hell with it. He yawned and felt the ice crack around his mouth. Jesus, I'm tired. He was falling into a dangerous reverie and might well have slept had there not been another toll of the church bell. It chimed the hour, stirring a childhood memory of a song, "Turn Again, Dick Whittington, for You will be Mayor of London." He looked up and saw through encrusted eyes the street sign above him click from Don't Walk to Walk.

Slowly, painfully, he staggered to his feet and began to move defiantly forward again, tramping like a man demented down the middle of Broadway.

5

For several hours that evening the supertanker heaved and rolled in the storm, her safety dependent on the skill of her helmsman who sat, tightlipped with concentration, watching the bank of instruments in front of him, correcting the sway of the ship with a small lever three inches long, which controlled the *Jersey Lily*.

Two other men sat on the bridge: a radio operator at a computer terminal keyboard, punching out an endless stream of messages, and the first officer who was watching a large, illuminated chart on which the ship's position was flashed every 30 seconds. Pushing a button, he could verify the position from the movement of three bright-red lines which represented the signals from three radio beacons.

On the powerful radar scanner he could see the dark outline of Long Island, 20 miles to the north.

The radio operator took off his earphones and turned to him.

"Coast Guard querying our position, Chief."

"Tell them we are seeking shelter, with minor engine trouble."

The radio operator talked quietly into a microphone, then turned back.

"They say we're too big for these waters."

The first officer said: "Repeat your message and sign off."

He looked again at the position of the ship and then at the electronic chronometer on the bulkhead of the bridge. It read 2000 hours.

The radar-illuminated chart was now showing clearly the outline of the approaches to New York harbor. He could see Sandy Hook and Rockaway Point. The distant tip of Coney Island was now visible. The shoreline of Staten Island was now more than just a muzzy blur.

He walked to the computer keyboard. He glanced quickly through the printouts and tapped out a coded message. The machine flashed back an acknowledgment. The one-second exchange meant that in exactly 30 minutes the entire radar system of New York harbor would be blacked out.

6

The two policemen on duty at City Hall had spent most of the evening shoveling snow from the steps and trying to keep open the semblance of a path to the subway. It was after midnight when they looked up from their shovels and made out a big, shambling snowman. The apparition came closer through a flashlight beam, then stopped, trying to wipe snow from its face.

One of the policemen, a gray haired veteran with a paunch, said: "Ben Boyle? Jesus, it's the new mayor himself!"

Ben Boyle fell forward, helpless, as they leaned out and caught him. They sat him on a bench in the granite-lined lobby, and the older policeman took a hip flask from his pocket. He eased Boyle's mouth open and poured whiskey into it.

Boyle gagged, his eyes opening on the two men bent anxiously over him. Tipping the contents of the flask again into Ben's mouth, the older policeman said: "Strictly against the rules, Mr. Boyle, but it's New Year's Eve." They watched as the color slowly came back into his face. He felt the alcohol burn his throat.

"That must have been a bitch of a walk," said the younger policeman. "I've never seen snow like this, sir."

Ben looked up at their name tags.

"Sullivan. Karminski. Thank you."

He stood up unsteadily and tried to loosen the buttons on his overcoat. But the pain in his fingers was too much. Karminski moved to help him.

"Oh, no," Ben croaked, "I can manage."

Karminski smiled. "But it's our duty to help you, sir."

Ben smiled, too, at his self-consciousness. "Okay."

They pulled off top layers of clothing and removed the boots from his nearly frozen feet.

Without embarrassment, Ben stood in the foyer in his new fifty-dollar swearing-in shirt and underpants and let the City Hall central heating system restore warmth to his body. "Is there a shower in the building?" he asked.

"It's in your antechambers, Mr. Mayor," Karminski said. "Shower, sauna, whirlpool, and gymnasium."

"No kidding?" Ben said. "So how come Macey got so fat?"

"He had a big dining room and kitchen put in, too," Sullivan said.

Ben made a face. "Thousands of people homeless in this city, and the mayor builds a palazzo. Okay, lead me to it."

As he stood under the shower, the water as hot as he could stand it, Boyle questioned the two waiting policemen. "Who else have we got in City Hall tonight?"

"Just the two of us," said Sullivan. "Our reliefs didn't show. And the night switchboard operator. She's bushed, Mr. Mayor. Collapsed. She's been getting a thousand calls an hour."

Ben stepped out of the shower. Karminski handed him a terrycloth gown he'd found.

"Okay," said the mayor. He was feeling human again. "Let's get this city moving. I need people. I want a direct line through to my office. Then I want to talk to the police commissioner."

"Sorry," said Karminski. "Headquarters had been trying to raise him all night. Half the city's phones are out of order. He's almost certainly been trying to call us, but that switchboard out there is lit up like a Christmas tree."

"The traffic commissioner?"

"He's trying to get in," said Sullivan. "He was in Bronxville. I don't know how he's going to do it."

"Jesus Christ," said Ben. "Sanitation? Somebody's going to have to start clearing these streets."

"We got a call from his wife four hours ago, Mr. Mayor," said Karminski. "Commissioner Nagel started out to walk to City Hall like you, but he had a coronory three blocks from his house. The sanitation men are still out."

"Looks like we'll be needing the army, then," said Ben Boyle. "On the other hand, there's no point in clearing anything until this snow eases. Now where can I get some clean clothes?"

"I'll find some," said Sullivan. "There's just one other thing, Mr. Mayor." He led Boyle into the mayor's oak-paneled office and picked up a thick manila envelope from the leather-inlaid desk.

"This young guy, about half an hour ago, walked through the snow outside, handed it to Karminski, and ran like a scalded cat. We didn't know what to do with it."

Boyle looked at the envelope. It had been addressed with a thick marking pen which had smudged with wetness.

"To Ben Boyle, Mayor of New York. *Strictly private and for the Mayor's eyes only.*"

"He came in this weather?" said Boyle. "With this?"

Sullivan shrugged. "Yeah, I thought it was pretty funny myself."

7

Ben sat down at the big, bare desk and opened the envelope. The letter inside was thick, typed on regular size bond paper.

Dear Mr. Mayor:

This letter is addressed to you personally for reasons which will quickly become obvious. We realize that what it contains will add considerably to the almost insurmountable problems which face you. We must tell you at once that the blizzard which has brought your city to a standstill was not of our making.

A tanker named the *Jersey Lily* was brought into New York harbor under cover of the blizzard, but also under a radar blackout which *was* of our own making. The *Jersey Lily* is now moored approximately 500 yards from the Manhattan shore, immediately facing the World Trade Center.

This ship contains the following:

100,000 tons of high-octane aviation fuel.
100,000 tons of natural methane gas.
100,000 tons of Arabian crude oil.
50,000 tons of naptha.

We must tell you immediately that this ship is equipped with a comprehensive range of highly sophisticated electronic devices. Any attempt to board this ship will result in instant death to the boarder.

For the next forty-eight hours a number of coded signals will be sent to an IBM computer on board the *Jersey Lily*. It will activate a number of primers which, in turn, at the receipt of one final coded message, will activate a series of magnesium flash detonators in the two holds containing the volatile substances which, combined with air in measured quantities, are now at their most explosive.

The resulting explosion, Mr. Mayor, will devastate your city with substantial loss of life. The attendant pollution will result in the closure of New York harbor, the Upper Bay, and the Narrows for at least a year with consequent massive damage to the city's economy.

Please make no mistake. This is not a hoax. This is a direct threat to your city and we are both prepared and capable of seeing it through to its conclusion, no matter how terrible the consequences.

To give some evidence of our technical competence to achieve our ends, we suggest you take note of the following: First, by use of our own lasar/microwave guide beacons, we have been able to navigate a 507,000-ton supertanker (through the most difficult weather conditions) through one of the busiest shipping harbors in the world and to moor it exactly in the position we planned—the position which, in terms of the explosion, will do the most damage to city property and its economy.

Second, we recommend that you turn to the transmissions of the Public Service Television Channel 13. You will notice, superimposed on its transmissions, the face of a clock. This is the clock in the computer room of the *Jersey Lily*. On each hour of the next forty-eight, that camera, which is remotely controlled, will pan slightly left to reveal a row of primers.

Your experts will have no difficulty in identifying their purpose. As each primer clicks into position the electrical circuit will near closure, and finally, detonation will take place.

Attached to this letter are two appendices which outline (a) the hazards you face if any attempt is made to board the ship, move the ship, or in any way pervert the carefully computerized system which we have outlined; and (b) the conditions under which we will deactivate the devices which threaten your city.

We had hoped you would be able to evacuate the greater part of Manhattan, it being our intention to strike at property rather than people. But it is too late now, storm or not, to change our operation, which has been intricately worked out over the past year. To paraphrase Dr. Samuel Johnson—it should concentrate the mind wonderfully.

We trust that you will be able to meet the conditions outlined in appendix (b). You may find them difficult. We feel, however, since your election campaign was fought on a front which promised true justice for the poor, the needy, and the oppressed minority groups, that you will appreciate the situation more clearly than your predecessors.

Sincerely yours,
Flaming Torch
for the League for Real Justice
for the Indian

8

Ben read the letter again and then glanced at the two appendices. There was a simple intercom machine on the desk in front of him. He pressed one button and it gave a shrill scream. He pressed another and another and nothing happened.

He walked quickly to the door, through his outer office, and shouted down the corridor. "Officer, either of you—come here."

Sullivan ran up the stairs and saw the look of anguish in his face.

"Listen," said Boyle, his voice strangely tortured. "Get that switchboard operator out of her pit. I don't care if she's dying. Wake her up and get her to get these phones working. I want to talk to the captain of the port. I want him now—not in five or ten minutes. I want you to stand over her and make sure she doesn't hear a word of anything that's said. Okay? And after I've finished with the captain, I want to speak to somebody in this city who knows computers."

The cop looked at him for just a second. "Right, Mr. Mayor."

The intercom on the desk buzzed in less than three minutes. Ben was rereading the appendices. The operator's voice was weary.

"You're through to Captain Robert Cusp, the captain of

the port, Mr. Mayor," she said. "I'll get off the line immediately."

The voice at the other end of the line was brisk and cheerful: "Happy New Year, Mr. Mayor."

"Could a supertanker weighing half a million tons be sitting off the Battery at this moment?" asked Ben.

"What'd you say?"

"Just that, Captain. Could it happen?"

There was a long pause.

"It could. At least I guess it could happen."

"Your radar. Any problems tonight?"

"Sure enough. It went on the blink for three full hours. Thank God nothing was moving. Nobody sails on New Year's Eve if they can help it."

"It has happened. Captain."

"I don't believe you, Mr. Mayor."

"It's your harbor, Captain."

"We had a strange echo from the starboard Hudson Channel. We guessed it was something to do with the snow or a freak reflection from the World Trade Center. I'll send a boat to look at it as soon as this damn blizzard stops."

"Don't do that, Captain."

"Don't what?"

"Don't send any boat near that ship."

After a pause, the captain's voice was no longer brisk. It was a voice not accustomed to taking commands.

"Mr. Mayor, we haven't met, but I'm afraid I'll have to point out before we do that the U.S. Coast Guard operates in this port with complete autonomy. The city has no say in the way we run the port."

"Captain, that ship, as of now, is the responsibility of this city. No one is to try to board her or go anywhere near her."

"Now look here—"

"Captain Cusp, I have every reason to believe the ship is primed to explode at a given time; this city is being held for ransom."

"Christ."

"I'll tell you a lot more later. I'm going to need a great deal of help from you. But in God's name, stay away from her until you get the go ahead. Understand?"

"I'm beginning to."

"There are several million people trapped in Manhattan tonight by this damn blizzard. That ship might explode if it's tampered with. That's what the ransom note says, and I believe it."

"Okay, Mr. Mayor. I'll comply."

"Good. One other thing. Not a word to anybody, especially the media—a leak could start a panic which would kill thousands."

"Right. For now I'll just make sure that a ship like that could get into the Hudson River. I still find it damned hard to believe."

"Thanks for your cooperation, Captain."

"Any time, Mr. Mayor."

"And Captain."

"Yes?"

"Happy New Year."

Ben sighed loudly as he hung up. Immediately the phone buzzed again. The switchboard operator said: "Mr. Van Horn, Mr. Mayor."

"Who's he?"

"Head of the City Technical Services."

"Thank you. How are you feeling?"

"Better, thanks, Mr. Mayor."

"Mr. Van Horn, where are you?"

"At home, Mr. Mayor. In Chelsea." His voice was deep, cultured.

"I need you at City Hall urgently. Can you get here?"

"In this weather?"

"Are you married, Mr. Van Horn?"

"Yes, Mr. Mayor."

"Children?"

"Three."

"And you live in Chelsea?"

Ben looked at a map of the city which covered one wall of his office. Chelsea was close to the Hudson.

"Mr. Van Horn, I want you here. I want you to walk to the 14th Precinct house. By the time you reach it I'll have arranged for some kind of transportation to get you to City Hall."

Van Horn didn't question the authority in Boyle's voice. "The 14th Precinct. Tell them to expect me."

Ben Boyle stood up from the desk and walked slowly over the carpeted floor to look out the window. Even the double glazing didn't muffle the sound of the wind outside. Directly in front of him was Murray Street, reaching to the river. He closed his eyes and visualized the supertanker there, straining at her anchors in the swollen Hudson.

He spoke aloud to the window. "*Jersey Lily*," he said, "the *Jersey Lily*." What a pretty name for a goddamn disaster. He turned.

She stood in the doorway. Huddled in a sheepskin coat and hat, enough of her face showing for Ben to see that she too had been exposed to the full force of the blizzard. She blinked several times to free her eyes of ice particles and shook the snow from her coat.

"You?" said Ben incredulously.

"I called City Hall just to congratulate you, Mr. Mayor," she said. "No luck at all, so I packed and was going home. Then I saw the blizzard. Ben, I was worried to death about you. Those policemen told me you walked. Walked—in this?"

"How did you get here?"

"By snowmobile. I mean, that's logical isn't it?"

"Where the hell do you get a snowmobile in the center of Manhattan?"

"Jim Bessemer-Smith had asked me two weeks ago if I was interested in a ride to Vermont on New Year's Day. He had his snowmobile all ready on the trailer when the blizzard started. So I borrowed it. It was a hell of a ride in this wind, especially with deserted cars everywhere."

Ben smiled. "Glad you came. That makes five of us to run this city."

"As bad as that?"

He looked at the document on the desk.

"Worse."

"What can I do?"

"I'll start dispensing my patronage by making you the personal assistant to the mayor of New York, an unpaid post, until the real one gets here. The first thing you can do is to find the liquor cabinet in this office and pour a big drink of anything and take it down to the switchboard operator. Then give similar drinks to those two cops. Then, and I hate to do it to you, I want you back in the snow. Take that snowmobile and drive like crazy to the 14th Precinct and bring a man called Van Horn back here to City Hall.

"And while you're at it, get one of those men downstairs to get me a complete weather forecast for the next 48 hours. It must be on tape somewhere."

"Okay," she said. "Anything to help the new boss."

Mary took off her sheepskin coat and threw it on the floor. Ben turned to the papers in front of him. He looked up momentarily and raised an eyebrow as he watched her put her hand up into her cashmere sweater.

She saw the look on his face and smiled.

"Don't worry," she said. She pulled a tiny bedraggled sparrow from between her breasts. "It was on the steps of City Hall. There are hundreds of birds dying out there."

She took a handkerchief and wrapped the bird in it tenderly and placed it in one of Ben's drawers.

"Now you can believe everything you've ever heard about the English," she said.

Ben sighed and started to read.

The first appendix was headed. "The *Jersey Lily*—Warning to would-be intruders."

Ben read quickly. It was a detailed account of the boat and its gadgetry. Numbered paragraphs warned that any attempt to move the ship more than 10 degrees from its present mooring would immediately activate a chain system and create an instant explosion.

It was made abundantly clear that any attempt to board the ship would be detected at once by electronic sensors and would result in death to the intruder or intruders. If these early-warning systems failed to detect any unwanted policeman or other person, the ship would be exploded by a second line of defense.

The ship's computer, the appendix added, was particularly well defended. It was encased in a heavy shielding of lead and heatproof chemicals.

The coded system by which it operated was foolproof; any attempt to feed false codes into it would be detected instantly. In fact, any attempt to derange the ship's computer program would bring about an explosion.

Boyle skimmed through this document. It called for specialized scrutiny. It was not for a plumber, that was for sure.

The second appendix was longer but in the same crisply polite style of the other documents. It began with a short, well-couched statement on the abuse suffered by the

American Indian people since the time of Columbus's first landing. Then it went into a series of general demands.

The television and radio networks of America would have delivered to them that day a series of video and audio tapes which dramatized these abuses. These tapes were to be broadcast exclusively and across the country for the next 48 hours, interrupted only by the news and weather.

"We anticipate that the Mayor will use his good offices to insure that this instruction is complied with."

The second demand was aimed directly at Washington. A number of agreements had been drawn up in negotiations over the years with the Secretary of State and the Bureau of Indian Affairs. These had been the subject of much tiresome vacillation on the part of the United States government. The signature of the Secretary of State was wanted immediately, together with a new agreement providing for the immediate disbanding of the Bureau of Indian Affairs.

"These are fair demands," the letter declared, "concerned with justice and equity. We will not bother you, Mr. Mayor, with the details—you will have enough other concerns. It is important, however, that the President and the Secretary of State be made to realize that the demands are not negotiable."

Boyle took off his reading glasses; he was beginning to feel relieved. Okay, he thought, we can handle the networks. A conference call in the morning. They'll scream, but they'll go along. They'll have to play, or I'll take them over at gunpoint.

The President might be a slightly bigger problem. But he'll sign. Christ, didn't he own half the property on that bank of the Hudson?

He read on. What he read now brought true fear. Ben's blood, just warming up after the long walk in the snow, began to chill again.

"Jesus," he said.

"Our third demand concerns the City of New York," the document said. "We seek, quite simply, the ground rent payable on the island of Manhattan since it was bought, illegally, from the Algonquin Tribe in 1626. Or roughly, the interest on that ground rent compounded over 360 years.

"Our computer has assessed this sum on the annual interest rates levied since that time. It has brought it to a round figure for the sake of convenience. The sum required is one hundred and thirty billion dollars."

"This sum is to be paid into a special United Nations trust fund within 48 hours. In order to avoid any abuse of trust, we insist that it be administered by the countries of Libya, Uganda, and Zaire.

"Obviously such money will not be found easily on such short notice.

"The fund *is* immediately available, however, in what you refer to as 'hot Arab' dollars and is payable immediately on the presentation of your mandate to the Dresdner Bank at Kaiserhoffstrasse 19, Frankfurt, West Germany, attention Herr Doktor Winkler. This fund is available on the following terms:

"It constitutes a loan to the City of New York at compound interest over 20 years, the whole repayable at the conclusion of the term; we have arranged for the favorable interest rate of 8 percent.

"It must carry irrevocable guarantees from the following corporations for the sums of ten billion dollars each: the First National City Bank; the Chase Manhattan Bank; the Bankers' Trust; the Manufacturers Hanover Trust; the Chemical Bank; the Marine Midland Bank; Exxon; IBM; General Motors; the Ford Motor Company; the Xerox Corporation; and Texaco.

"We are eager to achieve our aims quickly and not to wreak the havoc we most assuredly can wreak."

9

Ben Boyle closed his eyes for a moment and wondered whether he was still in that strange dream-like state that he had fallen into in that snowdrift on Broadway. He had been mayor for exactly two hours. His city had been paralyzed by the worst blizzard in its history. It was in grave danger of being half-blown to hell by a bunch of Indians. And now he was expected to hock the city for $130 billion.

He had won the election against all odds with the simple slogan "What This City Needs Is a Damned Good Plumber."

He said aloud: "What this city really needs is Merlin the goddamn magician." He took a deep breath and stood up quickly.

Officer Sullivan was in his secretary's office with the weather tape.

"They say that the blizzard will continue unabated all night, sir," he said. "It may ease, but it will probably freeze by morning."

Boyle said quietly: "Come in, Sullivan. Write down the names of these corporations." He called them off. "Get headquarters to find out for me exactly where the president of each of these outfits is now, where they're going to be for the next 48 hours, and what their telephone numbers will be. Make sure as hell that they stay at those numbers. Get Karminski to find the city treasurer and tell him to stay where he is. I'll want to talk to him shortly.

"And when you've done that, I want you to get a list of every snowmobile and snowcat owned in this city. Then tell each precinct captain to tell his men to requisition them. Hell, let them smash shop windows if they have to. But get them.

"One other thing. Find me a judge. Any judge. If I'm going to kick asses, I'd better be sworn in to kick asses—even if I have to be sworn in on the telephone."

10

The Hotel Marlborough stands ugly and unloved in a mean, sleazy street in midtown Manhattan between the tasteless black glassery of Sixty Avenue and the honest vulgarity of Broadway. It is not a hotel in any real sense of the word; a handpainted cardboard sign in the bare lobby declares, in fact: "No visitors aloud."

It is an old red-brick building, ornate with terracotta, which stands between a venereal-disease clinic and an all-male featurette moviehouse. It had once been an elegant place. But as successive owners went bankrupt and disappeared, it mellowed into a huge, yet discreet, expensive bordello before descending further into a common cat-house. Now it had become a caravanserai for the twilight people.

The police shun it and enter only in groups. The tenants do not sign registers; they pay rent to two large men who hold their hands out and ask no questions. In the heat of the summer some students sit on the steps and compare needle marks; occasionally someone freaks out and runs screaming into the street. Others slide from the hotel into Broadway and the streets below, flicking knives honed like razors in sweat-lined pockets. Some seek rape or some other pleasure. Most are looking for the price of a fix. No one left that hotel on the night of the blizzard, but it had a visitor.

Early that evening a small boat had made its perilous way up the swirling, angry waters of the Hudson River. A young man sat in the stern, hunched over the tiller against the snow, steering for a red blob on the direction-finding radio before him. When the blob became redder and began to bleep noisily, he took a powerful, rubber-covered flashlight from inside his clothing and shone it ahead. Through the thick, almost opaque, snow he could make out the wall of a pier. He brought the boat carefully alongside the wall and grabbed a rope that had been painted a luminous orange.

Holding the rope in one hand, he took a pistol with a silencer from his pocket and shot five holes in the floor of the boat. He put the pistol back in his pocket and climbed effortlessly up the rope and onto the wall. On the pier he found the transistorized radio beacon and threw it in the water below. Finally he untied the rope from the stanchion that secured it. Then he slipped into the pier shed and headed toward 45th Street.

Unlike Ben Boyle, he did not fall or stumble or curse or shout. He moved easily in the snow.

At the Marlborough Hotel he shook the caked snow from his clothing and kicked it from his knee-high leather boots. He walked into the elevator and turned a Yale key in the extra lock. He stood motionless in the filthy box, but his eyes saw none of the flotsam around his feet or on the walls; they stared directly ahead toward the doors of the elevator.

When the doors opened, the elevator was at the top floor of the hotel. On any other floor they would have opened onto narrow, sordid corridors, but on this floor they opened onto a large, airy room.

The room was cheerless and functional. At well-spaced intervals four men sat at individual black desks, each with a computer terminal on it. By one wall a fifth man sat monitoring a large tape recorder. On a raised dais facing the others sat the first officer of the *Jersey Lily*. A bank of miniature television monitors stood to one side of him; on the other side, clicking and whirring gently, was an IBM 360 computer.

11

The surrogate court judge was slightly drunk. The blizzard had brought business in the court to a standstill. No nightly parade of pimps and hookers, of petty thieves and vagrants, no quick fining, no wisecracks from the lineup. The judge had been free to sit in chambers with a bottle of gin and read from the police collection of obscene books impounded in more austere times.

He reeled slightly as he was brought into the mayor's office and blinked at the bright lights. Ben Boyle was sitting at his desk talking on the phone.

"No. For the last time, I don't want to know why this blizzard started. I want to know when the damn thing is going to end. The whole city is going to want to know why you didn't tell them. Now, when the hell is it going to stop snowing?

"Noon tomorrow at the *latest?* Good God. Can you guarantee even that?" Ben ignored the judge. "Okay, okay. Just as soon as you've got even the slightest idea that it's going to stop, call me. Talk to the police actions room and use the code word 'Crazy Horse.' Tell them to relay the message directly to the mayor."

He put the phone down and looked up at the judge.

"I want you to swear me in," he said.

"Huh?"

"There's the oath of office." He handed him a Xeroxed

sheet Mary found in a file marked "Mayor, Inauguration of."

"Is it constitutional?" The judge found it hard to say the word.

"You're the judge. At least you are at the moment."

"Very well, Mr. Mayor. Will you stand, please?"

Boyle stood up.

"Raise your right hand."

"I, Ben Boyle, do solemnly swear. . . ."

Ben repeated the words impatiently.

"That I will support the Constitution of the United States. . . .

"That I will support the Constitution of the United States."

"And the Constitution of the State of New York."

The judge slurred the word "constitution" badly this time. Ben glared at him.

"Judge," he said. "You are drunk out of your mind. Give me the form." He read the balance of the oath in a strong, impatient voice.

He handed the form back to the judge. "Okay, judge, sign it."

The judge signed the document with difficulty. Ben looked at Sullivan. "Witness, please, Sullivan. Then get this gentleman carried back to night court."

He looked at Karminski. "Would you say, Karminski, that I am now, without a doubt, the official mayor of this city?"

"Without a doubt, Mr. Mayor."

Ben picked up the telephone. "Honey, I want you to get me police headquarters—whoever is in charge there. I'll hold."

His intercom buzzed. "Chief Inspector? Good. Now, listen. I'm at City Hall in my office. I want you to come over here and bring the best detective you've got there.

"I *know* there's a serious blizzard, Inspector. But it's nowhere near as serious as what I'm going to show you. Get over here fast—hell, I walked from 14th Street. Bring anyone you can who knows anything about radios, computers, things like that. Another thing. Tell your switchboard that if they get any calls from someone using the words 'Crazy Horse' to take special note of it. You'll understand when you get here. And listen—send over as many switchboard operators as you can possibly spare."

He put the telephone down and looked at Karminski. "It's going to be a busy night," he said. "Now, I guess I'd better warn Jersey City. But they'd better understand that we are doing it our way."

There was a look of unconcealed curiosity on Karminski's face.

12

By all the laws, by all those traditionally well-greased rules that govern the political machinery of New York, Ben Boyle should not have been the mayor of the city that night. He was in every sense a political maverick, a man who had set himself apart from the machine, a man who spoke his mind too freely and too often in the wrong places. He spoke the truth at all times, not out of any built-in piety or evangelistic fervor; in fact, he loved honesty because it was easy.

The rank and file of the party loved him. They loved the way he would rise at a ward meeting and put the one question they had all wanted to ask with a brutal directness that often withered the speaker. The party bosses feared him, tried to court him; and then, finding him unyielding, to compromise him.

Six months before the election, the party suffered two scandals which shook the confidence of even the most cynical New Yorker. The major party candidate was brought swiftly before a grand jury and suspended from all political activities while they investigated the loss of $500,000 from the party coffers. Two weeks later the new frontrunner was photographed in a Brooklyn steak house with the head of the East Side Mafia.

With three weeks in which to find a candidate, the party, now in total disarray, picked Ben Boyle and presented him to the people with little confidence or enthusiasm.

The incumbent mayor, Joey Macey, dismissed Boyle contemptuously as a "fire hydrant philosopher" and tried to keep it a low-key election.

Macey underestimated the people of the city; equally, he had not reckoned with Ben Boyle. The city was running down. All the predictions were coming true. Whole streets had been closed because there was no money to repair them; the subways were on the point of closing after ten at night because of crime and vandalism; the number of homeless and helpless people in the city had swollen to a proportion which the administration could not cope with.

Ben Boyle's directness was infectious. The voters loved his powerful one-minute radio addresses. And when the mayor made the fatal mistake of appearing in a television debate with the plumber from Queens, the polls took a sharp turnaround. Now it was Macey who was on the defensive.

Boyle had become a celebrity. He was moving fast toward success, and the party knew it. Until this point, his campaign had been fought largely from the local headquarters in Queens, with Ben giving impromptu press conferences in his four-room walk-up apartment on Jerome Avenue. Now the party insisted that he move to a midtown Manhattan hotel suite and behave the way a candidate should.

Boyle resisted strongly, but as the coterie of press and media, of public relations men and party campaigners, grew around him, he acquiesced grudgingly and closed the apartment in Queens.

13

It was at a fund-raising party at the Plaza that Ben Boyle was introduced to Mary Fyfield. She had a martini and was talking to a political writer from the *New York Times.*

"Hey, Ben," the man said. "Come and meet Mary. She's the queen of the typing pool."

Ben was eating a cocktail sausage, wishing it was a giant Sabrett's frankfurter smothered in onions and mustard. He held out his hand automatically and smiled a weary candidate's smile. Then he looked at her. He was looking at the most beautiful face he had ever seen. More than anything, he liked the clear blue eyes; in them was a curious mixture of innocence, humor, and arrogance.

"Honored to meet you," he said as he had said a hundred times that night.

"It's my honor," she said. "After all, you're my boss." Her accent was English. Her voice was cut glass.

"You're *paid?"* he said. "What do you do?"

"Oh, I'm the girl Friday of the organization," she said. "I write press releases, answer phones, read all the abusive letters, and throw the death threats away. You'd be amazed how many people in this city don't like you."

"Hell, that's not a woman's job," he said.

"Come, come, Ben Boyle," she said lightly. " 'Press release number six: Ben Boyle on Women's Rights.' I typed it myself—and added a few choice phrases here and there."

"I've seen some of those letters," said Ben. "The language, I mean, it's nasty stuff."

"We get one every day that says the same thing. It's always pasted up from *National Enquirer* headlines and says 'Get out of town, you Irish motherfucker!' " she said blandly. "You'd be quite surprised to know about a lot of your other habits, too."

Her matter-of-factness bewildered him. "You know," he said. "I'm 50 years old, and I've lived in a tough neighborhood for much of my life, and I still don't like hearing swear words from women."

She smiled. "Mr. Boyle, you have a strong prudish streak. I don't think a future mayor of New York can afford that. I was born and raised in a racing stable in Berkshire. By the age of five, I knew every combination of colorful obscenity ever invented by man. That's how we bred Derby winners."

He was amused by the British pronunciations. "Future mayor of New York," he said. "I like your confidence, Miss. . . ."

"Fyfield," she said. "Late of the New York Stock Exchange. My company went bust. That's why I'm working for the party."

"Macey is still way ahead," he said. "We've got a long way to go."

"You're going to win, Ben Boyle," she said firmly. "I just hope you can mend this city."

"What don't you like about it?"

"I don't like the people who crawl out of the walls," she said. "I don't like the subways because they smell. I don't like not being able to walk in the streets after sundown. I don't like beggars. Too many beggars and drunks."

"What about the other seven million people—you don't like them either?"

"I'm one of them," she said simply. "It's my city too."

"You don't sound as if it were."

"Ben, you don't have to say dese and dose to be part of this city. For one thing you hear almost more Spanish spoken here than you do English."

She was making him feel uncomfortable, and he didn't

know why. He looked past her shoulder and saw a ward leader he had been told especially to backslap.

He waved and heard the English girl saying: "Don't get me wrong, Mr. Boyle." There was a mocking irony in the way she said "mister." "This city is ours. It belongs to those of you who were born here and also to those of us who have adopted it."

He was tired after weeks of campaigning. The air conditioning in the hotel was not coping with this mass of people. He felt a rising wave of irritation. It crept into his crisp, clear voice.

"You've adopted this city," he said. "Hells bells, sister, how high and mighty can you get? You've adopted *us? No* one adopts New York. *It* adopts *people*—Jews, Irish, Poles, Italians, Hispanics—hell, even the English. I'm sorry about the beggars on the streets. A lot of people have to beg in this city, because. . . ."

His face was flushed. He knew his voice had been raised too high because people nearby were looking. He was glad he'd stopped when he had. He turned away from her abruptly and made his way toward the party man.

For the first time since his nomination, Ben Boyle slept fitfully that night. The noise of a police siren woke him in the early hours, and he found himself thinking about Mary Fyfield, about the hurt in her eyes when he had shouted at her.

The next morning, he looked in at party headquarters. He found his way back to the typing pool.

Mary was standing at a Xerox machine, feeding paper into it with one hand and talking into a phone on the other. She was saying: "Four meetings in Brooklyn, two in downtown Manhattan, and then a rally in Central Park—in this heat? My dear Jim, what are you trying to do to him? He's only human. Why not cut out the first two in Brooklyn? They already love him there."

She looked up and saw Ben. He shuffled uncomfortably. She went on talking. The expression of concentration in her eyes did not change but she looked steadily at the candidate.

"Of course it's my bloody business," she said. "He's my boss too. He's got another six weeks of this. I mean, if you want a corpse in City Hall, just go on treating him like this."

Ben put his hand out and took the telephone from her gently.

"Jim? Ben Boyle. Keep Brooklyn the way it was. But where are the ball games you promised? And if you don't get me a day's fishing while the bluefish are still running, I'll break your arm. I tell you, there are 100,000 fishermen in this city, and I'm one of them. Sure, get the media there. They need a break too."

He listened for a few moments, watching the English girl operate the machine. Her movements were lithe and graceful. She took the Xerox copies to a collating table and his eyes followed her.

She moved well, he decided. There was a lot of grace about her movements.

"Okay, its a deal," he told his manager. "And one other thing. Find me a good driver. We took the door off a taxi this morning. I don't want to lose the cab driver vote. Who is this kid you've given me? The way he drives, you'd think he was driving for the mob or something."

He put down the telephone and turned to Mary. She was smiling now. He knew there was no need to apologize.

"Can we go out and have a cup of coffee?" he asked, surprised at the awkwardness in his voice. "I was rude last night."

"You were tired and I was being boring."

"I'm sorry."

"Please don't say 'sorry' again. It doesn't become the tough image, you know."

"I'll get along," said Ben. She had succeeded in embarrassing him again.

"Oh no you won't," she said. "I'll bring the coffee to you. You sit down there and put your feet up. I'll get it from the machine."

As she went out of the room she turned and said: "And then I'll tell you what a good driver I am. I made a good living in this city once—as a taxi driver."

14

The sallow-faced man at the tape recorder noted in his log: "Mayor sworn in 0125," and passed a note to the man on the dais who read quickly and said: "Okay. Now we have an official opposition. Stand by for a systems check."

He turned to the computer and pressed six keys.

On the screen came the fast-forming phrases:

PREDICTED RESPONSE BY MAYOR (AMENDED)
1. NOTIFY POLICE COMMISSIONER
NOTIFY CIVIL DEFENSE
ALERT SANITATION
ALERT COAST GUARD
ALERT FBI
2. NOTIFY LIEUT. GOVERNOR
ALERT PORT AUTHORITY
ALERT NATIONAL GUARD

ACTUAL RESPONSE BY MAYOR
NOTIFY COAST GUARD
TRACE BANK PRESIDENTS AND COMPANY PRESIDENTS
ALERT CHARLES VAN HORN. ESTIMATED ARRIVAL
CITY HALL 0145.
CALL DEPUTY COMMISSIONER TO CITY HALL.

CALL DETECTIVE (UNIDENTIFIED) TO CITY HALL CONDITION GREEN.

George Mahle, the man on the dais, was pleased. The new mayor, he decided, was thinking the way he had wanted him to think. The immediate call to the Coast Guard showed the right kind of respect for Mahle's letter; and the immediate move to trace the 13 money men was better than he had anticipated.

"Charlie," he said to the man at the tape recorder. "Let me know when this Van Horn arrives. I'd like to hear that conversation."

George Mahle spoke softly, but it was a voice that commanded attention in that room. "Let's check the systems," he said. He picked up a card from the console in front of him. "Sound systems. Sensor one."

"Negative sounds."

The man who spoke was small; he had the build of a strong lightweight boxer. He was small and ugly, with a well-spread Mongolian nose and widely spaced, huge brown eyes. His name was Mick Dull Knife; he was a full-blooded Sioux and a graduate of Princeton.

"Sensor two?"

"Negative aircraft or helicopters."

"Sensor three?"

"Wind noises approaching 240 dbm which is 20 percent under acceptable safe limit."

Mahle considered this. He lit a cigarette and blew the smoke out ahead of him.

"Deactivate sensor three," he said. "We don't want the wind to blow the place up."

He turned to the second monitor, a tall, lean man, the only one wearing glasses.

"Pete Stole Knife," he said. "Give me your data."

"Ship's position is A-Okay," he answered in a flat monotone. "She is veering three degrees maximum, which is acceptable. Wind gusting sixty to seventy-three knots, dropping slowly in velocity. Tide at slack water. Moorings registered as fully secure."

"Eagle Heart?" said Mahle.

The third man was nervous. Mahle noticed the moistness of his forehead, even in the cool of the control room.

"Warning electromatting is negative, except for snowfalls from rigging," Eagle Heart said. "Deck-approach radar negative. Sea and air radar negative. All radar systems working at 30 percent of capacity because of snow."

"Camera check."

The man called Eagle Heart pressed a button on his console, and a picture of a digital clock appeared on his and Mahle's screens. It read 46.24. The seconds were rapidly being subtracted. Eagle Heart pushed a second button, and they watched the camera pan to the left and then zoom slowly in on a row of metal teeth. One tooth at the extreme left of camera was closed on the tooth below.

"Engineering?"

The fourth man in the group was the young man at the Marlborough Hotel. There was nothing nervous or unsure about him. His eyes retained the same fanaticism that had brought him so easily, apparently, along the Hudson that night, and through the blizzard to the middle of the city.

"All systems are functioning properly," he said.

George Mahle spoke to this man with something akin to respect.

"Thank you, Jack," he said.

He stood up at the dais. "It's going well for us," he said. "Perhaps the great blizzard was more providential than we realized."

The tension in the control room eased. Eagle Heart rolled himself a cigarette.

"Will you take over?" said Mahle to Jack. "I'll get Evie to make us some coffee. Charlie, punch anything between the mayor and this man Van Horn into the apartment, will you? Can we dial through to the City Hall budget computer and see just who Van Horn is?"

Mahle stepped down from the dais and walked through a door at the side. The room he stepped into contrasted sharply with the bleak stringency of the control room. This was a room warm and vivid with color. Except for a thick maroon carpet, it could have been a priceless museum of Indian arts and crafts. The walls were rich with tapestries depicting all the tribes of the Americas, extant and extinct. There were lively, intricately worked pictures of the Sioux, Cheyenne, and Apaches, at war and at peace. There were ancient, unknown paintings of the great warrior chiefs, of Cochise, Red Cloud, and Sitting Bull; feathered headdresses, still multicolored and brilliant after a hundred years of aging.

The furniture was entirely in keeping. The chairs were carved from rosewood and covered with cushions died with multihued Navajo patterns. Against one wall, dominating the room, was a huge tepee made from soft deer hide, emblazoned from top to bottom with traditional Indian motifs of air, sun, soil, crops, harvest, sunset, night, and death. It was a room which needed the music of distant wardrums. Instead, two concealed stereo speakers carried the muted piano music of Scarlatti.

A girl sat cross-legged at the tepee's entrance. She closed the heavy book she was reading and rose to her feet in one lithe movement as Mahle came into the room.

She was tall, with long black hair braided into a tight pigtail. Her face, with its strong high cheekbones and mahogony skin, fitted naturally into the room. Her large, firm breasts tightened the suede blouse she wore; her heavy thighs made tight creases across the matching skirt.

She was a magnificent, powerful woman; a sexual animal. Her dark, almost black eyes were ablaze with excitement as she faced Mahle.

"How is it going?"

"Better than we planned," he told her.

"The mayor will be talking to the money people tomorrow. That's what I wanted to hear. He's taking us seriously, right from the start."

"So the bastard should," the girl said venomously. "Those pigs owe us all that money and a damn sight more."

Mahle picked up a copy of that day's *New York Post* and studied a picture of Ben Boyle on the front page under the caption: "New Mayor at Midnight." He looked carefully at the deepset eyes and the handsome features.

It was a picture taken that morning at a press conference at which Boyle had been persuaded to smile. Most pictures of him showed him as a serious man.

The girl said: "I bet the Mick sonofabitch isn't smiling now." Mahle, thoughtful, ignored her.

"Get them some coffee in there."

He was still looking at the photo as the girl padded barefooted across the carpet and into the kitchen.

15

The snow stopped almost suddenly, and the wind eased, but few of the seven million people trapped on the island of Manhattan that night knew about it or cared.

The New Year was in. Now they slept, some restlessly in the absence of traffic and sirens and the emptying of garbage cans, familiar noises to which they had been accustomed. Some slept in the arms of men or women who had been strangers a few hours before. Some slept drunk and misshapen on the carpets of bars and restaurants; some were on subway platforms, sleeping only because of the desperate fatigue which overtook them.

The city had never been so silent, so still, as it was on that chill morning. As the snow stopped and the storm center shifted out to the sullen ocean, a full moon caught the city for a few wondrous minutes when the whole, magnificent spread of the devastation could be seen.

The snow lay fast and thick, engulfing the island. In some places it was melting against the warmth of the subway below; steam geysers played in the streets. Here and there, heavy falls of snow crashed in noiseless explosions from the tall buildings where the snow had been stuck by the force of the wind.

The moon caught it all. It was a sight a few people would remember for the rest of their lives.

Some did care that night.

The police were among them.

In the 97 precinct houses of the city, from the moment the blizzard had hit, men struggled to keep order in their neighborhoods. Immobilized, they watched incident after incident go unattended. They built huge, frightening lists of the missing; except that they guessed that most of the missing would be found when order was restored.

The fire department cared. They watched and fumed with impotence at each fire station as lights flashed on alarm boards. They fought with brutal desperation to move their engines through heavy, unyielding snow. A tenement burned in the Bronx that night; the operator in the firehouse threw his earpiece at the wall rather than listen to the screams he and his colleagues were helpless to stop.

The subway men cared. They knew that theirs was going to be the only system working in the city the following morning, and a strange pride, after so many years of civic abuse, took over. Above ground, they hurled express trains at giant banks of snow, fighting the snow along the lines with shovels and steam hoses.

At City Hall, Ben Boyle cared. He knew just how vulnerable the city was that night.

16

In his first two hours in office it was the waiting that was the worst part for the new mayor. It heightened his own feeling of helplessness. He sat at the long desk and read the terrorists' letter again with great care, searching hopelessly for some kind of loophole.

He knew he had 46 hours, indeed, more. Yet he glanced at his watch over and over again. In his mind he saw the shattered city and heard the cries of the maimed. He had a cruel vision of a funeral procession stretching the length of Fifth Avenue, himself taking the salute on the steps of the Public Library.

He was impatient for people to arrive, to feel life in that gaunt, echoing building.

Sullivan came in, carrying coffee which he placed in front of Ben Boyle. He saw the Mayor gazing directly ahead of him and turned to leave the office.

"Sullivan."

"Yes, Mr. Mayor?"

"Where do you live?"

"In Brooklyn, sir."

"Children?"

"Six, Mr. Mayor. They've all grown up now. The two boys joined the force—one of them is a detective with five commendations—and the others are all married women now."

"Grandchildren?"

"Fifteen, sir,"

Boyle sipped the coffee. Sullivan looked uncomfortable.

"You lost your family, Mr. Mayor?"

"Ten years ago. My wife and two small daughters in front of a delivery truck driven by a drunk." Ben looked up at the officer. "I suppose I would have had grandchildren by now, too. Better than sitting around at City Hall, that would have been. I would have been lying there in bed in Queens, thinking of all the plumbing business this snow would have brought in, and waiting for some guy in City Hall to sweep the goddamn streets."

The intercom buzzed loudly on the desk.

"Ben Boyle."

He listened, and Sullivan watched his face relax into something near a smile. "Thank you," he said.

"Sullivan, tell headquarters that the wind has stopped and we might get a full half hour without any more snow. I need people here. They've got the choppers. I need the deputy mayor badly. I need the traffic commissioner, the civil defense commissioner. And more than anyone else, I need Frank Schenk of the Uniformed Sanitation Men's Union.

"But one thing. Make it very clear that on no account must any of those machines fly over the Hudson south of Chambers Street.

"Tell Schenk the Mayor says to get a move on. I want that lawn out there to look like JFK."

Even as Boyle talked he could hear the shuddering of helicopter rotors. Then he saw the powerful landing lights of a Coast Guard helicopter on the lawn outside his window.

The captain of the port was a small man, almost dumpy, with a strong, jutting jaw and a face with the deep, healthy tan of a man who spends his life with the sea and ships.

He exploded into Boyle's office, showing little outward respect for the mayor except for the removal of a braided cap which he threw casually on a chair.

"You were right, Mr. Mayor," he said. "You were too damned right. There *is* a supertanker there, five hundred thousand tons of her. I saw her in the moonlight—and I'd make a guess that she's fully loaded. Mr. Mayor, what the hell is going on?"

17

The inside of the tepee was hot and airless, the way George Mahle liked it. It was, he told himself, part of a deep-rooted womb fixation. He did not mind in the least. He lay staring at the leather interior of the tent. He was almost relaxed now; it was the first time in several days. The worst part, he reflected, had been the journey through the Narrows.

They had come in fast, much faster than they had planned; but they needed that speed to be able to maintain steerageway against the strong winds, which buffeted even a ship of this size and threatened constantly to ground her on the Jersey shore.

Most of the radio beacons which they had had planted ashore had worked well, but the radar-jamming system they had installed on the forward bridge had distorted signals. At times, George Mahle had found himself the captain of a 507,000-ton supertanker traveling at seven knots through the lower bay and relying entirely on a computer for safe navigation.

The beacons on the Verrazano Bridge had worked well, and they shot the huge span with the ease of a speedboat; but then in the total blackness of the bay they had waited for the steady pulse of the second bank of beacons, a bank on each side of the bay.

Charlie Strong Heart sat quietly, emotionless, at the radio console and twisted the dials in front of him.

"Anything?" Mahle had asked.

"Nothing but static—and our own jamming," Charlie told him.

The bridge of the *Jersey Lily* had suddenly become very quiet at that moment. The only sounds high up there were the soft whining of the turbines far below and the gentle click of the computer.

Mahle had walked over to the chart table and lit the bright lamp that illuminated the chart from below. The ship was being steered automatically by the computer, which took note of every wind and tide change, which assimilated the radio beacons and plotted the programed course from them.

Now without the radio beacons, the ship was in grave danger. There would soon be two major anchorages on either side of them, and Mahle knew that the ship must make a thirty-degree turn toward Manhattan.

Even a minor error by the computer would have brought the tanker at speed into a mass of other shipping.

Mahle had looked at the computer. Its green light glowed confidently. He breathed a deep sigh. This was the first time he had distrusted the machine that had become his god.

The computer clicked softly, sending instructions to the automatic pilot. Mahle and Charlie Strong Heart looked up at the gyrocompass repeater on the bridge's bulkhead. It swung gently, lazily, from the original course and came to a stop; the new course was exactly 30 degrees to starboard. Manhattan lay directly ahead.

From the radio console Charlie Strong Heart had said: "I'm getting Liberty ten tenths—and Pier 14—as clear as mountain water."

Mahle wondered then why he had insisted on a radio beacon on the Statue of Liberty; it was a risk they need not have taken. He put it down to foolish bravado and dismissed it from his mind. He had felt the speed of the ship lessen slightly and heard a change of pitch in the engines beneath him. The computer had decreed that they were nearing their target.

The rest had been relatively easy, he remembered. The tanker was so well automated that the seven men were able to moor her securely under the cover of radar blackout and blizzard while he sat in his cabin and typed a new letter to the mayor. It allowed for the blizzard and gave Boyle an extra 12 hours.

Mahle lay there on the soft mohair blankets, feeling exhilarated at what they had achieved so far. The leather flap of the tepee opened, and the girl slipped through it noiselessly, kneeling on the blanket beside him.

"It's quiet at City Hall," she said. "Ben Boyle, the soft punk, is telling his life story. Did you want coffee?"

He shook his head. His right arm moved toward her. He grasped a leather-thonged bow on the tight suede blouse and pulled it loose. He did not speak as he undid four more bows and watched her large breasts fall loose. Already there was the soft sheen of sweat on them.

The girl held her breasts gently toward him and his two hands reached out towards the large dark nipples and held them between fingertips with a featherlight touch. It brought a distant glaze to the girl's eyes.

She moved closer. "George, baby," she said.

She hitched up the short suede skirt and slid her heavy thighs astride him. She undid his belt and loosened the trouser zip, then guided his erection into her.

At no time had his hands left her nipples; he continued to stroke them with a gentle, soft, practiced rhythm.

"It's been such a long time, baby," she whispered. "Jesus, such a long time."

She pulled open his shirt. Her hands wandered over his brown, hairless chest, her fingers fastening on his nipples. She clamped them fiercely between forefinger and thumb and squeezed in a grip that whitened her knuckles. She began to move her body in a slow, easy motion. The man beneath her remained entirely still as she began to speed her action, clutching and clawing harder at his nipples as she moaned with pleasure.

George Mahle enjoyed pain. As a child he had allowed other children to stub cigarette ends on the soles of his feet and watch with amazement as he took the agony with the detached stoicism of the Indian.

Later, as an athlete, he had endured the pain of marathon running, the sheer ecstasy of the torture of the last few miles in the race, when every muscle, every fiber, every nerve end of his body screamed for release.

The same high tolerance—but it was really enjoyment—had stood him well in the hills of North Vietnam when he, then an air force captain, had made his way through the Vietcong, his leg lashed in a homemade splint and a hole in his head. It had served him well, too, in the NASA training center for astronauts.

18

Soon after one o'clock that first morning the central computer in the police actions room at downtown headquarters had relayed a message to the miniature computer terminals on each of the four launches patrolling the Hudson and East rivers:

REPORTEDLY LARGE VESSEL NOW ANCHORED ILLEGALLY IN MAIN HUDSON SHIPPING CHANNEL. ON NO ACCOUNT REPEAT ON NO ACCOUNT MUST THIS VESSEL BE BOARDED. ALL PATROL VESSELS TO STAY MINIMUM TWO HUNDRED FEET FROM SHIP AND PASS AT HALF REVOLUTIONS.

The operator in the PAR watched the screen in front of him as three of the patrol launches acknowledged receipt of the messages. He turned to the sergeant sitting next to him. "P.32 isn't answering Sprint message on the tanker, sergeant."

The sergeant, tired from a night in which the whole force had been helpless, looked at the screen.

"It's a top-secret priority. We can't send it in plain. Tell them to stay north of Pier 45 until they hear from us. That is, if they know where the hell they are."

Out on the Hudson the crew of police launch 32 were huddled below decks, trying hard to stay warm in the poorly heated cabin. The storm had hit them in the center of the river, and the sheer weight of the freezing snow had crippled their two communication attenas and radar. Now completely blind, they lay at anchor off the Hoboken shoreline and waited for the snow to ease.

It was a long wait.

The sergeant who was in command, a young man newly promoted, had tried several times to climb onto the iced-up deck. Each time he had been driven below by the wind which was at its most strident on that exposed shoreline.

Finally the storm eased. The tide had turned. The sergeant ordered the engines started, and the small launch moved south, downriver toward the Battery.

The sergeant was standing in the cockpit, beating his arms against himself in the bitter cold, when he saw it.

The tanker, almost in midchannel, loomed ahead of them like a cliff, all navigation lights burning, an island where an island couldn't possibly be.

The sergeant said: "Holy God—how the hell did *that* get here?"

On the top floor of the Marlborough Hotel, Pete Eagle Heart, still sweating with tension, watched the electronic sawtooth on his computer screen begin to change patterns. He pushed a series of buttons on the console and stopped at the screen which repeated the *Jersey Lily*'s close-inshore radar. He watched a small blip appear on the outer ring on the screen and then slowly approach the center of the monitor. "Echo bearing zero-zero-five."

The man called Jack punched a second repeater at the main computer. "What's your reading?"

"Small boat, probably a police launch, moving at six knots." Sweat was beginning to form on Pete's face. He saw Jack looking at him.

The man on the dais spoke into a microphone: "We have a red alert. Can you come in?"

The police launch, its two powerful engines almost idling, made a long, slow circle around the massive bulk of the *Jersey Lily* as the sergeant yelled at the gaunt wall of the hull through cupped hands.

"Christ, I wish the megaphone was working," he said.

He filled his lungs with freezing air and bellowed: "Ahoy! What ship is that?"

The three policemen looked up, craning their necks in the darkness. They heard the engines humming quietly within the great mass of metal; otherwise there was silence.

They had turned on the launch's spotlight. Now its heat was beginning to melt the thick covering of snow and ice. Using remote control, they beamed the spot on the tanker's hull and along the rails. They read the name of the ship, painted bold and white, and the sergeant yelled again:

"*Jersey Lily*—ahoy! Call your master!"

He stopped the launch's engines and stood thinking in the cockpit. "No one, but no one, could have brought a great bastard like that up this river," he said. "Not in that snow. Come, let's go and see if it's real."

He started the engines and the small boat moved slowly toward the tanker.

Mahle watched the radar "blip" hover uncertainly off the ship and then move slowly toward it. There was an odd look of fascination on his face.

"He's alongside," said Pete Eagle Heart.

"Companionway warning system positive," said Jack. "Two men are climbing up."

"Activate the rail," said Mahle quietly.

The sergeant was 40 feet up the companionway when the shock hit him. The effect of 30,000 volts passing through his body from his bare hand on the rail to the metal steps of the ladder was instant and horribly final. His body convulsed. His hand stuck firmly to the rail as he began to dance and leap, already dead. Then the body crashed down the companionway, bringing with it the other policeman who had climbed up.

Mahle watched the galvanoscope on the console as it changed slowly from a jagged green line to a normal one.

"Deactivate," he said. He turned to Charlie, the radioman. "Still nothing from City Hall?"

Charlie said: "They're beginning to arrive now."

19

Slowly and noisily, with the shuddering chatter of helicopter engines rattling every snowlined window frame, City Hall was coming to life. A squad of policemen, huddled deep in furlined jackets, had scraped and pressed down paths through the snow to make movement easier from the headquarters building to the mayor's office. Others had stamped a big circle into the lawn outside Ben's office, to indicate a helicopter landing spot. The cafeteria was open; two policewomen were brewing coffee and making sandwiches.

Ben heard it all happening around him and felt relieved. The utter silence of those first few hours and the eerie feeling that only he and Mary, with two cops and a switchboard operator, were left alive in the world was replaced by a new feeling of confidence. He had considered moving the entire operation to the police headquarters building. "But why should I?" he asked Mary. "I'm the mayor. This is City Hall. It wouldn't be right; it certainly wouldn't seem right. Hell, let them come here."

He sat in his office, facing the hastily gathered emergency committee.

George Altmeyer, the first deputy mayor, a small, slight man who peered with difficulty through heavy, pebble-lensed glasses, sat impatiently, drumming fingers on Ben's desk and making nervous coughing noises.

Ben had been reluctant to reappoint Altmeyer. For one thing, he did not like him. He did not like the first deputy's tart, irritating manner, the lack of humor, the determination to go only by the book. Altmeyer was a model civil servant. Yet, for all his fussiness, he was a strong administrator who worked hard for the city.

Next to him sat Jim Crotty, the fifth deputy police commissioner (night), a giant, raw-faced Irishman whose hard cynicism, born of a lifetime of fighting a losing battle against the city's night crime, was reflected in a tight, cruel mouth.

Jane Landesmann, the deputy commissioner for traffic, was a small, attractive, darkhaired woman in her forties. She ordinarily appeared at City Hall in severe, dark clothes and now felt uncomfortable to find herself in the Mayor's office in sweater and slacks. She crossed and uncrossed her legs uneasily.

Ben liked her. She was a Jewish girl from a poor Bronx family who had studied law at night while working as a secretary in City Hall.

Only Michael Canaletto, the commissioner for civil defense, felt at ease in that room. He was a fattening, florid man, completely bald, with a long cigar in his mouth. His heavy jowls shook when he laughed, which was most of the time.

"Sorry to keep you waiting like this," Ben said. "But the first deputy mayor here says, quite rightly, that nobody does anything until all the commissioners have been sworn in. They're bringing the judge over now."

"Should have been done hours ago," said Altmeyer.

"I was here hours ago," said Ben. "And sworn in."

"Still don't know how you did it, Ben," said Canaletto. "I started walking, but got only two blocks before I was stuck in the snow. Stuck so I couldn't move. The wind blew my hat off—God, the cold. If I hadn't got out of that drift, I'd have frozen there. This city would have had a free, fat, deep-frozen Michelangelo on Second Avenue."

Behind the commissioners, sitting at a respectful distance, were the two experts whose presence Ben had demanded.

The deputy chief of detectives, Owen Owen, was hunched in a worn leather jacket. He was a thin man with a thin, weasel-like face and the sallow, unhealthy complexion born of thousands of snatched sandwich meals, of too many hours spent sitting in warm cars on cold corners.

Charles Van Horn, the head of the city's technical services department, did not fit in. He paced Ben's office nervously, examining the pictures, unwanted souvenirs left by the previous mayor.

Ben wasn't sure about Van Horn. He was too damned young for one thing; and he had long, straggly blond hair which Ben did not like and which Commissioner Crotty clearly held in considerable distaste. His plump, boyish face, still red from the wild ride with Mary on the snowmobile, was owlish and abstracted. It was not the sort of face that gave Ben the confidence he needed in a situation like this.

"Do we need to be sworn in to know what a hell of a state this city is in?" said Crotty.

"Go ahead," said Ben.

"Okay, Mr. Mayor. Well, I'll tell you that New York, and Manhattan in particulary, is a disaster area. Central computer indicates the following from the precincts. There are eight thousand missing persons, for a start, although we estimate that most of these will be accounted for safely. They're holed out in hotels and other places where the telephones don't work."

"No wonder the emergency lines were tied up," said Ben.

"We know of 112 certain deaths," said Crotty. "God knows how many more people are buried under the snow. Some died in accidents, some from heart attacks. Asthmatics and others were hit by the cold and that wind.

"The rest—and remember these are only the *known* figures—are deaths from exposure. The homeless, bums, drunks—that kind of thing."

"Jesus Christ," said Ben.

"This is a very imcomplete report, Mr. Mayor. We might get a clearer picture by morning. You see, our cars can't move. There are a lot of people trapped in their own cars all over the city. Some will be frozen to death, that's a fair bet. It always happens. It did in the last three blizzards. And this one came in real fast."

"What else?" said Ben.

"Port Authority says JFK is in chaos. The place is jammed—no food, no power. People are rioting there. And again, how many people were caught in the blizzard on the way out there?"

"What next?" said Ben.

"Fire commissioner reports that there are six bad fires, one in Harlem, two in the Bronx, two in Brooklyn, and a real bad one over in Richmond. They can't move." Crotty took off his reading glasses and looked directly at Ben. "Somehow, Mr. Mayor, we've got to get these streets cleared. What the hell are Traffic and Sanitation doing about it?"

Jane Landesmann had listened coolly. Her eyes were icy as she turned to Crotty. "Traffic," she said, "is waiting to be sworn in. And Traffic is also waiting for the combined police force of this city to find Frank Schenk so that we can persuade him to get the Sanitation men back at work with the snow plows."

"So why wait to be sworn in?" said Canaletto. "Civil Defense is already operating. I've been using the red telephone since eight o'clock last night. Emergency food supplies, readying the hospitals to clear nonessential cases, getting the volunteer transport services ready to move. Hell, clear the streets and we'll be ready to operate at dawn."

Altmeyer was clearly outraged. "By whose authority?" he demanded.

"By my own damned authority!" Canaletto said. "Okay, to determine condition red, I've got to get the agreement of the mayor, you, and three members of the City Council. So Ben was in a subway or trudging through the snow like Admiral Byrd, you were at a farewell party for Joey Macey—where no one would answer the telephone. The only city councillor I could grab onto told me to do whatever the hell I liked."

"Hold it," said Ben. "You've done the right thing, anyway. You'll be a damn sight busier in a few minutes, but you're going in the right direction."

There was a knock at the door. Mary came in, clutching a heavy pile of paper, and walked over to Ben's desk. "It's all copied, Mr. Mayor," she said. "The original and six others." She was not smiling now. Her face was pale and her expression was serious.

"Thanks, Miss Fyfield," said Ben. "Can you find out where the hell that judge is?"

20

It began to snow again. But it was not the icy, savage snow of a few hours ago. This snow came in great wet flakes which fell heavily onto the frozen layers beneath. The police details outside City Hall cursed it with casual obscenity and started to clear the paths all over again.

It fell evenly and heavily all over Manhattan. It fell with the same impartial silence on the supertanker in the Hudson River. In an hour it added another foot to the snow which had blocked the city. Then, capriciously, it stopped, and the city was again silent under a dark brooding sky.

The surrogate court judge was almost helplessly drunk as he administered oaths of office to the deputy mayor, to Jane Landesmann, and to Michael Canaletto (who found it hard to keep a straight face as the judge slurred his words and swayed slowly back and forth through the ceremony). Altmeyer, who had snapped out his oath like a series of military commands, was scowling lividly.

"A drunk judge," he said. "No prayers. We always have prayers. It's all too irregular, Mr. Mayor."

Ben, already furious with the man for spoiling the simple dignity of the ceremony, turned angrily to Altmeyer. He had an irrational desire to take his deputy's thick glasses and grind them under his feet.

"He's a judge, right? He can send some poor guy to

the Tombs for stealing, can't he? Okay, then, we're sworn in. Let's get down to business." He looked at the judge, who was having difficulty focussing his eyes on the three forms of oath and even more difficulty signing them.

"Get this man out of here," Ben said to the two policemen who had escorted the judge. "Take him across the road and lock him in his own tank."

The judge swayed perilously. One of the policemen grabbed him and swung him up over his shoulder in a fireman's carry.

Upside down, the judge looked around at Ben, his eyes glazed, his glasses nearly falling off his face.

"Moshuncoshitutional," he said and hiccuped.

Caneletto laughed. Mary, watching from the door, suppressed a giggle. Altmeyer snorted.

"Sonofabitch," Ben said. "To think that a jerk like that can have so much power."

"Okay, Ben, let's have it," said Canaletto. "What else is on your mind?"

Ben looked at Mary. "Send that Coast Guard captain in now, please. Then close the door and make sure there's a cop outside and that no one comes in until we're finished."

When the door was shut, he sat back in his chair and said: "We've wasted a lot of time. I'm going to hand each of you a copy of a document which was brought here at midnight. I want you to read it carefully. Then I'm going to tell you what has to be done."

As Ben was handing out the papers, the Coast Guard captain arrived. He was flushed, obviously ready for a fight. "Now look, Mr. Mayor, I can't wait any longer—"

"You can wait, and you can sit down, Captain," said Ben. "This concerns you. Gentleman and lady, this is Captain Robert Cusp of the U.S. Coast Guard."

Cusp sat down heavily between Altmeyer and Landesmann.

Ben watched them as they read. Altmeyer studied the document with scrupulous care, as though he were reading a balance sheet. Jane Landesmann put on a pair of tinted glasses and read slowly and deliberately. Canaletto read quickly; Ben watched his mouth forming oaths as he did so. Captain Cusp read with horror in his eyes.

Detective Owen instinctively held the paper by its edges to avoid smearing fingerprints.

Ben was beginning to think he had done the wrong thing.

Van Horn sat down on the carpeted floor and read. He read quickly, almost skimming through the pages; then he stood up languidly and walked around the room. He stood behind Ben's chair. He leaned down and looked at the Mayor's desk top. He crouched behind the Mayor and looked underneath the desk. Then he stood and walked to the door and silently motioned Ben outside.

Ben complied with some reluctance.

"That room," Van Horn told him, "is bugged. I'd lay a dollar against that ransom they want. There's been every opportunity all day. Always is when the city changes mayors. Moving men in, whole crowds of people."

"Where are the bugs?"

"That big paperweight on your desk. It's a French antique. I can't imagine Mayor Macey leaving you that. And there is a small microphone diaphragm on the top of it. There's another behind the picture of Mayor Walker. You can see the aerial penciled in along the side of the frame. That's all you need, Mr. Mayor. A microphone and transmitter can be combined in a matchhead these days. You just draw the aerial."

"Sweet spring violets," Ben said.

"That pair of bugs in there will give off low-powered transmissions that can be picked up by a more powerful receiver which will then amplify the message and send it for miles."

"So what do we do?"

"I'll tell you what I think. Then it's your decision. These people, these Indians. They're clever, make no mistake. It's a hell of a project they've brought off. That tanker. To get it in on a night like this . . . oh boy. Crazy."

"Okay, they're damn clever. I just hope we're more clever. Now what about these bugs?"

"Sorry, Mr. Mayor. Don't forget, I'm a scientist. These Indians will have heard everything said in your office. I suppose nothing's been said so far about how we're going to handle this situation? The psychological condition of these terrorists is an important factor. They've done a big thing, and they've a deadline. They'll be keyed up—in short, in a dangerous emotional state. So one very edgy guy could maybe press the wrong button and blow that ship sky high. I think that it would be a good idea to leave those bugs in your office alone and let them know what you want them to know. That'll keep them at ease. They'll think they have the upper hand. Then they won't be as likely to make mistakes."

"Makes sense," Ben said. "Except that I don't see why they should feel they're on top."

"It's going to take some time to think out an adequate technological answer to this one. But I'm sure we will eventually. We should talk about this and the police work involved in a different place. Doesn't matter where. It could be the ladies' room—as long as *it* isn't bugged. Meanwhile, I'd handle the city business as you would normally. Let the Indians listen."

Ben thought about this for a few moments. "Oh, no, oh hell, no," he said. He smiled at Van Horn; there was a malicious glint in his eyes. "We'll use those bugs—sure. I can talk to them. They've given us a readymade radio station."

"What are you going to tell them?"

"I'm going to tell them that they're not so damn clever as they think they are. That's one thing. I'll think about the rest. Go and find an unbugged room, and we'll come and find you."

Ben opened the office door and found a near dogfight going on inside. The captain of the port, small as he was, was standing on his tiptoes, trying to get on the same level with the big police commissioner. An agitated Altmeyer was trying hard to keep between them.

"Now you listen to me, Chief," Captain Cusp was shouting. "The patrolling of New York harbor is my responsibility, the sole responsibility of the United States Coast Guard. I don't give a monkey's damn about what you say or what anyone else in this room says. That ship out there is our job. Got it?"

Crotty towered over the captain. "As I understand it, Captain, the mayor of this city doesn't agree," he said. "This is a crime. Blackmail. Extortion. Call it what you like; it's a crime. And policemen handle crimes."

Altmeyer succeeded in pushing his way between them. "Gentlemen, please," he said. "Technically, you are both right, so there's no point in fighting."

"Goddamn right," said Ben. "The trouble in this city is that everyone wants to put his nose into any crap that's lying about. Police, Coast Guard, State, Port Authority, Triborough, the Feds—hell, we're going to be fighting them all off in the next few hours. Okay, so what I say is that it is a matter for us in this room. You, Captain, you're part of it. You know the water, you've got ships; anyway, you're the only person in this room who has actually seen this damn tanker.

"And you, Commissioner. You've got the force and the finest police communications system in the world.

"And Van Horn out there. He runs the most complex computer system of any city anywhere. So let's not fight."

The little Coast Guard captain was on his toes again, this time to the mayor.

"Mr. Mayor, the Coast Guard is fully equipped to deal with this situation. We know about ships."

Ben exploded. "Well, you didn't know about *this* ship! And it's *our* city that may get blown up, Captain."

"It's not necessary to shout at me, Mr. Mayor."

"And what the hell do you know about computers, Captain?"

"We have experts."

"Where *are* they? In Baltimore, I bet."

"We can get them here."

"In this snow? Look out of the window, Captain."

The snow was still falling heavily. Cusp's lips trembled, but he stayed silent.

Ben sat on his desk and looked at the others. "Now then," he said. "As I see it, this is a fight between Indian terrorists and the city fathers of New York. With Manhattan as the prize.

"We can't waste time on the kind of interference we'll be getting, so we're going to have to fight people off. We'll have the FBI on our backs, for a start. Then the State of New York, then the President, then the Bureau of Indian Affairs. Before we know it, every damned agency in this country will be in here treading about in the snow and making one hell of a mess. This city is ours. We are going to have to do our own thing, just as we always have. Now here's what I want—here's what I'll answer to the voters for."

They watched him intently. Ben was new, but he had to give them the right kind of confidence because each of them was going to play a vital role in the next two days. Jesus, he thought, it wasn't even two days. He glanced at his watch.

"We've been given a deadline which expires forty-four hours from now," he said. "There's a lot to be done. Mr. Deputy Mayor, I want you to get down to organizing three things. First, I want you to get together with Civil Defense here and start preparing for the evacuation of the city from an area which we can define more clearly when we have studied the potential damage. But assume that it will be every living soul between the Battery and 23rd Street. There are a lot of people, and we can't move them until the streets are cleared.

"Second, I want to start getting the ransom money together. If any of these companies or banks hollers, lean on them—and hard. Third, you will handle liaison in New Jersey throughout.

"Jane, I want you to take over Traffic and Sanitation until the others manage to get in. I want you to get the avenues cleared. That means Fifth, Sixth, Seventh, Eight, Ninth, and Tenth. And Brooklyn Bridge and the West Side Highway."

Canaletto laughed. "You'll lose a hell of a lot of votes on the East Side, Ben."

Ben smiled. "They always think they're a safe area," he said.

Jane Landesmann looked up at Ben. "Just one thing, Mr. Mayor," she said with studied simplicity. "How do you expect me to clear these highways?" She opened her purse and took out a small hairbrush. "With this?"

"Jane," said Ben. There was a weariness in his voice that had not been there before. "Somehow—God knows how—we are going to get the Sanitation men back to work. If only we could get Frank Schenk here."

Owen, who had stood back from the rest until now, said: "Mr. Mayor, we had a line on him when I was leaving headquarters. He was due at a meeting in Queens tonight, but he never made it. He spends a lot of time in massage parlors, especially one on 45th Street."

"Find him," said Ben. "Get him here, and you'll see the fastest piece of union negotiation in the history of this city. Even if it means me beating him to a pulp."

Owen left the room.

"Mickey. Civil Defense. We need you badly. I want every hospital north of 23rd Street cleared for a disaster, a real disaster. You must have plans for this somewhere. I want the hotels up there prepared to take in a lot of refugees. And I mean the Plaza and the Waldorf, a much as any of the others. Get orders ready for requisition of empty office blocks, empty apartments—the whole damn works."

"Mr. Mayor, do you know what you're saying?" Altmeyer's face was a study in horror.

"I sure as hell do, Mr. Deputy. Where else do we put those people? In Central Park?"

Owen came back into the room. "We're turning the massage parlors over, Mr. Mayor."

"Good."

Altmeyer glared up at the mayor, his eyes huge through glasses.

"One hundred and thirty billion dollars in the time allotted to us is quite impossible. In the first place, we can't get these guarantees. The SEC rules won't allow it."

"Then maybe they'll have to change the rules," said Ben. "I want that money available."

"Impossible," said Altmeyer, "Mr. Mayor, do you realize how much this ransom represents? Something like the equivalent of the budget of this city for the next eleven years. The interest on it will put New York into a position of total bankruptcy for the next hundred years, probably forever. All this on top of a twenty-four million-dollar deficit which you have inherited. Impossible, Mr. Mayor. Quite impossible."

"Go out and get the money, anyway," said Ben. "Make sure that these guys will put up the collateral. Hell, they've taken enough in the past."

Ben shifted himself off the desk. "We'll meet again at 10:30 in the morning. My God, it *is* morning.

"Crotty and Owen, I'd like to talk to you in another room. Just one other thing. If we are dealing with

Indians, I'd like to know more about Indians. Have we got any experts we can get here to fill me in on them?"

"Right here in this room," Crotty said. "Owen here. His mother was a full-blooded Sioux."

21

Ben was nervous when he went back into the empty office. He was very much aware of the microphones, loathsome and cockroachlike, in the room. He walked softly, almost cat-like, across the carpet, anxious, for no rational reason, not to make any more sound than necessary. He had spent a lot of time in recording studios all over the city during the preceding weeks. He had talked with ease and fluency and never a hint of microphone fright.

Now, as he paced the floor, his hands deep in his hip pockets, he longed for a script, for technicians, for a red light to flash, for men in shirt-sleeves to cue him.

The past mayors of the city watched him from the walls of his office. Some were sepia-stern; others, the more contemporary, looked on with smiling compassion. La Guardia, his hero, seemed ready to speak to him. John Lindsay looked ready to burst into song. Abe Beame seemed ready to burst into tears. He paced and thought and was very much aware of them as a silent, sardonic audience.

None of you guys ever had this problem, he thought. I wonder what you would do.

He took a deep breath and stood over the paperweight, gripping the edge of the desk tightly. He spoke directly at it.

"This is Ben Boyle," he said. "We found your bugs. You've probably placed a lot more. We'll find them, too. Okay, I'll use them."

The silence around him was devastating. He wanted to shout and swear and rant his feelings into the microphone. He wanted to call them a bunch of crazy pricks, Redskin psychopaths. Instead, he talked very calmly, making an effort to keep the tension out of his voice.

"Now, then," he said. "I'll tell you guys one thing. I like your style; we all like your style.

"It was damn clever of you to get that ship into the Hudson. The whole setup is clever. I've got to hand it to you. But there is one thing you didn't count on. You didn't count on this snow. You thought you were going to blow up property, and that industry and the banks would cough up the cash. Right? You thought I'd evacuate the area. Damn right, I would. But now I can't. And you know why.

"That ship out there is threatening the lives of several million people. To hell with the property. These are people, innocent people, men, women, and a lot of children. A lot of Indians, your own people, are out there with them."

His knuckles were white now as he gripped the desk.

"So I'll make a deal. I could take a big chance in the belief that you are really too humane to do what you plan. I could ignore you, forget your threat. But I'm taking you seriously. You know that I've worked hard for minority causes, including yours. And it hasn't just been words. So I'm sympathetic. Not sympathetic to having a 500,000-ton supertanker held against my head—oh no. You've got a good cause—you've been screwed. For too damn long.

"So, okay. You extend the deadline and give me a chance to get the people out of here. Do that, and I'll put the arm on big business to get you the money. But I can't promise all of it. You're asking a helluva lot."

Ben paused. Jesus, he thought, I shouldn't be so damned cozy.

"Listen," he continued. "I'm not General Custer and you're not Sitting Bull. This is the twentieth century and New York City, not the nineteenth century and Little Bighorn. But if you insist on playing cowboys and Indians, you'd better remember what happened after Little Bighorn. The army went after the Indians as though you were animals. They hunted you down and killed you by the thousands. They did that to avenge a handful of soldiers. So what do you think might happen if you murder maybe half a million people? Will it help the Indian cause? Not a bit. You know that. You know what people are like—you should know better than anybody except maybe the blacks and the Jews. People can be cruel and vindictive, given the slightest opportunity. You'll give them every reason to turn on you, like the savages *they* were in the past. And the frightening thing . . ."

Ben paused, coughing to give himself time to think. "The frightening thing is that I, a liberal who has always fought for minorities—I'll be in the forefront of that fight if you harm so much as one of my citizens. Keep listening on this channel. I'll have more to say."

22

There are three kinds of massage parlors in the city. There is the high-class, well-run, licensed luxury house that prefers to be known as a "health spa." Here, for an annual subscription and a fat fee, the tired executive can be scrubbed, sauna-bathed, stand in tingling cold showers, and have his aching body caressed in a whirlpool bath. Then, for a big tip, he can watch a porno movie and have sex. The second kind is a less expensive version of the first. There is no sauna, no whirlpool, no quadraphonic stereo. There's a brisk body rub and, again for a tip there is sex. The third type—and here the euphemism is stretched to the breaking point—is a room with a bed and a girl in bra and panties equipped with a bottle of Mazola and a few paper towels, who does not ask for a tip but sells sex.

It was in the second kind, on the tenth floor of an apartment block overlooking Central Park, that the police found Frank Schenk.

At 4:30 that morning he waked and oozed his fat bulk around in the bed where a girl lay sleeping, snoring quietly, her body twitching occasionally. He looked at her in the red gleam of a small night light which glowed on the headboard. He put out a fat arm and pulled down the coverlet, exposing her big white breasts which drooped, flaccid and ugly, in the sideways position she slept in.

Schenk felt his body begin to stir. He pushed the weight of it against the girl, cupping her right breast in his left hand, squeezing it until he felt the nipple harden in his palm. Her saw her eyes open and gaze at him, not quite focussed, and then come to angry life. She pulled her body away from him and put her clenched fists in his huge stomach, pushing at him angrily.

"Jesus, not again, fatso," she said. Her voice was harsh, her accent Brooklyn. "Four times since five o'clock yesterday. Four times! Hell, you only came for an hour. Forty dollars. Ten dollars a time. If this bed was metered, I'd be on the streets tomorrow."

"I couldn't move, baby," he said. "It was that goddamn blizzard."

She climbed out of bed and put on a thin, red nylon negligee. He watched her fat body as she crossed to the window and looked out.

"Oh Christ," she said. "Fifth Avenue. Fifth Avenue neck high in lousy, stinking snow. How the hell am I going to get home to Flatbush? I've got kids in Flatbush. And I've gotta see my accountant."

Frank Schenk lay in the warmth of the bed and smiled ironically. So the snow was still there. He'd hoped it would be. Snow and the piles of black garbage bags lying under it. He was meeting the new mayor at twelve o'clock. The snow and the garbage would have to crack the city into paying.

He looked at his fat hands. Hell, he thought, I've got all of New York in these. Seventy-five cents an hour, he reckoned. Not a penny less before his men went back to work. And thirty bucks a day hardship money to clean this mess.

The girl was still talking. "I mean, who's in charge of this mess? Who's supposed to be cleaning these streets? Where are the sanitation men? And how am I going to get rid of you, fatso? I mean, one more time, baby, and you'll have a coronary, and I'll be up on a manslaughter rap."

"Sweetheart," he said, his voice purring. "Come on back. Daddy wants you. You'll get cold there looking at all that nasty snow."

"It'll cost you," she said.

"I thought it was all-inclusive."

"Sure, for an hour. Thirty bucks, cash on the table. And right now."

"Thirty bucks? Make it twenty."

"Thirty."

The negotiator in him was taking over. "Look at it this way, baby. If I wasn't here, you wouldn't be making so much as a dime. All you got to do is lie down on the bed."

"Oh yeah," she said. "And who did all the work the last time?"

She was slipping off the negligee, coldly and reluctantly, when the knock came at the door. It was a loud knock. It got louder as Schenk and the girl looked at the door.

"Who is it?" she said.

"Police." The voice was strong and meaningful.

"What do you want?" she shrilled.

"Open up," the voice said.

She unlatched the guard chain and slid back two bolts. The door opened and two policemen, their furlined jackets and caps streaked with snow, seemed to fill the room. One of them looked over at Schenk, who was sitting up in the bed.

"You Frank Schenk?" he asked.

"What the hell is it to you?"

"Are you Schenk?"

"So I'm Schenk, so what?"

The girl stood back from the three men, bewildered and frightened.

"I gotta license, you know," she said.

"The mayor wants you, Mr. Schenk."

"I'm meeting the mayor at twelve o'clock. Not before."

"The mayor has ordered us to bring you to City Hall, Mr. Schenk."

"Tell the mayor, tell the whole damn City Council, to shove City Hall."

"Write that down, Joey," said the first policeman.

"Spell it A–S–S," Schenk said. He exuded confidence and self-assurance.

"Mr. Schenk, I've got orders to bring you to City Hall."

"Officer, if you so much as lay a finger on me, I promise you, it'll take a year to clean up this city."

The policeman walked to the window and took a two-way radio from his hip.

"Oscar romeo to sprint one," he said.

"Sprint one," said a voice they could all hear.

"We've found Mr. Schenk. He won't come. Say's he'll see the mayor at twelve o'clock."

"Ten two. Hold it."

The girl had watched all of this with growing amazement.

"The mayor?" she said. "Who *is* this guy?" She nodded toward Schenk who sat back on the bed, hands behind his head, looking at the police with disdain.

"This guy is Frankie Schenk, honey," said the first policeman, holding his radio close to his ear. "He runs the Sanitation Men's Union. His men are going to have to get these streets clean just as soon as he gets out of your sack."

"Big Frankie, they call him," said the second policeman. "Big, bad Frankie, the protector of our environment."

The girl looked at the fat man in the bed. "You big shit," she said. "Laying there all night—dirty hog you are, too—when you could have been getting the snow cleared. I gotta get back to Flatbush, you know that. You ain't staying here, baby; I'll tell you that. Not for twenty—or thirty—lousy bucks, you ain't."

The first policeman told her to shut up.

The voice on his radio said: "Bring him in."

Reluctantly, with a contemptuous look at the radio, Frank Schenk pulled back the bedding and lifted his fat and shuddering bulk from the bed.

"Ben Boyle," he said evenly. "Ben-fucking-Boyle sends the cops to fetch me. That snow stays. And that garbage can sit there until summer, until the stink drives the whole damn population of New York out of the city."

Schenk stepped ponderously into his trousers and reached into his pocket. He pulled out some loose change and handed it to the girl.

"Here's your subway fare to Flatbush, honey," he said. "Get there soon, before the subwaymen go out on strike, too."

23

They heard the helicopter heading toward City Hall as it flew low over the computer control room. They watched it on their radar and sound monitors as it moved quickly down the length of Seventh Avenue and disappeared.

It was one more indication of increasing police activity that morning. Within a few hours, certainly from daylight on, the whole city would be turned upside down in the search for the Indians.

George Mahle was confident that they would not be found. He was sitting on the dais, watching the individual systems register automatically on the screens in front of him. He continued to show no more emotion than the computer at his side. But he felt deeply grateful at the way each stage of the operation had worked.

The blizzard had greatly increased their chance of success. Mahle thanked the Great Spirit for the gift of the snow, then dismissed the thought from his mind as banal and superstitious. It was a scientific, intellectual pleasure that glowed in his brain—condition green. He had a good brain, one that could adjust in milliseconds, that could concentrate with amazing clarity on any given subject, that could reason and process swiftly. It was a computer of a brain, one that shifted rapidly, that was capable of urgent and impeccable analysis, of thought uncluttered by wasteful emotion. He had few emotions. A professor of nuclear physics at MIT had once called him a "cold, calculating fish," an insult that gave him pleasure.

He had never really considered the injustices done to American Indians until a few years before the elaborate planning of this operation began. He was an Indian, certainly. His parents had been Cherokees living in Brooklyn where he was born. His father drank too much and had fallen 30 stories on a construction site to his death. His mother had died soon afterward of tuberculosis in a drab charity hospital. He had been raised in an orphanage in which cruelty was abundant. Kindness there was shown so rarely that he came to view it with suspicion, then hostility, and finally with contempt.

The emotional damage had been done by the time George won a place in a school for gifted youngsters. The scholarship which followed this was generous. He became an outstanding student at MIT, but the frigid aloofness he always showed to people caused him to be thoroughly disliked by the staff and students.

Mahle came back from Vietnam, like so many thousands of young men, an unsung hero unwanted by his depressed and disillusioned nation. He found a teaching job in a small public school in Kansas, but he and the school board soon discovered that he could not talk to, let alone teach, the children in his care. He wrote a book based on a computer study thesis he'd done at MIT. The book became an immediate success—with the 300 people in the country who could understand it. The book did find him a job, however, and he became a designer for a computer network. Once again, though, his icy arrogance lost him the position. He worked his way quietly through the lean years that followed, programing computers for a small Madison Avenue advertising agency.

It was there that a computer found him.

In Washington the government had decided to commit the country once again to a space program in which a rejuvenated NASA would build a moon base from which manned flights into the solar system would be launched.

In the search for potential astronauts a computer traced hundreds of Vietnam veteran flyers. George Mahle was among the 50 who presented themselves at the NASA training school. Within weeks he was the star trainee.

It was there that the hurt started; it was the beginning

of the cruel and ravenous fire that burned inside him and caused him to select New York as the target of his vengeance.

It happened one afternoon when he and three other trainees emerged from a moon-walk simulator. As they climbed from the tank and switched off the air-conditioning packs and loosened their helmets, they felt the humidity of the Texas air and began to sweat freely. For the first time in his life, Mahle was feeling almost happy. In the simulators—in all training, indeed—the language of the astronauts was the language of pure technology. Wisecracks and ordinary mortal language were ruled out. Mahle suddenly found a way of communicating with his fellow men that they understood.

As attendants removed the unwieldy spacesuit, Mahle heard his name being called over the intercom.

"Looks like the moon for you, sir," said a technical sergeant.

Mahle smiled, one of the few times in his life that he did. He was walking lightly, filled with confidence, when an orderly ushered him before the three-man medical board. The senior doctor, a marine colonel, wasn't smiling, nor were the other members of the board.

"Mahle, I'm sorry," said the colonel. "I'm afraid you've flunked one essential test. We can't take the risk. Other men's lives are at stake."

"What test, sir?"

"Your vestibulary system is not adequate to cope with the kind of prolonged weightlessness you will be expected to endure."

George sat silent for a moment and felt a fury grow inside him which he tried hard to still. Anger was new to him; he could not cope with it.

"The truth would be better," he said. "I know, and you know, that I am the healthiest man on this station. After two years of flying the most sophisticated fighter aircraft in the world at supersonic speeds, after six months of training and processing in this station without the slightest hint of an earache, I know, gentlemen, that you are not telling the truth."

"It is the truth, Mahle."

"The truth? I know the truth. The truth is that I am an Indian, and the United States of America does not want a Cherokee standing on the moon. They don't want an Indian any more than they want a black man up there."

"Very well, Mahle, you shall have the truth," said the colonel quietly. "Without any doubt, you are physically the finest specimen at this center. It's just unfortunate that you have a psychological problem that makes you unfit. You are, to put it bluntly, mildly schizophrenic."

Mahle considered this. Strangely, his brain processed and analyzed the information and accepted it as correct. His anger decreased.

"It took you a long time to find out," he said coldly. Then he stood up and walked out.

The colonel turned to the crew-cut psychiatrist on his left. "You made your point, Dr. Fleming," he said.

Fleming said: "Most extraordinary case. An IQ like Albert Einstein's, yet the guy's unbalanced. And it took six months to dig out the truth."

Mahle left Houston that evening. On the plane to New York he met Evie Martin. Evie's father had refused an offer from an oil company for the small Midwestern valley ranch he had farmed all his life. Instead, on the basis of two cents for every barrel of oil pumped from his land, he became a multimillionaire.

Evie was the only child of his marriage to a pretty Sioux. Her father lavished money on Evie's education. From Vassar she went to Cornell, then took up a career as a lecturer in political science at Berkeley. It was there that she became a ruthless, totally dedicated revolutionary.

The wave of bombings along the West Coast, always aimed at the bigger corporations and inevitably casual where human life was concerned, brought on the biggest search ever conducted by the FBI and the State of California. Evie was found finally and arrested. Her father hired the best lawyers in the state. His daughter, faced with a life sentence, was jailed for a year as an accessory. Her parents were flying to meet her on her release from prison when their private jet crashed in the Rockies.

Now rich, she turned her attention to the American Indian Movement which, since the siege of Wounded Knee, had been weakened by internal strife and political indecision. There had been a number of similar demonstrations, but, certainly since guns had appeared, the organization had also been well infiltrated by the FBI.

Evie was jailed again, this time for plotting to blow up the Bureau of Indian Affairs in Washington. This time the sentence was two years, with no parole. She emerged from prison a martyr and formed a small, fanatical group which she called the League for Real Justice for the Indian.

As the plane in which she and George Mahle were traveling entered the approach to New York, which took them over a brightly-lit Manhattan, Evie looked out over the city and said: "That's our property down there—Indian property. They stole it from us. Wouldn't it be great to hijack New York?"

She turned to Mahle, who was leaning over her. He saw the lights of a small tanker making its way down the Hudson.

"We could," he said.

That night Evie took George to the secret apartment at the top of the Hotel Marlborough; it was there that he began to outline the plan which they had now put into effect.

It took the former astronaut a year to move through a rapid series of promotions from deckhand with the Eftyvoulos Line to become a qualified first officer. Evie's money was there to help train the other Indians as seamen, although each had been selected by the underground organization for their technical abilities.

Mahle had traveled throughout the United States in search of this handful of highly skilled graduates, each with a grudge against a society that continued to deny good jobs to Indians. Evie, who had an almost hypnotic capacity to imbue men with her cause, did the rest.

Their task was made easier when the tanker companies signed an agreement with the unions that allowed for minimal crews to operate the supertankers. Ships almost as big as the *Jersey Lily* had become so automated and computerized that eight men were all that was required to maneuver the giants in and out of port; most of the work was done from a control room on the ship's bridge. But the shipping companies and oil combines had not foreseen the danger.

The computers had been bought in the name of a Topeka market research company which Evie registered. The same company purchased the infrared intruder systems, the field surveillance radar and the geophone monitors from war surplus supplies. This equipment, together with the electromatting, was stored in a vast pump room in the *Jersey Lily*.

It had taken them four days to make the ship ready during that voyage from Houston. Others in the group had set up the elaborate system of radio beacons that had guided the ship through the Narrows and into the Hudson. The beacon placed inside the torch of the Statue of Liberty proved to be the most difficult. A guard who had surprised the young Navaho was now lying inside the torch, his throat slit.

Four deaths so far, thought Mahle, and there may well be many more.

The systems he and the others had worked for so long to perfect had functioned with a smoothness which he, the technician, had anticipated, even in this blizzard, which had been allowed for in their planning but only as a remote possibility. Despite the snow each component of a highly complex set of instruments was operating efficiently, competently, well within the limits he had set.

They had done the one thing no one had thought possible: they had brought this ship, 507,000 tons of metal, to the very heart of the most vulnerable city in the world. It was an operation which made anything else achieved by the Indian movement look like a mosquito bite on a white man's arm.

The systems were silent now. The light under the computer glowed green. It had been that way since the two policemen had tried to board the tanker and been wiped out of existence by that intricate machine at Mahle's side.

In the cool, rarified atmosphere of that room, the policemen's deaths had meant no more than a sudden surge of a needle on a dial, the straightening of a jagged line on a screen. The systems had done their work. Mahle was neither elated nor saddened by the deaths, which were no more than a conclusion to the closing of a circuit by a piece of electronic machinery that had been programed to kill.

He was a technologist. If there was any question in his mind, it was to wonder whether this computer, which could now, at the simple movement of a piece of magnetic recording tape against a minute light, take a million lives, whether this computer was an extension of him or whether he, by reason of his own total detachment, was a slave to it. It didn't matter which, he decided.

He could have pressed an override on the console; he could have cut the power that surged through the intruding policemen so that it stunned rather than killed them. But it was important to prove conclusively to the mayor that they were business-like and purposeful.

The computer had made this decision; it had been fed every possible scrap of data; it must react by itself. In a few hours it would be in a position to make the final decision. Twelve punch cards, carefully coded, would be fed into the master computer which, in turn, would relay instructions to the slave computer in the tanker's control room. Mahle and the others would evacuate the hotel six hours before the tanker was due to explode. From that moment on, the primers would continue to click into position. The sensors and monitors in the ship would continue to guard against what by then must be a powerful onslaught by the city and probably the entire federal government.

Only one thing would stop the process at that point, and that was a coded signal to the computer that $130 billion had been paid into the United Nations account.

24

"I guess this is a secure room," said Van Horn, ushering Ben into a committee room lined with maps of the city's neighborhoods and well filled with scale models of the city's buildings. Ben was followed by Commissioner Crotty, Captain Cusp, and Detective Owen.

"It's been locked for the past three days and the janitor has the only other key," the young man continued.

They sat at a long conference table, Ben at the head. The Coast Guard captain, still clearly discontented and edgy, sat some way down the table.

Ben smiled at him. "Now look, Captain," he said. "I know how you feel. It's a ship, and you handle ships. I'm sure that you are the best ship-handler in the business. I'm a plumber, if you remember anything about my campaign, and I'd be just as mad if some damn sailor came along and tried to mend a ballcock in my apartment. But we are talking about a whole city. Now let's listen to Van Horn here, who was the only one among us to have the sense to think of the bugging."

"Okay, Mr. Van Horn—Charles, isn't it?" Ben said. "You're the scientist. What do you make of the letter?"

"I'm sorry to repeat it, Mr. Mayor," said Van Horn. "But from what I've seen, those guys know what they're doing."

Commissioner Crotty was not the sort who took easily

to long-haired young scientists. His face showed that. It was the face of a New York cop, one who had grown hard and unyielding in his years on the force. "Okay, we know what they're doing," he said. "But how are they doing it?"

"I've only got the document to work on, like everybody else," said Van Horn. "But, as a first guess, I'd say, looking at the kind of hardware they're using, that they are feeding that computer in the ship with instructions from a shore base, almost certainly using another computer to do it. They could possibly be using a land line. They're probably using radio. Possibly a microwave circuit."

Captain Cusp, who shared Crotty's views on young men with long hair, said: "Computers talking to computers by radio? You're kidding, son."

Crotty said: "Why not? Each of our prowl cars has a computer terminal in it. They work by radio."

Ben raised his voice to intervene. "Hold it," he said. "Let Mr. Van Horn finish."

"Well, as I said, Mr. Mayor, this is the only theory I can offer at this point. If I were in their position, it's the way I'd do it."

Crotty made a noise in his throat.

"What can we do about those computers?" Ben asked. "Can't we bend the signal or something?"

"Sure, you can bend a microwave," said Van Horn. "But would that do any good? The slave computer—that's the one on the ship—is almost certainly programed to go through with the routine, right up to the explosion. The other one must be governing it. If they get the money, the master computer will tell the other one to abort the explosion.

"What we have to do is find the master computer and, if we can decipher the coding system they use, screw their system up. It can be done—if we can find the computer." He looked questioningly at Crotty.

"So where are we likely to find it?" asked the commissioner heavily.

"If they're using microwave, it will be somewhere in the direct line of sight with the ship," said Van Horn. "As soon as we get a chance to look at this tanker, we will probably see a bowl-like aerial high up somewhere. The direction that bowl faces is the direction to start looking in."

"What sort of distance?" asked Detective Owen.

"Anything from five hundred yards to three or four miles, depending on the strength of signal. They need to be sure of what they're doing. They won't be too far away. Either here in Manhattan or in Jersey."

Ben swallowed hard. "You know," he said, "I keep forgetting New Jersey. Should I tell them?"

Detective Owen, his voice heavy with cynicism, said quietly: "After the event, Mr. Mayor."

For the first time that night there was laughter.

Ben turned to Van Horn. "Just one other thing, Charlie. Suppose this damn tanker does go up. How much damage would it do?"

Van Horn pulled a piece of paper from his coat pocket. "I did a quick calculation just now. With that amount of highly volatile fuel on board, and given the mixture, which they seem to have right, with oxygen, the detonation would be somewhere in the neighborhood of a fair-sized atomic explosion."

"How much?"

"The equivalent of the explosion at Hiroshima," said Van Horn, his voice bland.

The others sat silent.

"That isn't to say that the damage would be quite the same," Van Horn went on. "The explosion in Hiroshima was detonated in midair. Here the effect might be considerably less."

"How much less?" Ben asked.

"Well, for one thing, a great deal of the blast would go upward and expend itself in the atmosphere," said Van Horn, still in the same even tone. "But it would create a vacuum of several billion cubic yards which would, in turn, create a sudden inrush of air representing a wind of about six hundred miles an hour."

"And that would mean?"

"The World Trade Center would come down and quite a lot of high-rise buildings would certainly either come down with it or be badly damaged."

"How much of the city?"

"Hard to say, Mr. Mayor. But I'd guess there would be very few windows left south of 42nd Street, although most of the real damage would be in this part of town."

"People?"

"There was a similar explosion in Halifax harbor in Nova Scotia in 1917 that killed 2,000. But the size of that one was nothing compared with this."

"How many people died in Hiroshima?"

"If I remember rightly, the figure was 91,223," Van Horn said very quietly.

"You've got a good memory for figures," said Crotty.

"For that one I have," said Van Horn. "There is another factor which might make any explosion much more devastating than the one at Hiroshima," he said. "This tanker carries liquified natural gas. There are few more dangerous cargoes. It is stored in refrigerated tanks and will vaporize quickly into a low-lying cloud that will burn more easily than gasoline. A cigarette end would ignite it. I'd assume these terrorists have designed their explosion to allow for just such a cloud to form before detonation.

"This, combined with the blast, would create an explosion and fireball that would make Hiroshima look tame, indeed. Mind you, Mr. Mayor, tankers carrying LNG—which is what the trade calls it—have been plying the harbor and the East and Hudson rivers for years without incident."

They looked at Ben, who was staring along the length of the table. His face was impassive.

"That's a hell of a lot of humanity," he said finally. "I'm sure we're not going to let it happen here. Commissioner Crotty, will you and Detective Owen find out from Mr. Van Horn just what technical equipment is necessary and then go out and find this master computer. It's imperative not to tell the public anything yet, so I'm pledging all of you to secrecy.

"Captain Cusp, I respect your views, but I'm afraid that this is a problem for the city of New York. We must do it our way. We'll need a lot of help from you. I hope I can count on your cooperation."

"I'll have to talk to the Coast Guard in Washington, Mr. Mayor."

Ben's voice was weary, but none of them missed the fury in it.

"Now listen, Captain," he said. "It's five in the morning. I have 43 hours in which to save this city. In about four hours I'll be talking to the President of the United States about the other demands these people are making. I shall tell him that I am not receiving cooperation from a certain Coast Guard captain. For the last time, Captain, are you going to cooperate with us?"

The captain looked down at the table and said: "Okay, Mr. Mayor. After all, I do live in the Battery."

They were getting up from the table when a gentle bleep sounded from Crotty's breast pocket. He looked around and found a telephone.

"Crotty," he said. He listened. "Right," he said quietly and put the phone down. He turned to the others. "Two of our men didn't get the word and tried to board that tanker. They're both dead."

25

"Tough about those two cops," said Ben to Crotty. They were walking through the City Hall corridors, Ben striding quickly, the big commissioner trying hard to keep up with him. "One thing for sure. We aren't going to be able to keep this from the public very long. My worry is panic, and as long as those streets are clogged with snow, sure as hell, that's what will happen."

"The message came through on a restricted circuit," said Crotty.

"Cops have wives and kids and friends," Ben said. "It'll have to leak out. This is no city for secrets, you know that." He bounded down one of the simple stone staircases that led to the lobby.

The main door opened as Ben was passing. A policeman held it wide, and Frank Schenk was ushered in with perhaps exaggerated politeness. Schenk was smiling and friendly now. He walked up to Ben immediately, a fat hand outstretched towards the mayor.

"Hi, Ben," he said. "What a night."

Ben had not expected this. He knew Schenk and had seen the famous tempers, the walkouts, the tantrums that had made this man the most powerful union leader in the city. He shook the hand and felt like counting his fingers.

"How are you, Frank?"

"Fine, fine, fine. Pity you had to arrest me to get me down here."

"You weren't arrested."

"Those cops wouldn't put the handcuffs on me. But I was arrested."

"I want to talk to you. So I sent transportation."

"Forget it. I won't."

"Let's talk. There's a room over there."

While they were standing in the lobby Ben had noticed two reporters by the door of the City Hall pressroom. They were coming toward him and Schenk.

He grabbed Schenk and took him by the arm, walking him firmly into the office.

"Frank," he said. "Don't say a word until I've finished. This city is at a total standstill. You've got the power to get it moving. Okay, so your men want a raise. I'm not in a position to raise any wages now. This is a new administration; the people of New York are taxed to hell, anyway. We agreed to talk at noon. I want to talk to you now."

Schenk smiled, not a pleasant one. There was an element of triumph in it that Ben didn't like.

"Seventy-five cents an hour, Ben, and you can have every Sanitation man on the streets by eleven o'clock."

Ben looked at him coldly. "Fuck your seventy-five cents, Frank. You've already broken one contract, and now you want to blackmail the city."

He saw the famous temper begin to rise in Schenk's face. The union man started to rise ponderously from his seat.

"Now hear me out," said Ben. "You know damned well that the settlement will have to be with the Office of Labor Relations, not with me. I've got a reason, a good reason, which you'll know about soon enough, a damn good reason for getting your men on the streets and getting this snow cleared."

"Of course you have," said Schenk. "You promised the voters you'd get the city moving. Christ, you've only just been elected. What's the hurry?"

"It has nothing to do with politics, Frank. Nor my popularity, nor people getting to work. It's important and it's crucial and I need your help as a citizen of this city and not as a union leader."

Schenk recognized the sincerity in Ben's eyes and swallowed his anger. "Tell me."

"I can't."

"No dice."

"On my own authority, I'll arrange for triple overtime for the next two days."

"No way."

"The streets stay like they are?"

"Damn right they do. And the stinking garbage."

"Frank, I can help a lot in those negotiations."

"So help. But don't make the mistake, don't ever make it again, of arresting Frank Schenk. It's going to cost you dear, Mr. Mayor. And screw the taxpayers of New York."

Schenk finally struggled to his feet. He stood over the still-seated mayor, and his great body trembled with anger.

"No. No way, Mr. Mayor," he said. "No fucking way. Bad mistake you made. I've got fourteen thousand members to look after, remember. Nobody likes the garbage man, nobody talks to the garbage man, everybody complains about the garbage man. Those poor, stinking, filthy sonsabitches have the worst job in the city. Nobody loves them until the shit piles up and the snow starts falling and white-collar workers can't get to their carpeted offices. Then they love them. Jesus, they even start arresting their own union men."

Schenk turned away from Ben and began to waddle towards the door.

"Frank."

Ben's voice was very quiet and conciliatory.

"Your wife, Gertrude. She was a great friend of my wife, did you know? They went to school together."

Schenk stopped but did not turn.

"So?" he said.

"Until I got into this particular rat race, Frank, I used to see a lot of Gertrude—you know, at the A & P and the delicatessen. Come to think of it, I seem to remember plumbing a washing machine in your place. Nice place, Frank."

Schenk turned and faced Ben.

"So?" The jowls of his face were trembling.

"So if we're going to play it dirty, Frank, if we're going to play at blackmail, I'm going to play it real dirty. I know Gertrude well enough to know that if she ever found out where you were found this morning, your Gertrude would kick you into a great, blubbery, messy pulp. Right?"

"Hey, now Ben. Come on. There are certain rules in this game."

"Rules, my ass. She's a big girl, Frank."

He watched with some fascination the collapse of the fat man.

"What's the deal?" asked Schenk.

"Double overtime for the next 48 hours for all your men as long as they're on the streets before eleven. The city's radio service is at your disposal. Pretape your instructions to your men and issue a statement to the press outside."

"You said triple."

"She's a big girl, Frank."

"And the pay deal?"

"The city undertakes to listen sympathetically to every request made by the Sanitation Workers Union, especially in view of the fine public spirit shown during this emergency."

Schenk smiled again, a defeated smile.

"You've got a deal," he said. "You bastard."

Puffing heavily, Schenk walked out of the office. Ben sat still in his chair for a minute and tried to visualize 90,000 dead people. He looked at his watch. It was six o'clock.

Outside in the lobby, Frank Schenk, beaming now and fully confident, was talking into two microphones simultaneously.

"I just felt that it was a matter of public importance that we should be prepared to suspend negotiations for a couple of days and get this city cleaned up," he said. "So I call on all Sanitation men to report to their depots as soon as possible so that we can all get to work."

A reporter asked him: "Was this on your own initiative, Mr. Schenk?"

"Of course, Pete," said Schenk. "I just felt that this

was a time for every citizen to play his part. The Uniformed Sanitation Workers are the very lifeblood of this city at such a time. I'm sure the city will recognize that public spirit in the proper way at the proper time."

26

The hour before the city became gray with the dull even light of a dawn that struggled against the brooding cloud mass was the darkest hour of that night. The winds, which had played such havoc with Manhattan through the hours of darkness, had dropped to nothing now. No snow was falling, but the stone-black sky was charged with the menace of more.

For Ben it was a time of intense physical tiredness. Every joint in his body ached; his eyes were red and felt as though they had been pricked with red-hot needles. It was a reaction to that walk to City Hall and, more so even, to the hours of sitting in smoke-filled rooms.

It was also a time—almost the only time—when his tired mind swam anxiously through a sea of self-doubt. Had he done the right thing? Of course he hadn't. He should have been on the line to the White House within minutes of reading that letter. Just hand the whole damn thing over to the President and go to bed.

The President had the National Security Council, the best brains in the nation to handle this one. He had the whole army and navy and could whistle up nuclear subs and the whole air force.

And what have I got? Ben thought. A long-haired Dutchman who knows computers and a handful of cops who can't even move on the streets of their own city.

He walked over to the window facing the Hudson River and stared into the blackness outside.

He had brought his family to this part of town one Labor Day when the city was bathed in sunlight and there were few automobiles to be seen, and the air was clear and smelled good, like the air in the mountains upstate.

His wife had packed a huge picnic. They sat there on the grass watching the girls run wild. They had eaten chicken and drunk cold white wine and Ben had waked from a deep sleep on the grass to find that his daughters had covered his face with flowers. He remembered the way his wife had laughed.

Then they had walked around City Hall and the municipal buildings and Ben had tried to explain the workings of a system to two small girls who wanted nothing more than candy and Coke. Then, as the sun started to drop over New Jersey, they had sat among the graces of Pilgrim Fathers and the country's heroes in Trinity churchyard, and listened to a group of black soul singers, and he had held his wife's hand.

He wiped the memory from his mind. It was replaced by a vision of 10,000 children lying dead out there, of destruction and carnage, of 50-story buildings leaning into the wind and crashing against each other, of the screams and shouts of the people who lived out there. He made the sign of the Cross and turned from the window.

Mary was waiting for him as he came out of his office. He marveled at her freshness and vitality.

"Come on," she said. "You're bushed." She held out her hand. "Come into Mayor Macey's massagerie, and I'll rub your back. You must be dead tired."

Ben would have argued. He would certainly have looked around to see who was looking. But he took her hand and followed her into the suite unprotesting.

"A shower and shave," he said. "That's all I need to wake me up."

"I'll run the shower," she said.

A few minutes later he lay on the bed and let Mary knead the muscles on his neck and shoulders, which felt as though they had hardened into knots of heavy wire.

"You were not supposed to read those copies," he said.

"And needless to say, I did," she said.

"It's a damn mess."

"You're right, Ben Boyle," she said. "Right in your lap."

"All that campaigning, would you believe it? Just to get to City Hall. Oh boy, who'd have City Hall on a night like this?"

"You would." There was a force in her voice. "You would because you know it's a situation custom-built for you. That last mayor, Macey, he wouldn't have been here. He'd have been directing operations from Florida."

The bedside telephone rang.

"He even had a sexy telephone in here," said Ben, picking it up. "Boyle."

"Altmeyer, Mr. Mayor. The press wants a statement for the early bulletins. Can you come out?"

Ben yawned. "Be right with you," he said.

"Mr. Mayor, how come the city wasn't prepared for the worst blizzard of the century?"

"You'd better ask the last mayor."

"What are you doing about it?"

"The cleaning operation starts as soon as the Uniformed Sanitation men are ready to go," said Ben.

"When will that be?"

"This morning. Remember that the problem is one of getting them to work through this snow. We're using helicopters, every possible means, to get them to the trucks."

"I take it there will be an inquiry about this?"

"There'll be an inquiry."

"Mr. Mayor, were you at City Hall when the blizzard started?"

"No."

"How did you get in?"

"I walked from the subway."

"What advice have you for the people of New York?"

"This is important. I want the people of New York to stay indoors, keep warm, and wait for further announcements from the city. Everything is being done to get the streets cleared of snow. People will just have to take their turn."

"Are you declaring a state of emergency?"

"Let's face it, there isn't much point in declaring anything. It *is* an emergency, a real emergency; it may turn into a disaster. I hope not. But people have died in this blizzard already. I want every assistance given to the emergency services. That's why no one should go into the streets, especially in automobiles, until they've been cleaned up."

"Thank you, Mr. Mayor."

Mary was asleep on a settee, fully clothed, when he got back to the suite. He leaned down and put his arms under her and carried her to the bed. She woke up and looked at him and put one hand behind his head and pulled his mouth to hers. He felt the other hand unbuttoning the sheer nylon blouse with an urgency he hadn't known in her before.

He felt her mouth open under his. Suddenly she was arched in the bed, unfastening her skirt and sliding it with her pants and brassiere over her body and kicking them away from her in a series of jerky, frantic movements.

With that same urgency she grabbed at his bathrobe and tugged it from his body and then thrust the softness of her body against his. She felt the hardness of his penis against her and grasped it hard in her hand and pulled it toward her, pulling the weight of his body over her with her other arm and opening her legs wide so that they gripped hard around him. He sank himself deep into her.

While his body pounded into her he forgot everything, and knew only a deep and abiding love for this slender girl who had come into his life and who was threatening to go out of his life, who was making strange animal noises now as she bucked and fought under him.

But as his love exploded into her, in a fierce, long, devastating orgasm, the visions of the dead and the shattered city flashed again through his mind. As the girl cried out beneath him, her legs threatening to crush him, he smelled the flowers and the grass and heard his children laughing and saw his wife's face. She was smiling.

27

On the Jersey Palisades, a very old man stood in the thick snow and looked over the island of Manhattan. Age had carved deep grooves in his mahogany face. A confused mass of wrinkles had pulled the brown eyes deep into their sockets, so that only the irises could be seen glowing fiercely. He wore a heavy, quilted coat of synthetic fiber, zipped tight around his neck, and long buckskin trousers tucked into furlined boots. Two black pigtails extended from his fur cap which was butttoned under his gnarled chin. He stood very still, seemingly oblivious to the cold.

His name was Peter Brown Bear. He was 100 years old. Standing there above the Hudson River, he remembered another blizzard so many years before, the blizzard that had engulfed the dead at the first battle of Wounded Knee. He had been a young boy then, too young to join the handful of braves who had defied the federal cavalry. He had been in the wilderness for four days and four nights, to starve and thirst himself in preparation for manhood and to secure a sacred vision, which was the custom of the Sioux tribe.

From a hillock which overlooked the encampment, he had seen the cavalry avenge the general they called "the man with long hair"—shooting first the braves with Hotchkiss guns, and then pursuing the women and children across the plains, killing all of them with pistols and sabres, sparing none. He had seen the soldiers re-form into lines; they were laughing and proud of their victory.

Peter Brown Bear had this vision. He had seen it through the clarity born of hunger and the agony of grief —there alone, a small boy beating his breast and crying his anger—he had seen a day when the Indian people would wreak a terrible vengeance on the white man.

He had often talked about his vision, but his people scoffed at him. The wild girl, Evie, had not scoffed.

Stand on the Palisades on New Year's Day, she had told him: "Stand with patience and pride in your people, and you will see that vengeance, old man."

And becuase he had lived for so long and had waited so long for that vision, he waited now. His breath steaming from his mouth and nose, he watched the city of New York.

The thickness of the fur cap around his ears, combined with his deafness, hid the sound behind him of snowplows and machines clearing rudimentary lanes to the clifftops, hiding, too, the sound of excited voices of young men who were clearing the lanes. There on the Palisades the greatest gathering ever in this century of Indian tribes, a gathering organized behind an impenetrable screen of secrecy by the Indian activist movements, was about to take place.

But only a few of the most militant and dedicated young knew that it was a gathering that could end in the revenge which so many of these people had promised themselves over the centuries.

28

"Right, ladies and gentlemen," said Mary. "I'll read the checklist just to make sure you are all present and correct."

She was sitting at a telephone in Ben's anteroom. It was 8:00 A.M. Ben sat on a nearby desk, eating a bacon sandwich and drinking coffee from a paper cup.

"NBC, Mr. Martinez?"

"I'm here."

"ABC, Mr. Platt?"

"Present."

"CBS, Mr. Buckhardt."

"All bright and bushy-tailed, Miss Fyfield. Good morning, George. Hi, Dennis."

Mary scolded him lightly. "Please don't waste time; we have a lot of people to talk to. Channel 13, Miss Grosschmidt?"

"Here."

Mary finished reading the list of television channels, cable TV channels, and radio stations.

"Thank you, ladies and gentlemen. I have the Mayor of New York here at City Hall. Will you please listen to what he has to say without interruption. Then would you please announce your name and station first and try not to talk over other people. Sorry to be so bossy at this time of the morning, but there are a lot of things to talk about."

Ben walked into his office where a microphone and two loudspeakers had been placed. A tape recorder on a side table was turned on.

"Good morning," he said. "Sorry about this method of having to talk to you. It would have been good to have had you at City Hall for the inauguration, but that will have to wait. I don't have to tell you about the effect of this blizzard, except that it's more serious than anyone could have imagined. Several people have died, and most of the police force has been crippled by the snow.

"That's only part of it. If you can bear with me, I'll tell you the rest."

Ben outlined the whole story of the tanker, keeping back nothing except the amount of the ransom. Unemotionally, he quoted Van Horn's assessment of the potential damage.

One of the 14 voices listening said "Jesus" very softly.

"There is one other party to this conference call," Ben said. "The terrorists. They have this office bugged, and I'm keeping it that way. They can hear what you say. They've got their fingers on the button. So it would be a good idea to keep this conversation cool."

Ben turned to the picture of Jimmy Walker. "I hope you're listening, Crazy Horse," he said.

"Okay, gentlemen, this is what the city is doing. The good news is that the Sanitation men are back at work, and I'd be glad if you would say a few kind words about them in your bulletins. Hell, you can even give some violets to Frank Schenk. We have been assessing the snow situation since dawn, and we estimate that the average depth in the streets is something like four to five feet, drifting to 15 to 20 feet. You see the problem.

"The top layer of snow is frozen hard. Clearing is going to be difficult. In the first place, we have to get the snowplows to the right places, and they're going to have trouble moving. We're spraying now with salt. We may use more drastic methods later."

Ben paused for a moment and looked at a map of southern Manhattan on the desk in front of him.

"Now this is desperately important. I know it's a hell of a story and that I'm asking a lot of you. But we've got to try to stop panic. I've got forty hours to evacuate the whole of southern and southwest Manhattan. That isn't long. It means we have to clear the West Side Highway, Hudson Street, Broadway, Sixth and Seventh avenues. Then the streets, so that we can get people out. We don't want them to know—not yet. First we take the people whose lives are definitely in danger. There are a lot of them in this part of New York. Then those whose lives *may* be in danger. Then the rest if need be. Okay?"

The deep, familiar voice of George Martinez, program director of NBC, once the best-known face on American television, came on the line.

"What you're saying, Mr. Mayor, is that you want radio silence on this supertanker?"

"Right, George."

"You're asking an awful lot."

"I know. But if it gets out now, there could be the worst panic this city has ever seen. It won't just be southern Manhattan. It'll be the whole city trying to get out at the same time. You see?"

"He's right, George," said Mike Buckhardt of CBS, a cheerful man who had started as a radio comedian. "Anyway, if the whole city went scuttling to Connecticut, think of the ratings."

Nobody laughed.

Ben said, forcefully now: "Can I rely on you not to mention this threat to the city, certainly for the next few hours?"

Martinez said: "The mayor is right. Is there any point in discussing this further, gentlemen?"

"You're damn right, there is," said a new voice. "This is Pedro Gomez of Station WXYR. Why the hell are we being dictated to by the networks? Who lives in that part of this city? My people do. They're in danger, right? They should know *now*. Where is all this free speech, civil rights, all this freedom you talk about? To hell with the big networks."

The loudspeakers on Ben's desk burst into a cacophony of argument. He listened for a few moments and smiled. Then he took a deep breath and yelled into the microphone: "Hold it!"

The voices stopped.

"Thank you. Mr Gomez, I sympathize. I'll save time. Will you go along with a vote?"

"I should bother, Mr. Mayor," said Gomez. "It's a city

license, anyway. You can take us off the air. I'll go along, but you'd better give me a big police guard afterward."

"Thank you," said Ben. "Are we agreed, ladies and gentlemen?"

No one spoke.

Ben said: "Thank you."

"What about these video tapes?" said Mike Buckhardt. "I mean, what are they—replays of the Lone Ranger?"

"Are the Indians still listening in?" asked Orville Platt of ABC.

"Yes," said Ben. "I hope so."

"That's a very different matter," said Platt, whose voice was slow, deliberate, New England. "We're prepared to cooperate with the city to save lives, but we don't like being told by some outside source what we're going to put on our channel."

"You're damn right," said Martinez. "But, like Boyle says, they've got the button."

"Maybe it's good entertainment," said Buckhardt. "Let's not make a decision now. Why not look at the tapes and see what we think then?"

"This is Boyle," said Ben. "I'm asking you to play the tapes. There's too much at stake to argue about it."

"I'm not committing ABC until someone has heard them," Platt said.

"As long as they're serious and not inflammatory, NBC will cooperate," said Martinez.

"Count me in on that," said Buckhardt. "That is, if anyone can make it in to get the damn tapes on the air."

Ben relaxed back in his chair. "I'm very grateful," he said. "I don't want to ask for questions because there are too many things happening here at City Hall and too few people to do them."

Martinez cut in. "I've got a question," he said. "What about the rest of the country—hell, the world?"

Ben answered: "The only thing that worries me is the fact that we will have half the roads leading out of the city blocked by rubbernecks. How much can you black this out to stop people from driving in to watch the bang?"

"Whew," said Buckhardt. "Well, suppose we edit transmissions in Jersey, Connecticut, and the whole of New York State? How would that be?"

"If you can do it, fine," said Ben.

"That means that a lot of people are going to hear it on shortwave transmissions," said another.

"Not enough to worry about," said Ben. "People aren't going to move a lot today, not for a while, anyway."

"I've got a question, Mr. Mayor." It was a woman's voice, languid and drawling. "Patsy Grosschmidt of Channel 13. What about this damn clock that keeps coming up on our transmission?"

"Keep it," said Ben.

"Your audience will think it's all part of 'Sesame Street'," said Buckhardt.

"Crazy Horse!"

Evie Martin spat the words out.

"Sonofabitch mayor. He's taking liberties, George. Watch him."

Mahle padded barefoot across the heavy Indian carpet. Using a remote control switch, he turned on a large-screen television set.

"He's just trying to rile me," he said. "Boyle is no fool. He's using that bug well. What I want to know is, what is this Van Horn doing?"

With a button, Mahle went around the clock of New York's television channels.

A blond girl was saying: "That's the only advice we are getting from City Hall. Stay home and wait for the roads to be cleared. Have you ever tried Hormonex toilet soap? It's the one natural soap supplemented by hormones. . . ."

Mahle pushed the button. ". . . and this certainly means the Knicks won't be playing tonight or for some nights to come. It's bound to hurt their chances. . . ." ". . . Macy's great New Year's Day sale has had to be postponed, but you can expect ever better bargain value. . . ." "If the whole goldarned Apache tribe is on the warpath, General, what we going to do?"

The next channel was showing cartoons. The all-Spanish channel had soccer.

On Channel 13 two black men and two white men were talking earnestly about the influence of African primitivism on modern sculpture. Mahle glanced at his watch. "They're too damned slow," he said. He padded into the computer room and took his place on the dais.

"We advance the program by one hour," he said. "Paleface talk too much, does nothing."

"Now hook me into the City Hall computer," he said. "Redskin parley with paleface chief."

"Your next conference call is ready," said Mary briskly. "The editors of the *New York Times,* the *Daily News,* and the *Post.* Associated Press, INS, UPI, Reuters. Don't you think it's time you appointed a press secretary?"

"I did," said Ben "I called his wife. He got lost in the snow last night."

In her room on the eleventh floor of the Municipal Building, a short distance from City Hall, Jane Landesmann was directing the snow-clearing operation with a coolness and firmness that enraged her six deputies but finally earned their grudging admiration.

"No, Mr. Morris," she said into the phone. I want plows 7, 8, and 9 on the Manhattan side of Brooklyn Bridge, and I want them to sweep the bridge, the causeway, the causeway to Fulton and from Fulton to Broadway. No, Mr. Morris, the contingency has been changed. Please don't argue, Mr. Morris, I'm very busy."

She put the phone down, and it rang again immediately.

"Mr. Kratzmeyer, I want your team of plows at Broadway and West 14th and at Seventh Avenue and 14th, sweeping south. Mr. Kratzmeyer, please do as you are told."

Her slim, delicate hands picked out another number on the pushbutton phone. "Twenty-third Street depot? This is Landesmann. How many men have you got now? Too bad. Just as soon as you get a team together, I want Tenth Avenue swept to 14th, and then south down Hudson Street."

At no point did she raise her voice. She talked to her men with calm authority and earnest directness. It melted their harshness. Then it had them talking to their own subordinates in the same even-toned, icily polite way.

Mahle's message on the City Hall computer circuit arrived while the mayor was 800 feet over the Hudson

River, strapped and helmeted, in a police helicopter. The pilot talked to him through his headphones.

"There she is, Mr. Mayor," he shouted and wheeled south, away from the giant tanker which lay in the green waters of the Hudson, gaunt and slug-like, its bulbous bow structure evenly parting the fast-rushing current.

Now for the first time Ben realized the enormity of what had happened. It took the sight of this obscene monster lying so close to the city, his city, for him to shudder, even in the heavily vibrating aircraft. The helicopter was over New Jersey now. Ben could see the whole of Manhattan spread out before him.

"Hold it there," he shouted.

The helicopter jerked back and hovered. The tanker was directly ahead of them now, the World Trade Center behind it. Ben remembered the publicity which attended the launching of the *Jersey Lily*.

"If you stood it on its end, it would be taller than the World Trade Center," the blurb had claimed.

Damnit, he thought, even on its ass it was as big as most apartment blocks in the city.

"Okay," he said to the pilot.

He turned to Cusp, who was sitting in the rear seat. "How are we making sure that no one goes near that ship?" he asked.

"Civil Air Authority has banned all flying over the Hudson," said Cusp. "Only police and Coast Guard helicopters are allowed to fly anywhere for the rest of the day. We have four cutters lying half a mile off each quarter of the ship to warn off any approaching craft."

Ben nodded. "What about tides and the currents? Couldn't she break up on the bottom there?"

"That's the real danger," said Cusp. "She's in a deep-water channel now, but she may well be touching the bottom at low tide. They're big ships, but they're more than vulnerable to breaking in two if they bottom on anything uneven. Anyway, it's only a small drop in the harbor."

"What about the bottom there?" shouted Ben.

"The charts show it as being particularly even," said Cusp. "With luck, she will be lying on soft silt from the river."

"Any other dangers?"

"My biggest worry is ice flow," said the captain. "Not too likely at this time of year, but it's been pretty cold upriver. One of those could do a lot of damage to her moorings."

Ben looked downriver toward the piers and cranes and the normally bustling Brooklyn waterside.

Cusp said: "We are deploying every antipollution measure we have, Mr. Mayor. If the equipment can be got here in time, we can have an oil-containment boom right across the river, just in case she does break up. I've got 90,000 drums of detergent loaded on six spraying ships. That's about all we can do right now."

"You've worked hard, captain," said Ben "Thank you."

He turned to the pilot. "Okay, let's look at Manhattan."

The message read: "To Mayor Boyle. Too many treaties have been broken in the past. Because of the reluctance of the networks to cooperate fully we are advancing our schedule and propose now to detonate the tanker at 2300 hours on January 2. A study of the primers on Channel 13 at 0900 today will confirm our intentions."

The message was handed to Deputy Mayor Altmeyer who turned on the television set in his room and watched. Over the discussion on modern sculpture, he could see the outline of the digital clock. At nine o'clock exactly, he watched, hypnotized, as the camera moved to the primers. Eight of them had already clicked into position.

Now two more locked into place.

"Oh my God," he said aloud. He turned the television set off and dialed for the fourth time that morning the home number of the President of the Manufacturers Hanover Trust.

29

From heights that ranged dramatically from 3,000 to 400 feet, swooping dangerously low over the skyscrapers and the tall apartment blocks, dipping from the bottom of the cloud base into the valleys and deep chasms of the avenues and wide streets, the police pilot took the new mayor of New York for a guided tour of the snowbound island.

It was Wednesday, a morning on which certainly by this time the streets below would have been a maze of automobiles and people, streaming ant-like, avenue by avenue, street by street—ant-like, indeed, tidy from the air, disciplined and anxious, stop on red, go on green, walk on "Walk," stop at "Don't walk," into the store, into the subway, up from the subway, correct change for buses, cabs that weave, cabs that cheat, drunks in the bars, beggars who bully, early morning gospel, too early for muggers, the winos sleeping while the ordinary people of the city, with the help of effortless small talk and wise-cracking, saw the day through—kind, plain people who made this place a city, who made it a city of power and unrivaled glory.

From those heights, Ben Boyle looked down on his city and thought, not about crime in the streets or the rat race or the chaos he had inherited, but about the people down there.

The scene below was not *his* New York. It was a

monumental wasteland of buildings and streets piled high with last night's snow, a deserted, empty, barren place where people should be. It was bereft of people now, no one moving in those streets, neons flickering at chain stores and supermarkets, the high, fine buildings still caked on one side with frozen snow, the new, glass-coated boxes standing stark and unlovely; the whole city beckoning with its beauty. But there were none but its captive inmates that day to look out of high-rise windows and capture that momentary exhalation when Manhattan was stilled and quieted and tamed and cleaned by a force bigger even than itself.

Boyle spoke into the radio headset: "North, toward the Bronx." The control stick went forward, and the helicopter dipped lightly, gaining speed. They were over Central Park now. Ben watched with fascination as a polar bear plowed happily through the snow in search of food or the water in the frozen pond beneath it.

In two minutes he saw what he had hoped for. In the center of the Triborough Bridge, three snowplows were cutting their way through the thick, frozen mass, making a thin, dark swath as they charged and hacked away, much too slowly for his liking. Two more vehicles were smashing their way south at the head of Fifth Avenue.

Jane Landesmann was working well, he thought. But how long would they take to get the avenues clean in the southern part of the city?

"Back to City Hall," he said. "And don't stop for any lights."

0930 SITREP

HEAVY SEA AND AIR TRAFFIC WITHIN APPRECIABLE BUT SAFE DISTANCE OF JERSEY LILY. SENSOR ANALYSIS INDICATES COAST GUARD CUTTERS HELICOPTERS.

CBS, NBC, ABC ANNOUNCE MAJOR PROGRAM RESCHEDULING.

CONDITION GREEN

Mahle looked at the printout and handed it back to Peter Eagle Heart. The young Indian had grown appreciably more edgy during the night. Mahle now noticed a tremor in his hand as he took the sheet of paper.

"Pete," he said gently, "you're too tense. This in no time for tension."

The younger man said nothing.

"We've spent a lot of time and money and thought on this," Mahle said. "I chose you and the others because you had the finest brains among the Indian people. You worked excellently on the preparation of the sensors and other warning devices. As you can see the operation is going well. In a few hours we will be in a position to take back—to buy back honorably—the land that was taken from us by trickery and deceit."

"I am not nervous, Flaming Torch," said Eagle Heart.

"I have fought in wars, Pete," said Mahle. "And I've seen stress in all its many forms. Some men talk too much and drink too much and some men have considerably increased sexual appetites. Some men have frequent bowel movements. Some men, like you, Pete, sweat freely and cannot hide the shaking of their hands." He looked hard at Eagle Heart.

"I hope we don't have to detonate the tanker," he said. "But I am prepared to let the master computer go ahead because it's the culmination of a struggle by our people against their people. To force the mayor of New York to arrange the ransom money, we must show no fear, no hesitation, no compromise. Throughout the centuries, our leaders have been tricked and made impotent through their own guilelessness and by the greed of others. Have no doubt that Ben Boyle will try the same—he already has. We must remain rock-like. We will not yield."

Pete Eagle Heart said, almost defiantly: "There is no fear in me. There is apprehension and expectancy, which are very different."

Mahle turned and walked silently away from the younger man and took a black cigarette from a box on a carved sideboard. He lit it and puffed it gently.

"The cause of your anxiety is not what worries me. It's the simple fact that you show your emotions so readily. It is in the nature of our people to endure suffering with something akin to scorn."

Mahle sat at a rosewood table and looked up. "Watch my face," he said. He put his left hand on the table and ground the cigarette directly into his palm. His face did not change. Eagle Heart said nothing, but stood looking into Mahle's eyes. They showed no expression.

"It hurt," said Mahle. "Don't think otherwise. The pain was the same pain that you or the others would have felt. The important thing is the ability to control your feelings and not to allow the pain to show. In that way you are contained within yourself. It is this containment which will give you confidence. Your sweat and your trembling may be an expression of apprehension and excitement. But the fact that you show them is a sign of weakness. And we cannot accept weakness."

Pete Eagle Heart walked into the control room and sat at his computer console. He was gripping the edge of the desk very hard to stop himself from trembling. But the sweat had started to flow now, and he knew that he was indeed frightened.

"You had calls, in order of importance, from the President, the Secretary of State, and the Governor," Mary said. "I told them you were busy. The fire chief called and asked for priority in clearing fire lanes. And this message arrived from the Indians just after you left. They've moved the deadline up. You could have watched it on television."

"Where's Van Horn?"

"Locked away with Detective Owen."

"Altmeyer?"

"Talking to banks."

"Okay, give me some good news."

"The good news is that the Transit Authority called Mickey Canaletto a while ago and said they would be able to operate limited service on the IRT and IND by midday."

"Good."

"Except, who's going to make it to the subway stations?"

"Now I'll talk to the President."

"Just one other thing, Ben. And this isn't good news. The U.S. Weather Bureau called and said the barometer is falling, and the temperature is rising slightly. There is a good chance of more snow before too long."

Ben bit his lip.

"Wouldn't you just know," he said. "Still, they were

wrong last night. Some guy was talking about a lover's moon."

"How the hell can they use the City Hall computer?" asked Detective Owen.

"They dialed it," said Van Horn. "On the Bell system. It shouldn't happen, but all they need is a code of 12 figures and they can link their computer to ours. No trouble. We do it all the time."

The two men were oddly contrasted, sitting there in the Planning Committee Room on opposite sides of the table. Detective Owen Owen, a sparse, tough, crew-cut figure, his small, alert eyes watching the bigger, younger man with impatience. Van Horn was slow in speech and meticulous in thought. His mannerisms annoyed the detective; he did not like the way Van Horn bunched his hair together behind his head while he thought. He didn't like the endless taking on and off of heavy hornrimmed glasses. He just didn't like longhaired young men who were cleverer than himself, he decided.

"How would they get the code?"

"Search me," said Van Horn. "Maybe they have someone working in my department. Or they may have stolen the program yesterday when they bugged the mayor's office. I don't know."

"You mean they can tap into the City Hall computer just like that?"

"Until we change the code. Mind you," said Van Horn. "It's only that computer. None of the others used by the city, I hope. We have twelve working in this city, you know. One for hospitals, another for education, traffic, sanitation. They're all quite separate units, linked only when instructed to do so. So they can't have learned anything confidential, except maybe the city budget plans. And if they're anything like those in the last twelve years, they'd be offering us money, not taking it."

"Could we trace them through this message?"

"Not a chance. There would be no record left of the origin of the message. You see, the whole thing would have been passed from one machine to the other in a millionth of a second. Not at all like an ordinary phone call."

Owen stood up impatiently.

"So what are we going to do?"

"Find the master computer."

"Okay, I've got helicopters going from precinct to precinct, bringing in every cop of Indian origin in the city—and that's not many. There's no such thing as an Indian ghetto here, so where are they going to do the routine inquiries? In one or two known apartment blocks and small hotels where we know that Indian activists have been living. All this while everything's thick with snow, and nothing moves."

"I can't see that you can do much more in terms of police work," said Van Horn slowly.

"So what about the technical side of it?"

"Well, we can do a lot of things. The first move is to get hold of that master computer with one of ours at the other end."

"Then?"

"Then talk to it, feed it trivial information, make it answer. Keep it locked onto our computer and confuse it so it doesn't have a chance to pass on any instructions to the slave computer on the ship."

"That would stop the explosion?"

"It will if they haven't given final instructions to the slave. My bet is, they haven't."

"Can we do that?"

"If we can find the frequency and the code they're using, certainly. But there's a better way. If we can get the Mayor to provoke them into sending another message to our computer, we can lock onto them immediately from our own computer room. We could keep their machine busy. Hell, we might even be able to trace the location from their coding."

"What if the Mayor provokes them and they cut the time again?"

"I'll ask the Mayor."

"Good morning, Mr. Mayor."

"Good morning, Mr. President."

"Okay, Ben, tell me all."

"You've read the telex, Mr. President. We've got big trouble. You can see that."

"I can see it, all right. How can we help? The army?"

"I could use ten thousand men to clean these streets.

But they'd never get in. Kennedy, La Guardia, Newark—they're all closed. Apart from that, the roads are impassable."

"I mean use the army to help catch these Indians."

"Oh no, Mr. President, not that. Remember American history? No soldiers, except to clear the streets."

"The FBI?"

"Not yet. The deadline is too short, and these bastards have just lopped an hour off it because ABC wasn't sounding too friendly about the tapes. I don't want to sound uncooperative, but there's a limit to the number of people who are able to do the police work in this city. I don't want to confuse those guys who are working."

"Ben, you're taking a hell of a lot on yourself."

"I know that, Mr. President. But hell, it's my city."

"I was born in the Bronx, Ben. It's mine, too. Supposing I override you, Ben. I could."

"Like hell, you could, Mr. President. The federal government telling New York City how to run its affairs. Wow. I'm sorry, Mr. President, but no."

"Ben, Governor Day and I are very old friends. And you and he don't quite hit it off, if I remember right."

"So?"

"So, Governor Day can declare New York a disaster area and call for federal help."

"Mr. President, I'll be frank. If you want to prevent the deaths of thousands of people by panic, if you want to give us time to find these Indians and stop them from blowing up Manhattan, you'll tell Governor Day to keep out of New York long enough for us to sort this mess out."

"Ben—"

"What's more, Mr. President, I hate to sound disrespectful, but this is an election year, and it wouldn't be particularly good for you if the people knew that you overrode the mayor of New York."

"I'm only trying to help."

"Okay, Mr. President, then let's get on with the demands from this group, give them what they want. We can sort the rest out later."

"Do you realize what they want, Ben? They want the abolition of the Bureau of Indian Affairs, they want admissions from the government that the bureau has been continually corrupt since it was created. . . ."

"So?" said Ben.

"And they want an option to buy back the Black Hills and six other former reservations at the going price. That's a helluva ransom."

"Give it to them, Mr. President."

"I've called a cabinet meeting for eleven o'clock, Ben. I'll see what we can do. And what about the money? How do you raise that?"

"I seem to remember that your bank has a fair piece of real estate on that part of the waterfront. Your total assets are sixty-five billion bucks. Can I put you down for ten?"

"Ben, you know damn well that I'm not the president of the bank anymore, nor do I have any say in its affairs."

"But you owned it."

"Okay, I'll talk to my sister."

"We already have, Mr. President. She's going to talk to you."

"I'll call you after the meeting. Good luck, Ben."

"Thank you, Mr. President."

30

After three hours of solid talk and countertalk, Owen and Van Horn stared gloomily into their paper coffee cups.

"It's this damn snow," said Owen fitfully. "On any normal morning I'd have fifty detectives, the best in the city, out there in the streets, checking names, checking alibis, talking, questioning, making notes. Sooner or later there'd be a lead, some kind of lead, any damn kind of lead to chase. So I'm sitting here in City Hall at the end of a telephone that doesn't ring and when it does it tells me 'inquiries negative.' "

Van Horn looked at him almost dreamily.

"Who was it?" he was asking himself out loud. "Who was it who wrote about microwaves?"

Owen picked up a photostat of the original letter to Ben. "It must be somewhere in here, the answer. But we've read this until we know it by heart."

"I was only a kid when I read it," said Van Horn. "It was a book. Called—wait a minute—it was a book called *Computer Interactivity and Microwaves.*"

"The money," said Owen suddenly. "The money. Who arranged for Herr Doktor Winkler to have a hundred and thirty billion bucks? Somebody must have fixed that cash."

"The book was by a man called, oh, what was it? Mahle. That's him. I remember now, there was a picture of him. Dark hair, aquiline nose. He could have been an Indian."

"Of course," Owen was saying. "Herr Doktor Fuckin' Winkler. What name did you say?"

"It took a long probe back into my memory bank," said Van Horn. "The man I'm thinking of was a war hero. Lord, that's right, he was an astronaut trainee."

Van Horn stared at Owen. The detective realized that the other man saw nothing at that moment, nothing but a screen in front of his eyes with words written on it.

"The first name was George," he said. "George Mahle."

Owen took a small black notebook from his inside pocket.

"Spell it, baby," he said. "Spell it."

"The president of the Chase Manhattan Bank is in the anteroom," said Mary.

"That's my bank," said Ben. "I've never seen more than a manager. Tell her to wait. I'm with a client. What's she like?"

"Incredible. Flew her own helicopter in from Long Island, landed in the middle of Chambers Street and finished her journey on snowshoes. I like her. You'll hate her."

Mrs. Amy Stonybridge, who was wearing a heavy leather jacket, was old, very old. Her small wizened face was tucked away inside a vintage leather flying helmet. She was hectoring a frightened young policeman who kept edging away from her toward the wall.

"Just do as you're told, young man," she said. "Go and find a glass, fill it halfway up with bourbon and then top it with hot water—hot, not boiling. Then bring it to me. Now."

"Ma'am," the policeman managed to say, "this is City Hall. I don't know. . . ."

"Hell's bells," she said. "What's the point of having a brother as president if you can't get a drink in City Hall?"

She caught sight of Ben standing in the doorway. "Mayor Boyle?"

"Yes, ma'am," He turned to the policeman. "You'll find some Jack Daniels in the liquor cabinet in my office. Look after the lady, will you?"

"That's more like it," she said. "You're a big fellow,

Boyle. Not at all like your pictures. I like the girl out there. Pretty. You married? No? She'd make you a good wife. Good childbearer, I'd say. Okay, Mayor Boyle, what's all this about ten billion dollars? Been in office ten hours and already you're trying to borrow our money. Not a hope in hell. We haven't got ten billion dollars. That's a good painting—Van Dyck, isn't it? Yes, of course, we gave it to the city.

"Ten billion bucks. You're out of your mind. Thank you, officer. Hope you didn't use boiling water. Nice-looking boy. Ten billion? Hell, Mayor Boyle, I don't think we've got more than thirty billion in the bank. I like girls with blue eyes and small breasts. Like that one out there."

Ben shifted his weight from one foot to the other, put his hands in his pockets, took them out of his pockets, flushed slightly, and tried to speak. But his mouth only moved.

"That's the trouble—putting a plumber in charge of New York City. I've never heard of such a thing. Ten billion bucks. For pot-smoking parties in Central Park, I guess. This isn't Jack Daniels. This city needs a real boss. Hitler, no, not Hitler. Didn't like him. And he *did* use boiling water. Met Hitler, you know. Tried to borrow money from us. Not ten billion dollars."

The shrill, squeaky voice did not stop. Her face, on which at least two surgical lifts had retired, was animated; her sparrow-like eyes fixed Ben mercilessly. He waited for her to draw a breath. It was a long wait.

"Ask my brother for it. He's the President. They've got plenty of money in Washington. We haven't. Goes in taxes to keep you people in office. Nice office. And what about this snow? My people won't get to the bank. Whole city a damned disgrace. Just like Lindsay. Remember when he let it all snarl up? Nice man, Lindsay. Too smooth though."

"Ma'am!" roared Ben. The pent-up violence in his own voice surprised him.

"No need to shout, Mr. Boyle."

"Ma'am, can I get a word in? Please?"

"Talk, talk, talk, you politicians. Came from a political family, you know. All talk and no action. What is it, Mayor Boyle?"

"We are looking for one hundred and thirty billion dollars to pay off a ransom on this city."

"Well, we haven't got that."

"I need a number of guarantors on a loan of that amount. You are one of them. This city is in danger and so is a great deal of your property, certainly valued in excess of ten billion dollars."

"What do you mean, danger? Has someone hijacked the city or something?"

"In a manner of speaking, yes."

"Can't do it anyway. SEC regulations."

"Mrs. Stonybridge, I'd be very grateful if you would speak to your brother and ask him, as we are asking him, to rush a bill through which allows the banks and major conglomerates to guarantee such a loan."

"He'll do what I say. I want to know more, though. Ten billion dollars. It's all too much, Mr. Boyle. You're a good-looking man, aren't you? I'm eighty-one years old, four husbands behind me, all dead, all dead in bed. Used to find them there, tired them out. I've got a hyper energy-producing chromosome, Mr. Boyle. Not a chance of ten billion. One billion, maybe. What security, anyway?"

"The deeds of New York City, ma'am."

"Hmm. We own most of that anyway."

"Would you mind very much if I leave you with my first deputy, Mr. Altmeyer? I have an urgent conference starting right now. Mr. Altmeyer understands money. He'll explain."

Ben began to usher the small leather bundle toward the deputy mayor's room. Mrs. Stonybridge opened an old vinyl handbag and pulled out a cigar.

Ben lit it.

"And, ma'am," he said. "There are many lives at stake as well as the property. We need your cooperation desperately."

He saw Mary standing protectively in the background.

"Miss Fyfield, will you take Mrs. Stonybridge to the first deputy's office?"

"Ah, there's that lovely girl," the old lady said. "Just told the mayor to marry you." Mary took her arm and led her away. "Nice man, good-looking for a plumber. Talks too much. You should always wear that deep blue outfit child. Goes with your eyes. Pretty eyes. Bit sad. Still, he'll put some cheer into them."

Ben watched them down the corridor and went to find Owen and Van Horn.

"We're approaching this on two main lines," said Owen. "Criminal and technical, with Mr. Van Horn here handling the computer side. We have one lead and one important thought. First, thanks to Charles here, I think we know who this Flaming Torch might be. We're checking him out right now.

"We are also waiting, and it's a hell of a long wait, for the crew manifest from Piraeus. That should give us more names."

"Who is this man?"

"Mahle, Mr. Mayor. George Mahle. Very talented Indian."

"What's the important thought?"

"The money, Mr. Mayor. I have an inspector from the Special Fraud Investigation Department on his way in. We want to know more about that fund in Frankfurt."

"Charles?"

"We have a ship sitting behind the *Jersey Lily* at the moment with a broad-spectrum receiving aerial which scans the entire series of wavelengths at high speed and which should pick up the frequency on the hour. This is connected by our own microwave to the World Trade Center, which, in turn, is connected to us by land line. If we can get that frequency, we can start worrying their computer with our own. If we can't get it, I'll be making a special request of you, Mr. Mayor, which you may not like. But we have to get them talking."

31

Detective Inspector Michaelson of the Special Fraud Investigation Department was unlike any cop Owen had ever seen. He was a fat little man with a cerubic face and curly white hair and an aura of supreme confidence. When Owen handed him the ransom note, Michaelson took a pair of gold-rimmed pince-nez from his breast pocket and studied it carefully.

"How intriguing," he said when he had finished. "Do you know, Owen, that these people have found the perfect ransom method? I didn't think anyone ever would."

"Explain," said Owen.

"Everything has been tried. Used bills in telephone booths, air drops over the desert; we've seen it all. But in ninety-six percent of kidnappings, hijackings and the like, the money is recovered. This way is clever. The money is paid into a trust and it will be a hell of a job to get that money from the trust."

"Even when it has been secured under duress?"

"The trust has not been making threats."

"But this Doktor Winkler, he must know."

"Not at all. Herr Doktor Winkler is no more than a faithful servant of his bank. Probably not even a vice-president. He will be controlling this fund with instructions from clients.

"He'll be very careful with that money. Remember,

while it's in his bank it will be earning some twenty-five million dollars a day in interest. No, he'll have been told to expect the telex and to act on it only as soon as he's been assured that the guarantee is absolute and watertight."

"So who fixed this for the Indians?"

"You need to find the broker and the fiduciary."

"Come again?"

"The middleman who holds the money is the fiduciary. Probably one of the big English banks, Barclays or the National Westminster. You might get a lead from them, although they don't actually see the money. It just passes through them in the form of a paper transaction. They do, of course, pick up some commission along the way. Nice business."

"The broker?"

"That's the man you want. He's almost certainly in New York, waiting to pick up his commission. A half percent of this, even a quarter, is ample for him to retire on; more than that—enough to start a bank."

"So where do we find him?"

"I hate to tell you, Owen, but finding a money-broker of this sort in New York is like trying to find a cab driver in Brooklyn. Ever since the Arabs got clever with oil and dollars, New York has been plagued with people who think they can get hot Arab dollars and lend them at favorable rates. It's all quite legal. The SEC has tried to crack down on them; so has the Federal Bureau of Commerce, because the rates are extortionate and it's crippling some big industries."

"You can't help?"

"I didn't say that. I've got one or two interesting thoughts."

"Let's hear them, Inspector."

"I've got five names, each one of whom could be the man you're looking for. These are the brokers who work with funds like this—real big money. They're all being watched. Usually they fail to pull off the deal because the rates of emission are too high. Emission? That's the actual amount of money which is paid out. By the time this cash has passed along a daisy chain of the sheik, who always wants a cut, his son, who takes a kickback from the agent, the agent himself, the banks and the brokers, that's three percent of the money gone already. Then there are commissions on top of this."

Michaelson took a pad from his briefcase. He put on his pince-nez and began to write.

"Here's your list. I'll get my department to start nosing about in the finance world to see if anyone has been talking in billions lately. And we have some good friends in Frankfurt. We might even get Winkler in a whorehouse. It's been done before. Good luck, Owen."

The little fat man stood up, shook hands, picked up his briefcase and walked briskly out of the room.

The radio technician on the U.S.S. *Whaleback*, a high-speed ship whose usual task was to monitor signals from Russian trawlers in the Arctic Seas, shouted into the radio which was linked directly with Van Horn at City Hall.

"We've got her! A group of fifteen digits on two-point-eight kilohertz. Clean as a whistle."

"Good," said Van Horn. "Give me the digits."

The radioman read out a list of figures.

"Excellent," said Van Horn. "Standard IBM coding. Thank you. Please keep listening on that channel and relay any other signals immediately."

The sailor turned to the man sitting at the radio console next to him.

"This sea's damn smooth," he said.

"I should think so," said his companion. "I've just been on deck. We're moored between Ellis and Governors islands."

In the computer room at City Hall, Charles Van Horn was trying to explain to an impatient Ben Boyle the way he wanted to lock the IBM computer in front of them to the computer that controlled the ship.

"We know two things, Mr. Mayor," he said. "The code that this computer uses to talk to the slave computer. And we know the frequency they operate on. So what I'm going to do is use this City Hall computer as a rogue in the middle of their signals. When they talk to the ship, we'll answer."

"What are you going to say?" said Ben.

"We'll simply feed them a lot of trivial, erroneous information. As long as we are locked onto them and we can keep their master computer confused, so busy that it can't give the right instructions to the ship, we can mess up their operation."

"Won't they know this?" said Ben.

"No. The computer they're using has eight channels. My guess is that they're using seven of those for standard operational messages—that's to the sensors, and so on—and keeping channel eight for anything critical—like blowing the ship up."

"How do you know that?"

"From the last signal. The last one, you see, was manually operated. Punched out on a keyboard. Then the signal follows immediately at ultra high speed. If we lock on that frequency, we can both read their signal and reply during their transmission and keep them occupied.

"This computer instructs the other to keep transmission going. On channel eight, that is. Then we talk to it, feed it with nonsense, give it a list of city employees, you know. Do it all on a constant loop which I'm preparing right now."

"It sounds okay, Ben said. "But if it doesn't work?"

"Then we'll have to do it another way. Over the telephone."

"What?"

"You'll have to provoke them into replying as they did before, by dialing directly into this City Hall machine."

"Last time they took an hour off the deadline, Charles."

"It would be worth it if they did it again."

"We'll try anything."

But I hope you know what you're doing, Van Horn, he thought. You're so goddamn young. So confident. Please don't be too confident, Van Horn.

He looked at Van Horn and he realized, once again, that this man was not just extremely clever. He was in charge of the New York computer system—the most intricate and complex of any city's in the world. Ben felt much better about the long-haired young man who was feeding complex equations into the City Hall master machine.

On the top floor of the Hotel Marlborough, Charlie Green Bird, the radio operator, a member of the Crow tribe and, like Mahle, a much decorated war hero, heard the signals of a powerful transmitter from the direction of the *Jersey Lily*.

"We are receiving a strong scrambled signal from what appears to be a military transmitter," he said. "It is directly in line with the ship."

"Radar?" asked Mahle.

"We have an echo from a small craft at two-zero-zero, range two thousand yards."

"Moving?"

"Stationary. Strong radar impulses," said Charlie Green Bird.

"The navy has arrived," said Mahle.

At Rockefeller Plaza, in the tall building which houses NBC, the lone switchboard operator, who had been in the building all night, answered a stream of abusive telephone calls from angry viewers.

"I'm sorry, Mrs. Leibowitz, but 'Guess My Tragedy' has been pulled off the air for operational reasons. Nothing to do with me, Mrs. Leibowitz, it's network policy. Why don't you write in and complain?"

"Mrs. Magruder, I'm sorry, Mrs. Magruder, but we aren't showing 'Trauma Room' today for operational reasons. Sure, you're upset, Mrs. Magruder, why don't you write in?"

The girl turned to a tired videotape operator who had just brought her coffee.

"Jesus Christ, Jack, what are they doing upstairs? Indians, Indians all day and all night. It's driving everyone mad. Just look at those lights. Nothing like this since the abortion documentary.

"Sure, I understand, Mrs. McCarthy. I'll pass your complaint on. Well, I don't run the network, you know, Mrs. McCarthy. No, I'm too busy to watch Channel 7, Mrs. McCarthy. . . ."

32

Le Comte de Chaillot was a man of about 60 who felt obliged to hide a very bald and shining head with a poor and ill-fitting wig which he had bought during a period of financial depression and personal hardship. Given to overweight, he fought this equally sadly with a body corset which slipped frequently, allowing two or three inches of ugly fat to spring, squirming with relief, from beneath his bulging striped shirts.

He lived by money, by selling money, by selling very large sums of money and taking a small, but always useful, commission.

De Chaillot had the pallor usually associated with prison. His prisons, however, were luxury hotel rooms, in which he worked by night and slept by day. He lived thus in Zurich and Rome and Venice and Paris and London, sometimes all in one week. He maintained a permanent suite in the Plaza Hotel in New York, from which he often flew to San Francisco, Tokyo, and Singapore.

He was last in the long line of the Chaillot family, which had hardly distinguished itself in the history of France since Charlemagne had granted the rank of count to Jean-Paul Chaillot for perpetrating a particularly cowardly and brutal court murder. That the present Comte, Edouard Michel, was the last of the line was a certainty, and all France knew it, because he suffered from an incurable allergy to women, an allergy that was well compensated for by an insatiable delight in the company of young, well-built men.

He knew everybody who mattered in the world of finance, the world of entertainment, the world of high society and the world of organized crime.

It was this man who had arranged that the $130 billion in the Union Bank of Switzerland be made available to the Dresdner Bank in Frankfurt. He had done so at the request of Evie Martin.

Detective Owen Owen was glad to see that the managers of the Plaza Hotel had organized a group of bellboys and other staff to clear a path from the main door of the hotel to the nearest quarter of Central Park, no doubt on the assumption that refugees would be arriving by chartered helicopter.

Owen walked briskly across from the park through banks of snow piled high on either side of him.

He heard an assistant manager in the lobby say to the receptionist: "My dear, the most horrible thing—*we've* been named as an emergency reception center."

A minute later Owen was pressing on the bell of the Compte de Chaillot's suite.

He rang several times and then hammered on the beige door of the room. Finally he saw a shadow appear beneath the door and disappear again.

Owen was ordinarily a man of considerable tact and discretion. He was not given to sudden, violent impulses, but on this occasion he felt all the fury of a man who had been trudging through heavy snowdrifts and meeting with the rich.

He stepped back and kicked the door just below the lock. The door crashed open but only two inches. There was a chain guard.

A shrill voice from the suite shouted "Go away. Mel, call the police."

"I *am* the police," said Owen through the opening. "Open up."

The chain clicked, the door opened, and Owen found himself facing a young man who was tall and powerfully built. He wore a Kung Fu T-shirt and see-through underpants. The young man's hair was black and straggly, and his face was a mass of acne.

The young man said nothing, gaping at the detective in disbelief.

"Where's the count?" Owen demanded briskly.

The young man nodded toward the adjoining bedroom. Through the door, Owen could see the outline of a man in bed, the sheets pulled high over his head, with two large feet poking out at the bottom.

Owen walked over to the bed and said to the trembling form, "It's okay, I'm a policeman."

The dome of de Chaillot's bald head emerged first, followed by the pale face and finally a white, hairless chest.

"Police?"

"My name is Owen. You're Count Chaillot?"

"But, but this is an outrage. You smash your way into my private suite. I shall speak to your superiors. Mel!"

The young man stood at the doorway.

"Call the police."

"Don't bother, sonny, I'm a senior detective and the complaints department is closed." He turned back to the count, who was making strange patterns of outrage with his mouth.

"Get dressed."

"Not with you in the room."

"Get dressed. Or I'll dress you."

The count was more composed now. He pulled the sheets about him and arranged a pillow squarely behind his head and lay back, his hands behind his neck.

"Oh no," he said. "There is a law for citizens in this country as well as for policemen," he said. "You burst into my room without a warrant. I take it you haven't one, otherwise you would be brandishing it like your constitution, and your behavior is unpleasant and rude in the extreme. Kindly go away while I consider this behavior."

Owen walked around the bed. It was an emergency, sure, but the man was right. A divisional inquiry would crucify any cop who had done this.

There was an ashtray by the bed. Owen picked up a thin, brown cigarette butt and silently praised the Lord and the Great Spirit which governed his Indian blood cells.

"I'm taking you both to headquarters," he said. "Now,

will you get dressed or do you want a naked ride in a helicopter?"

"Threats, too," said the count. "What exactly is the nature of your business?"

"I'm taking you in on a charge of unlawful possession of marijuana, and there may be a further charge concerning minors. We will also be discussing the matter of one hundred and thirty billion dollars."

The count reached under the pillow and found his wig. He sat up and pulled it on with some dignity. Then he walked, otherwise naked, to his dressing table and stepped into his corset. The young man walked over casually and helped to ease the bulk of the count's body into it.

"A lot of money," said de Chaillot. "What am I supposed to have done—stolen it?" He giggled.

When he had finished dressing, the count put on a heavy lambswool overcoat and a pair of earmuffs.

"Very well, officer," said de Chaillot. "But I must warn you of one thing. I understand that your police force has a reputation for the direct and physical approach to interrogation. I should warn you that brutality in any form will not assist you. I have, you see, a prediliction for being ill treated by strong, handsome men.

"Come, Mel," he said, putting on a fur cap. "To the Bastille."

"What the hell's holding up the snowplows?" Ben demanded. "They should have been well over Brooklyn Bridge by now."

"Sorry, Mr. Mayor." Jane Landesmann's voice remained antiseptically cool "The trouble is that so many drivers abandoned their cars in the blizzard last night that they are blocking the roads. They have to be pulled out of the way before our men can move."

"Tell them to shove them aside."

"That would cost the city a fortune in claims."

"To hell with that. You know what the bill will be if that ship blows up."

"Very well, Mr. Mayor."

"Tell your men to go like crazy," said Ben. He put the telephone down and walked out of his office to look in on Altmeyer.

The deputy mayor was tapping at a calculator on his desk. "The compound interest on this ransom," he said to Ben, "will amount to the sum of six hundred and six billion dollars.

"I don't know if you realize it, Mr. Mayor," he said. "But this would mean hiking the taxes of New York by seventy-three percent for thirty years just in order to survive."

"Have you raised the guarantees?" Ben asked.

"That woman, that awful Stonybridge woman, has taken over," said Altmeyer. He pointed to his secretary's office. "She's in there."

"Evacuation?"

"We have a complete operational plan worked out, Mr. Mayor. Going on a block by block basis, starting at Battery Park, we have arranged for three hundred buses to be available to work on a simple circuit basis because there will be only one traffic lane open. Buses moving downtown will use the East River Drive and Fifth Avenue and Broadway; uptown they'll use the West Side Highway and Eighth Avenue. We'll turn Penn Station, Grand Central and the East Side Bus Terminal into clearing centers.

"Other refugees will be moved by subway to the two big stations and to Rockefeller Center, which is the fourth clearing center."

"How are they going to know about this?"

"The commissioner for civil defense is preparing a number of radio tapes which will be broadcast at selected times throughout the evacuation. The City Hall print shop is preparing two million leaflets in English and Spanish. They'll be ready by four o'clock."

"I like it," said Ben.

From outside he heard the ugly, nerve-jarring shriek of metal being pushed over asphalt.

"One other thing," he said. "I think we'd better make this an official state of emergency. The snowplows aren't worrying too much about abandoned cars. We'll have the insurance companies to face before very long."

The computer had been carefully programed by Van Horn to accept the next signal from the rogue master in the hotel. Then it would engage it, lock on to it, and tell it not to shut down transmission.

It was a system known as a remote job entry. There was no reason why it should not work.

The voice of the radioman on the U.S.S. *Whaleback* came over a loudspeaker.

"One minute from now, Mr. Van Horn."

"Okay."

He looked at the second hand on his watch. It went the full minute. There was no sound from the speaker.

The sailor's voice said: "I guess they've changed the frequency."

Van Horn said "shit" and went looking for the mayor of New York.

Ben found the tiny wizened figure of Mrs. Stonybridge sitting at a secretary's desk, her leather-clad legs propped on a chair, a glass of bourbon in one hand and a telephone in the other.

"If Chase can do it, Hanover can do it. I tell you, Jim Beedley, I know just how much money you've got in your bank. I read the figures, too, you know. I'm not telling you why, but the security is good. New York, that's the collateral. New York City, that is. I don't know what it's worth. No, you silly boy, you're just like your mother.

"It's not cash they want. It's a guarantee. I know all about the SEC and its rules. I've told my brother to change them. Now then, can I put you down for ten billion dollars? I've got Exxon and Ford so far, plus Chase makes thirty billion. How is your mother, by the way? Now look, Jim Beedley, I used to sit you on my knee when you were a little boy. Talk to me like that and I'll wish I'd put you over my knee. Hurry up and make up your mind, I've got a lot of people to talk to. There's a nice man here called Ben Boyle, a plumber you know, but he's good-looking and a widower. Just right for that ugly daughter of yours.

"No, don't tell me your problems. All right, call a board meeting. Tuesday? You silly man, I want an answer by three o'clock today. Fee? Of course there's a fee. One percent per annum, just what we usually charge. Well, have a conference call right now and call me back. I'm at City Hall, that's where I am. Hey Jim, listen. I happen to know because a little bird told me that the ambassador to France is about to retire with liver trouble and you speak French, don't you? Call me back, darling."

She looked up at Ben. "Phew, Ben Boyle, you're going to be very lucky to get this. I haven't told so many lies since I shot my first husband—and keep quiet about that."

"Are they coughing up?"

"Give me a week and I'll get it. But it's a lot of money for these guys and they've been taught to watch their millions, let alone their billions. Now I've got to talk to Bunderchook at Xerox. He wouldn't want to be an ambassador. Might offer him a cabinet position. What do you say?"

Ben smiled, and the smile broadened into a wide grin. "You're a crafty old lady," he said. "How many ambassadors to France have you appointed today?"

"Three, so far," she said. "And there's nothing wrong with Pete Younger's liver. Jesus, he can drink any man I know under the table, except me. Get me another bourbon, that's a good boy. No, straight. Ice spoils whiskey. Where's that pretty girl, anyway? I quite fancy you, Ben Boyle. Might make you number five." She picked up the telephone. "Darling, get me the president of the Xerox Corporation. I don't know where he lives. His name is Bunderchook and he's got gallstones."

Ben said, "Is your bank really in for ten billion?"

"Good Christ, no, man," she said. "I won't be able to persuade my board until all these others have agreed. Why do you think I'm so rich? Hey, where's that bourbon?"

"Name?"

"I am the Comte de Chaillot de Crotoy sur Somme au Touquet, il Principe di Capri, and the Duke of Zurich."

"First name?"

"Edouard Michel, Francois Charles. . . ."

"Edward Chaillot," said the desk sergeant. "Address?"

"The Savoy Hotel, London."

"Address in New York?"

"The Plaza Hotel."

"Go over to that desk and empty out your pockets. Then give your fingerprints to that young lady. Then sit on that bench and wait until I call you. In the meantime I must tell you that under law you are entitled to an attorney. If you are not in a position to afford one, we'll get one. Any statement you make won't be used against you unless it is made in his presence. Okay, I guess Chief Detective Owen told you all that."

"No."

"Too bad. Over there." He turned to the young man. "Okay, Pimples, tell me all. Name . . . ?"

33

The cigar-smoking driver of the twenty-ton snowplow reversed the giant vehicle for the hundredth time that morning, gunned his engine, released the heavy clutch and charged full tilt at a solid bank of snow. There was a bone-jarring, brain-numbing crash and the machine, its eight-foot high wheels screaming and smoking against the snow and road surfaces, moved forward another 12 feet until the impacted snow turned into the density of metal and stopped it.

The driver climbed down from the cabin and another man took his place.

"You can't take more than ten minutes," the first driver shouted up at him. "It's a killer. Knocks your eyeballs forward two inches every time you hit the snow."

Behind the snowplow, waiting impatiently in a line that stretched halfway across Brooklyn Bridge, stood a bizarre regiment of vehicles; garbage trucks with their snowplows poised; street-cleaners filled with salt solution; municipal and private buses; ambulances; fire engines and, in between them, the inevitable private cars driven by citizens who had chosen to drive to work that morning.

Ben Boyle had left City Hall to watch the operation and was talking to one such citizen, slumped low in the seat of his car.

"Just what the fuck do you think you're doing?" said

Ben. "Didn't you hear the appeals? Don't you listen to the radio?"

"I gotta get to work," the man said.

"What the hell sort of work?"

"I'm an undertaker. They said there was a lot of dead."

Ben looked at him coldly.

"Pity you couldn't be digging some of the poor bastards out instead of filling them in," he said.

The Mayor walked along to the third vehicle in line, a mobile canteen, where the snowplow driver was drinking coffee.

"How's it going?"

"Hey, Ben Boyle! I mean, Mayor Boyle. How're you doing, Mr. Mayor?"

"How are *you* doing?"

The man chewed on his cigar, took it out of his mouth, and spat into the snow.

"I'll tell you. There I was lying in bed this morning thinking who's going to clean up all this snow with the sanitation men on strike, and I'm thinking who the hell cares, it's warm in bed, and there's Frankie Schenk on the radio telling us to go back to work. Hey, Mr. Mayor, what did you do to Frankie?"

Ben's answer was drowned by the scream of the lead snowplow.

It was just after twelve noon. Ben found the note on his desk.

"Mr. Mayor.

I've gone to get you some chow. This is what's happening.

1. Captain Cusp wants you at a tanker conference at 12:30 in the planning committee room.

2. Van Horn says he's having trouble with the computer frequency and wants to talk to you about his second plan of attack.

3. Detective Owen says he may have a lead on the money source.

4. Mrs. Stonybridge says she's managed to raise 40 billion, but she isn't hopeful about the rest.

5. The Governor is on his way from Albany with a

retinue of experts. He's declaring a state of emergency and wants you to call a press conference. For him, that is.

6. Jane Landesmann says that her northern army has reached 42nd Street.

7. I love you.

Mary."

"What's happening is that these people are changing their frequency on each transmission, which makes it almost impossible for us to lock on to them and set up the remote job entry."

"Promise me you won't get technical," said Ben.

"What I want you to do is—and this is a very difficult request—to provoke those guys into talking over the telephone system as they did before.

"Then I can have Effie here"—he patted the City Hall computer—"ready to lock on."

"O.K. But suppose they shorten the deadline once again?"

"If we can confuse their computer in any way, Mr. Mayor, it lessens the chance of their closing the final circuit in that tanker. These guys are very clever. They've had a lot of time to plan this, to program their two machines to the point of being able to switch frequencies up and down the wavelength at exact timing, to operate all those devices on the ship and finally to blow up the city."

"And suppose we lose another hour and the scheme still doesn't work?"

"Then we'll have to take more drastic measures."

"Like?"

"Cutting the whole city's power."

"You can't be serious."

"I'm deadly serious, Mr. Mayor. They need electricity to run a computer."

"Yes, but in this weather?"

"We'll start first by playing games with the current, boosting it and dropping it at the critical times. But this can be dangerous. There are people in hospitals, for example. They'll have to be warned. That's a hell of a job in itself."

"How do we warn them?"

"Con Ed will have lists. They'll need help though—

their engineers have been working long hours without any relief and the office staff hasn't turned up."

"We'll use the radio."

"Do that and the Indians will be ahead of us again."

"Jesus."

"If you could provoke them, Mr. Mayor, it would be the best bet."

"Okay, Charles, I'll think of something real nasty."

34

The four men sitting around the end of the long committee table rose when Ben came into the room and he motioned them back into their seats impatiently.

Ben sat at the end of the table, which was covered with charts and photographs.

Cusp sat at his right hand.

"I'll introduce you, Mr. Mayor. Mr. Onodera of the Mitsubi Company's New York office. His firm built the *Jersey Lily*."

Mr. Onodera leaned forward in a slight, formal bow.

"Captain Bomboulas of the Eftyvoulos Line."

Bomboulas was a man in his early forties, although he looked younger, with close-cut, curly, black hair. He shook hands with Ben. Looking grave, he chain-smoked sweet-scented Pappastrados cigarettes throughout the meeting.

"Mr. Mayor, I wish to apologize on behalf of my company for the fact that it is one of our ships which has brought about this terrible dilemma. Needless to say, the company will give every assistance that you wish."

"Thanks, Captain."

Cusp spoke quickly.

"Captain Bomboulas has managed to get the crew manifest from Athens—the port office in Houston was broken into and their copy stolen."

Commissioner Crotty, the fourth man, said, "The FBI is checking the address of every one of them. What we're looking for is a strong lead to a New York address."

"But we know their names."

"That's right, Mr. Mayor. Captain, first offices, two engineers, a quartermaster and three seamen."

"Jesus Christ, is that all?"

Captain Bomboulas said: "That ship is so automated that it requires only a minimal crew. Everything is automatic and controlled by computer. The ship has the finest navigation systems in the world—satellite, radar, radio, Loran and Decca Navigator. It moors automatically and throws its own ropes by radio. It anchors and up anchors itself. And it pretty well steers itself in and out of the few ports it can enter."

"Holy cow," said Ben. "What you're saying is that these eight men have been put in charge of a bomb. Christ, no wonder they can hijack it and hold this city for ransom."

"Company policy," said Bomboulas apologetically.

"Well, fuck your company's policy," said Ben. "Just to make a few more bucks a week for shareholders, they'll put a lot of good guys out of work and take a great goddamned risk like that. Anyway, you may have to answer to the world, but what are we doing about this damn ship?"

"In the first place, Mr. Mayor," said Cusp, "we're waiting for young Van Horn to try to get that computer sorted out so that we can defuse the tanker. Second, we want to find a way of getting aboard her without activating those flash detonators. I'll show you the ship."

Cusp unrolled a heavy blueprint down the length of the table. As the blueprint unrolled the astonishing outline of the ship became clear; the giant bridge and tall stern appeared first, followed by the twelve tanks, and finally the bow section.

The blueprint covered the entire table.

"Now this supertanker, like most of the others, has a very simple but extremely effective system for prevention of fire or explosions," said Cusp. "Thanks to Mr. Onodera, we can pinpoint one possible method of defusing the *Jersey Lily.*"

The Japanese man spoke for the first time. "The company uses several kinds of fire extinguishers. Foam, chemical, oh, many kinds, according to the specifications laid down by the owners.

"The *Jersey Lily* uses the most common type, which is the inert gas extracted from the engine fumes, pumped into the tanks to stop the creation of volatile fumes in the tanks.

"In this case, the company applied a secondary system which is now demanded by several port authorities, including your own, in most tankers. That is a chemical foam system which is automatically pumped into the tanks in the event of the temperature's rising above a certain point.

"Each tank has a number of automatic sensors which relay the information to the ship's computer, and it instructs the pump room to pump the foam into the individual tank."

"Not another computer," said Ben.

"Well, now, here's some good news," said Cusp brightly. "Because of the danger of computer malfunction, possibly due to the fire, there is a bypass system which operates independently of the computer. That's the system we're relying on."

"But we can't get on the tanker."

"No," said Cusp. "What we are going to do is this. The army down at Fort Leavenworth has been working for some time on a laser ray system which can send a beam of heat for about a mile. We've got two of these LHBs on their way here by plane to Pittsburgh, with one of my helicopters there to meet them and bring them right here.

"Now, using this blueprint, and knowing just exactly from Mr. Onodera here where the sensors are, we reckon we can put enough heat onto them to get the foam pumped in. Then they can flash away all night and still not get the ship to explode."

"Sounds chancy," said Ben.

"It needs a direct flame to blow up those combustibles," said Cusp.

"I'll buy it," said Ben. "What about storming the ship?"

"According to Van Horn, they have yet to give that slave computer on the ship the final instructions to detonate the ship, although they say that our interference with the sensor devices would result in this immediately. So we've worked out a contingency plan that will knock out the sensors. We'll just have to take a chance."

Captain Cusp took a pile of large photographs from under the tanker blueprint.

"We've been doing a detailed photo reconnaisance all morning," he said. "These are the results."

The five men poured over the pictures. "These are blowups of the sensors, those which are visible, anyway. You'll see that they are spread evenly along the length of the ship.

"There are three kinds and we've indentified all of them. They are all in regular service with the infantry.

"Those big ones are field surveillance radar units, which will detect the approach of people. It's so damn good that the operator can even distinguish between men and women.

"These," he said, pointing with a pencil, "are infrared intruder systems which the army uses for guarding perimeters. Break the beam and the warning sounds. And these things lying all around the deck are TOBIAS geophones, which work by noise and vibration. Very sensitive.

"We've got to be ready to knock each of these out almost simultaneously, together with the ship's own radar systems, and to storm that ship before the Indians have had time to really know what's going on. Now that is chancy, but we have to be ready."

"Are you sure we aren't taking too much of a risk?" asked Ben. "As Van Horn says, these are clever people."

"We're working on one other possibility," said Cusp. "Can we get into that ship from underwater?"

"Tell me," said Ben.

"Okay, Mr. Mayor. There is a chance that they may not have guarded the ship from below. If they haven't, we might be able to flood those tanks from the outside or to pump them full of water."

"But, again, how do you know they haven't guarded the bottom?"

"We don't. We've asked the navy to send down a nuclear sub. The U.S.S. *James A. Lawrence* is on her way from New London."

"Now hold on, captain." Ben's voice was raised.

"We've already got one H-bomb out there in the Hudson. If she goes up, what about the warheads in that sub? And the radiation hazard?"

"They are disarming her before she leaves. We'll have to take a chance on the second eventuality. On the other hand, she has the best underwater detection equipment—real long-range stuff—of any ship in the world.

"She can tell just what kind of equipment they may be using, sonar or asdic, and she has jamming devices that might give us a chance to get real close to the tanker underwater."

"Good," said Ben. "I told you you would be needed, captain."

Cusp stood up. "I'll get along," he said. "There's a hell of a lot to do. I need some way to knock out those sensors.

"Just one other thing, Mr. Mayor. I think you should know that Captain Bomboulas here has offered to be the first man on that ship. He knows the layout better than anyone. It's a very brave offer."

Ben turned to the Greek captain.

"Thanks, Captain," he said. "Sorry I shouted."

"I've always disagreed with the company's small-crew policy," said Bomboulas.

When Cusp and the other two men had left the committee room, Ben turned to Crotty: "Commissioner, what about these Indians. Who are they?"

Crotty opened a manila folder in front of him and said: "The captain of that ship is, or probably was, a man called James Armstrong who had served with the line for thirty years and had an excellent record, completely unblemished. My guess is that the other seven have either killed him or have left him on that ship or, maybe, have made him a prisoner. Married, three adult kids, lives in New York."

"So who is Flaming Torch?"

"Everything points to the first officer, George Mahle. Owen came up with his name an hour before we got this list. Mahle is an MIT graduate, Vietnam hero, an expert on computers and, believe it or not, a former astronaut. Never got off the launching pad because they fired him as a psycho. He's a full-blooded Cherokee, born in Brooklyn, no known living relatives. Joined the tanker line two years ago as an able seaman and worked his way quickly to first officer. His conduct sheet says he's 'exceptional' and the line had him earmarked for the next captaincy."

"George Mahle," said Ben. "Now I've got a name to talk to. What about the others?"

"They're all Indians, all gifted, with degrees from first rate technical colleges, and they come from all parts of the United States. Not one of them has so much as a hint of a record, according to the 'national crime computer,' nor, strangely, have they been known to engage in covert political activities."

"What now?"

"As I say, the first thing is to try to connect each of these names, or any of them, to a New York address or contact. That's the present move. I'm getting pictures of all of them wired through and I'll get copies to you so that you can see what they look like."

"What's this lead of Owen's?"

"Owen has a suspect over at headquarters who he figures may be the money contact. Somebody must have fixed that fund in Frankfurt and that's our best lead so far in this business. I just hope he's right."

The two men were getting up to leave when the floor began to vibrate with the noise of a helicopter landing outside. Ben looked out the window and saw the Governor of New York leap out onto the snow and walk with long brisk politician's strides toward the steps of City Hall.

"The Seventh Cavalry has arrived," he said.

35

The Governor was a professional politician. He was impeccably groomed, from his stainless steel gray hair to his two-hundred-dollar shoes. He was healthy and suntanned and he oozed confidence from each thread of his light blue Savile Row suit. He was as big as his election posters and pledges, and Ben Boyle hated his guts.

"Gee, Ben," he said as they shook hands in the lobby. "What a hell of a journey. I was in the pool at the Barbados place when I got the message about this snow. Couldn't get in anywhere except Boston, then on to Albany by helicopter and then here. That's why I'm so late."

"You needn't have interrupted your vacation," said Ben, not trying to hide the irony in his voice. "We're coping."

The Governor did not hear him.

"Jesus, what a mess," he said. "I declared a state of emergency right away. I mean, that was the first thing to do."

"You might have asked me," said Ben.

"No need, not after reading your telex."

"Which telex?"

"The one you sent to Washington. The President had it relayed to me."

"He what? That was a top-secret message for the eyes of the President only."

"And he decided that the governor of New York should know what was going on in his own state," said the Governor. "Now look, Ben, I can see the trouble you have and I can understand your wanting to do your own thing your own way. But the state of New York is involved."

"Then give me a chance and do what the President did. Just be ready to help. I can't afford the confusion of everybody making the spaghetti. It's a matter of time, Governor."

"How can I help?" The Governor was unctuous, and Ben wanted to be rude and blunt in his answer.

"Get every upstate hospital ready for a disaster," he said. "Close all schools and have them ready as refugee clearing stations. Have the National Guard ready and briefed for antilooting and civil control."

"I've got the best technical brains in the state ready to move in," said the governor.

"The best brain in New York is already working in the computer room at City Hall," said Ben.

"And what do I say to the press?" asked the Governor.

"There is no press," said Ben. "Unless we can get these streets clear."

"Television?"

"The whole city is under a news blackout until we can move the people," said Ben. "But if you can make smoke signals, you'll probably get peak hour viewing. It's the big Indian spectacular today—and I haven't seen one show."

"Well, thanks for the briefing, Ben. It's been great talking to you. You seem to have it under control, but don't hesitate to call on me if you need me."

"Thanks for looking in, Governor," said Ben dryly.

He watched the Governor climb into his helicopter and turned back into City Hall.

"Sonofabitch," he said.

"Ah, Ben Boyle." Mrs. Stonybridge had seen him through the open door of the office she was using. "Come here. I want to talk to you. Bad news. Can't raise the money. Tried them all. Bribery, bullying, blackmail. Can't raise more than fifty billion. Not a hope."

She lit a fresh cigar.

"You'd better tell those Indians that they've asked too much. Tell 'em to lower their sights. Offer 'em thirty billion and work your way up."

"No other way of getting it?" said Ben.

"See what I can do. Know a lot of people. Old Eftyvoulos. Owns that damn tanker. He should be good for a couple of billion. Spends it all on those damn crazy kids of his. Wonder what his yacht would fetch? Not as much as ours, I bet."

A young policeman knocked on the door with trepidation.

"Excuse me, Mrs. Stonybridge, ma'am, but your helicopter is blocking Chambers Street, and we're trying to clear it."

"Well, get someone to move it," she said. "Can't you see I'm busy? Keys are in the cockpit. Now where was I? One three zero billion dollars. I've got an idea. It might work. But if I were you, Ben Boyle, I'd talk to those Indians."

36

Chief of Detectives Owen sat in the cheerless interrogation room at headquarters and pushed a button on the bare table in the center of the room.

The door opened and a policeman led in the young man whom he had surprised at a bedroom door of the Plaza. The young man was dressed now, in a heavy polo sweater and jeans.

"Sit down, Melvyn," said Owen gently. "Your full name is Melvyn Grayshott and you live in Richmond and you are nineteen years old, right?"

The young man said, "Yeah. I've told you that."

"How long have you known Count de Chaillot?"

Grayshott picked at his acne.

"Three months, I guess. We travel everywhere together. You know, to Europe and San Francisco."

"What's your job with him?"

"He calls me a 'P.A.' You know, personal assistant."

"You're booked on a charge of possession of illegal narcotics, Melvyn. It'll be your third. You'll get two years."

"Tough."

"Think about it for a minute and listen. I can drop that charge but I'll do it only if you talk to me about the Count de Chaillot."

"He's my friend."

"I know that. Just tell me one thing. Has he been talking about any large sums of money lately?"

"Ah, he spends all his time talking millions. He deals in millions. All day on the telephone talking to banks and big corporations."

"Okay, then, an extra large sum of money. Billions?"

Owen looked very hard into the boy's face. Grayshott looked down at the table.

"No, nothing unusual."

"You're lying."

"I said nothing unusual."

"I'm in a hurry, Melvyn. You won't just get the drugs charge. I'll tell you right now that you are in very grave danger of being charged with complicity in a multiple murder."

"Say that again?"

"You heard me, Melvyn. This is very serious and I'm running out of time. Now, an extra large sum of money."

Grayshott picked hard at his face and looked up slowly.

"Like a hundred and thirty billion?" he asked.

"This is Ben Boyle. I'm talking to George Mahle. I've got to tell you, and I'm pretty sure that you will understand why, being a highly intelligent kind of guy, that we can't raise the guarantees for that loan.

"Some of the banks you mentioned can do it. The others can't. The fact is that there is not the cash available. I'm asking you to cut the amount to, say, thirty billion dollars. Now that's a hell of a lot of money. It'll buy you a lot of land. It'll feed, clothe and educate a lot of kids. Take my advice and accept. Please.

"If you don't accept and you hold out for the full amount, I should tell you—and I'm damned sure you know—that I've got some equally clever people working for me and they can crack your system.

"One hour from now, I'm going to start breaking the news to the people of this city. And that's the moment that it won't be just me and my staff against you, it'll be all the people of New York City.

"We know a lot more about you now. And there must

be people who know you and know where you are and will be only too pleased to start talking.

"So take the money, George. Take my advice and the money and get the hell out of New York."

37

No one worked harder and with more gusto that day than the rotund Michael Canaletto. Unlike the Mayor, who was forced to stay close to the corridors of City Hall, the lively, gesticulating, bullying, cajoling figure of Canaletto, his bald head covered in a trapper's fur hat, was everywhere. He shouted, he pleaded, he bearhugged—and he brought the deputy mayor close to apoplexy with his total disregard of the rules.

Civil defense represented only part of his duties in running New York. Ben Boyle, who had known and loved Canaletto for years, had included in his bailiwick a whole lot of those city problems which had never really had a department before.

The extroverted Neapolitan would soon be handling the social needs of the homeless, the rehabilitation of reformed drug addicts, the counseling of dropouts. If there was a city conscience, it resided in Michael Canaletto.

Within a few minutes of his leaving that first City Hall meeting he had commandeered a police helicopter and was chattering from Penn Station to the bus terminals, hopping from rooftop to rooftop like an amiable bumblebee, slithering, laughing loudly through the snow, and getting the most confirmed cynics enthusiastic about the tasks he assigned them.

When the manager of one of the city's largest and most

exclusive hotels protested about the potential invasion by refugees from lower Manhattan, Canaletto burst immediately into a pleading Verdi aria. He sang (in a fine tenor voice) until the man capitulated. And when the owner of a fleet of privately owned buses started talking extortionate rates, the Italian, still smiling, lifted the man from his feet and shook him until his teeth rattled. The rates came down.

The entire Canaletto family—his mother, his sisters, his brothers, his aunts and uncles and countless cousins—were brought into the fray. They found themselves lifted from the Bronx and Brooklyn, from Queens and Staten Island, into Manhattan, to help prepare food for the influx of people expected.

Reporting to Ben, Canaletto sprawled a giant map of Manhattan over the mayor's desk and explained the details of his evacuation plan.

"Okay, Ben, now listen, we floodlight each street when its turn comes to be brought out so that they can see what they're doing. Then we get the block associations busy, the leaders going from house to house, apartment to apartment, making sure that everybody is out who wants to come. Then we get them into the buses and up the West Side Highway or Eighth Avenue, depending on which reception center they've been allocated to."

"How are you doing that?" asked Ben.

"Alternate streets won't work in the southern part of Manhattan. So we're doing it on an ethnic basis. You know, Italians to the West Side. I've got my family making pasta for 50,000 people. Then the Poles to Penn Station, the Hispanics to Grand Central. Like that. I mean, there may be quite a lot of people mixed up and a lot of Jews will be eating prosciutto, but it makes the organization much easier."

"What about the Irish?" said Ben.

"That's easy. When we move all the important people, we'll start a roundup in the Shamrock bars with forklift trucks.

"Get the hell out of my office, Canaletto," said Ben. "Is this plan going to work?"

"Sure it's going to work."

Ben pushed a button on his desk phone.

"Landesmann." Jane's voice was cool.

"Jane, what sort of deadline before we can start moving these people?"

"Look out the window, Mr. Mayor." It was snowing again.

"We'll keep going," she said. "We've cleared all of lower Broadway. Fifth Avenue is clear to Washington Park. The West Side Highway is pretty well clear to Chambers, and Hudson Street is looking good. Give me an hour and Civil Defense can start moving."

"Hey, Jane," said Canaletto into the mouthpiece. "If I get my buses moving down East River Drive, won't that help to keep the snow packed?"

"Oh, there you are, Commissioner," said Jane. "Forget East River Drive. The drifts there are up to 20 feet deep, and they've frozen. I'm clearing First Avenue instead."

"You might have told me," he said. "You've upset the master plan."

"It would help if I could ever find you, Commissioner."

Canaletto laughed.

"Jane, baby, one day, when all this is over, I'm going to take you out for a big Italian dinner and a lot of good Tuscan wine and I'm going to serenade you with soft Neapolitan love songs and then I'm going to. . . ."

She hung up.

Ben smiled. "Get out of my sight, you sex maniac," he said. "And for Christ's sake, keep in touch. Let me know exactly when you're ready to move."

Mahle switched off in the middle of Canaletto's conversation with Ben and turned to Evie Martin, who was sitting cross-legged on the carpet.

"He's up to thirty billion dollars," he said. "Not a bad start. Quite encouraging, indeed."

"I hope you aren't thinking of accepting the offer," said the girl. "They'll raise it. They can afford it."

"I wasn't thinking anything of the sort, dear girl," said Mahle. "I was thinking that maybe I should give Mayor Boyle a gentle prod. An incentive to get the other hundred billion."

The intercom buzzed.

"Boyle."

"Can you come down to the computer room, Mr. Boyle? There's a message for you."

Two minutes later, Ben was reading a printout. Van Horn, standing by his side, said, "We're locked in, Mr. Mayor. We're talking to their computer."

The tapes on the City Hall computer were whirling furiously.

"Looks as though they fell into the trap," said Van Horn. "Now let's see if we can put their machine off."

"You better had," said Ben. "Did you read the message?"

"No time."

"Read it now."

Van Horn took the printout from the Mayor.

The message read: "To the Mayor of New York City: "We appreciate your attempts to secure the sum of money required to save your city from the destruction which we are clearly in a position to inflict. We do not appreciate, however, the attitudes of those companies whose fortunes have been largely built on the exploitation of the Indian peoples through the centuries. We must make it clear that it is these people against whom this enterprise is directed. Accordingly, we have decided to assist you in your attempts to persuade these corporations to enter guarantees against the loan. We have decided to advance the time of detonation by five hours which, when taking into account the existing cut of one hour in the original deadline, means that New York will be destroyed at 6:00 P.M. tomorrow, January second."

Le Compte de Chaillot sat bristling defiance in the interrogation room while Owen paced behind his chair.

"The question is, who instructed you to have this money ready?" Owen asked.

"I have nothing to say until my attorney arrives."

"Your attorney, Count, is unobtainable because of the storm, and I do not have a lot of time."

"I am saying nothing."

"I have a sworn statement by Melvyn Grayshott, your personal assistant, that he has heard you on various occasions discuss the sum of one hundred and thirty billion dollars."

"I have nothing to say."

"And I have every reason to believe that this sum of money is earmarked in a conspiracy to obtain ransom from the city of New York."

"I have nothing to say."

"And furthermore, you, Count Chaillot"—Owen spat the name—"are a party to extortion and the threat of murder."

"I have nothing to say."

Owen walked around the table and sat down facing the count. The Frenchman was sweating. His wig was slightly askew.

"You realize that your refusal to answer these questions puts you in danger of a jail term of twenty to thirty years for obstructing a police inquiry into a serious crime?"

"I have nothing to say."

"And you also realize that you are hindering an investigation that may save the lives of several thousand people and untold damage to property?"

"I have nothing—"

"Shove it, Count Chaillot."

Owen was mad now. The blood pounded in his head. He felt an overpowering urge to hit the count very hard in the mouth. But his voice remained calm and he swallowed the fury.

"Now listen to me. There are a lot of very seriously applied rules in this force concerning the treatment of prisoners. We do not, Count, beat people up to extract information. Those officers who do indulge in such behavior face severe disciplinary procedures and are frequently dismissed from the force. Count Chaillot, I have been on the force for thirty years, during which I have never abused my position and never so much as twisted a suspect's ear. But in your case, I may make an exception. As I told you, I have little time. I am certain that my superiors would both encourage and approve any action I took."

"I am saying nothing."

Owen pressed a buzzer on the desk. A sergeant appeared at the door. Owen stood up and pointed to the count. "Book this man on a charge of conspiracy to defraud the city of New York of the sum of one hundred and thirty billion dollars on or about January thirty-first.

Find him an air-conditioned cell and have his clothes pressed."

The sergeant looked puzzled and then smiled.

"I'll give him the bridal suite, sir," he said. "With a nice northern exposure and three broken windows."

But Owen was already on his way out, in search of Crotty.

"Mrs. Stonybridge, they're not playing ball. What they've done now is cut six hours off the deadline, which means we're in big trouble."

"Well, now, just you hang onto your pants, young man, and I'll tell you what I'm doing."

Amy Stonybridge put her feet up on the desk in the anteroom and threw her dead cigar butt in a well-aimed arc at a wastepaper basket.

"I've just had a long talk with the President. He made a whole lot of clucking sounds—always does when he talks to me—but he agrees with me that New York City is worth saving. Other thing he agrees with me about is that New York won't be able to pay off this debt unless you triple your taxes, and that won't work, especially since it's property-owners like us who'd have to pay.

"So I said why don't you get the federal government to do the underwriting? And he said, well, that means calling a Senate Appropriations committee meeting. By the time they've digested this, particularly the radicals, the whole of this city could be in ashes. Anyway, it's New Year's Day.

"Now, I know that you're not too fond of my little brother, Mr. Mayor, but he's going to do a brave thing for your city.

"I'll get the money for you from a consortium of the biggest banks in the world. They'll put up the guarantees, but the only thing that will persuade them is the signature of the President of the United States of America on a government guarantee of the whole sum. He's a gutsy little fellow, my brother. So you'll get your money. But for God's sake, get your Indians. Mine is one of the banks that'll be guaranteeing you."

"I shouldn't have told him to mind his own business, I guess," said Ben.

"Don't feel bad about it, Ben Boyle," said the old lady. "He saw the point immediately. I mean, don't think that he hasn't got the army and navy and Marine Corps sitting off Sandy Hook right now. You can bet the last dollar in the city budget he has, and that he's turning the country upside down. He's got a lot of spies in New York City, and I'm one of the best of them."

"Can I get you another bourbon, Mrs. Stonybridge?"

"No, I'll have tea. It's afternoon. I drink tea in the afternoon and gin in the evening."

"When can we expect to have these guarantees ready?"

"What's your deadline?"

"Six o'clock tomorrow evening."

Mrs. Stonybridge reached into her old purse and pulled a small diary from a mass of papers inside. She put on a pair of ivory-rimmed reading glasses and opened it.

"Not a chance," she said. "Banks are closed here today, and they're closed in Frankfurt and in Zurich they have a two-day holiday. By the time we get through to the London banks, they'll have all closed. It looks like a telephone marathon again for dear old Amy. Make it a bourbon, Ben Boyle, I've changed my mind. Old girl's privilege."

The thirteenth Comte de Chaillot sat in a cell on the sixth floor of police headquarters, overlooking the Brooklyn Bridge, and shivered uncontrollably. His chill was not surprising, considering. The windows of the cell had been locked open, and the count was wearing only a pair of violet underpants, embroidered with his initials and the crest of the de Chaillot family.

He was too cold to think of anything but the threat by that girl Evie Martin of what would happen to him if he divulged her name to the police.

It had begun as a straightforward deal. At a cocktail party one evening he let it be known, as he often did, that he had access to a large amount of money. The following morning Evie Martin called him. Her request surprised him, but the fact that the loan would be guaranteed by the biggest banks and corporations in America, together with the added spur of $15 million payable to him on completion, was enough to send him on the first available jet to Frankfurt and from there to the sheiks of the Middle East and to the treasury of Iran.

On his return to New York, the fund successfully negotiated, he was met at Kennedy Airport by a car driven by Evie. He found himself sitting in the back seat with a powerful-looking young man who held a pistol. He and Evie carefully blindfolded the count.

An hour later Chaillot was in the apartment above the Hotel Marlborough, having the bandage removed. Evie was the first person he saw.

"I regret this drama," she said, "but it's important that you know as little as possible about your clients."

The count was angry. "I see absolutely no reason in the world why I should be treated like this. You ask me to arrange money for you, and that's exactly what I've done."

"Arrange money for whom?"

"For a consortium of development companies for major expansion throughout the United States."

"And you have done this?"

"I told you this in my telephone call. The money will be available in the Dresdner Bank in Frankfurt for three hours only, from 9:30 A.M. until 12:30 P.M. on January the second—just as you requested."

"Show me the confirmation."

The count opened his briefcase and handed her a letter.

Evie read the letter carefully and said: "Wait here." She went into the adjoining room. The count had a quick check of the technical equipment inside before she slammed the door. She came out three minutes later.

"I have talked to my associates, and I am assured that this money will be raised. We confirm that there will be absolute guarantees available for this loan between those hours from major banks and corporations in the United States."

"And my fee?"

"Fifteen million dollars payable within ten banking days of the successful completion of the transaction."

"And how can I be sure of that?"

"That's what I'm coming to."

Evie Martin's eyes, which had been only vaguely hostile until now, were absolutely meancing as she put her hand on de Chaillot's belly and pushed him into a chair.

"The money which you have organized is intended for development, certainly. It is specifically earmarked for the Indian population of this country. We are a terrorist organization, Count Chaillot. And we are utterly dedicated to that one cause."

The count tried to get up, but now there was a long, slightly curved, bone-handled knife in her hand. Its point touched the end of his nose and he sat back abruptly.

"We know a lot about you, Count de Chaillot. While you were away, I arranged for some inquiries to be made about your business activities. We now know enough to put you in a federal penitentiary for fifteen years, enough to have you deported to Argentina where you are wanted under an alias, and, worse still for you, we know that a crime syndicate has given you a month to return the sum of two million dollars which you had the temerity to embezzle from them."

The knife was poised close to de Chaillot's bulging eyes.

"You need the money. You'll get the money. But one last thing." She spoke very slowly now. The threat in her voice made him gasp for breath in a series of tiny gulps.

"One word to any law agency about this organization or about your role in it, or even the slightest hint of my name, being the only name you know in connection with us, and . . ."

Sweat was streaming from under his wig now.

"I believe in reviving as many Indian customs and traditions as possible," she was saying. "And this is why we need this money, to buy back our land so that our people may live in their own way without the harmful influence of the federal toadies of the Indian Bureau.

"There is one custom I shall revive for you. The women of my mother's tribe used to deal with traitors in a particularly satisfying way."

As she talked, the knife moved slowly down the length of his stomach and then was held an inch from his genitals.

"One word from you—or if that money is not available at the time promised—and I will cut off your balls,

Count Chaillot, and stuff them in your mouth and sew your lips with strips of rawhide. That's just for starters."

She nodded to the man standing behind the count. De Chaillot felt the blindfold being replaced. Ten minutes later he was standing in the lobby of the Plaza.

38

The cell door opened and Jim Crotty's bulk filled the doorway. The red-faced commissioner feigned horror. He did not feign it very well because Crotty, despite his other qualities, was no actor; nor, at that moment, was Count de Chaillot in a mood for further drama.

"Who has done this?" boomed Crotty. "What on earth have they done to you, sir? There will be an urgent and far-reaching inquiry into this barbarism."

He turned to a policeman behind him.

"Help this man get dressed," he said. The cop came in quickly, carrying a plastic bag.

"There has been a terrible mistake, my dear fellow," said Crotty. "Bring this gentleman to my office the moment he's dressed," he said.

Owen was waiting in the corridor outside.

"This must be the oldest and corniest one on the book, Chief," he said.

Crotty half smiled. "Look how many times it's worked," he said.

A few minutes later, in Crotty's office, de Chaillot was drinking coffee and chain-smoking from a freshly opened pack of Chesterfields on the commissioner's desk.

"Now, are you sure I can't get you something to eat?" Crotty asked solicitously.

"No, thank you, you are being very kind," said the

count. "The hotel knows exactly how I like my food. I'd rather wait until I get back."

"Of course," said Crotty. "Mind you, we do our best for visitors, especially people like yourself, from foreign parts; but police cooking is not really noted in the dining-out guides."

Crotty managed to conceal a slight belch, the direct result of a hurried frankfurter smothered with an excess of onions.

"How I'd love to be able travel like you," he said. "Big jets all over the world. I've always wanted to see Rome, you know—a sort of pilgrimage. But the most I've ever managed was a three-week package tour to Ireland. It rained the whole time."

The count lit another cigarette. He was sinking back into the one comfortable chair in the commissioner's bleak office. He was at ease now, warm again.

"If you get to Rome, Commissioner, you must see my cousin. I will give you a letter of introduction to him. A prince of the Holy See, very close to His Holiness."

"Wouldn't *that* be something," Crotty said.

"You know, I've always fancied the idea of high finance," the chief went on. "Take you, for instance—handling millions of dollars, just like we handle criminal reports."

"It is a business, yes. Supply and demand."

"Ah, but it must take a hell of a lot of know-how that other people don't have."

"It is true that I am an acknowledged expert on international banking. People seek my advice."

"They do? So, if I wanted to borrow some money, I mean a big amount, I'd come to you?"

"If by that you mean a sum in excess of a hundred million dollars, yes, you would."

"Well, well," said Crotty. "And you do this all the time? I mean, what sort of conditions do you put on these loans?"

"I don't put any conditions," said de Chaillot, warming to the subject. "The lender does that. He would normally ask for certain very strong guarantees."

"Guarantees?"

"From large banks or big corporations."

"A new world opens up in front of my eyes," said

Crotty. To anyone else, the edge in his voice would have been unmistakable. But the Comte de Chaillot was easily flattered.

"Tell me," Crotty pressed. "Would you like a guided tour around headquarters? We do a lot of them, you know, especially for foreign VIPs."

"It's very kind of you, Commissioner," said de Chaillot. "But I would like to pick up my things and get back to the hotel."

"Well, that's the problem. You see, with all this snow, we're very short on helicopters. I'm afraid you'll have to wait a bit. Anyway, sir, I'd just like to talk to you, I mean to get your advice on this question of a hundred and thirty billion dollars. You seem to know something about this sum that we don't. You see, we just aren't used to *talking* this sort of money."

The count stood up. "I really must insist that my attorney be present," he said.

But Crotty remained friendly. "Oh, come on," he said. "Sit down. I'm just looking for advice."

"What sort of advice?"

"Just how I would get together that sum of money, which is more than the budgets of half the small countries in this world put together?"

"That sum of money," said de Chaillot, "is about a tenth of the total sum in Swiss banks. It represents about a year's annual income from the major Arab and Persian oil-producing nations."

"Well," said Crotty. "But tell me how you get your hands on it."

"It is done by knowing people," said the count. "You have a client and you let it be known in the money market that he wants to borrow. If the money is there and the terms are right, the fund can be arranged very quickly."

"Tell me, Count Chaillot," said Crotty. "You put these people together, the lender and the client. I suppose there is a kind of reward for you?"

A sudden vision of fifteen million dollars floated before de Chaillot's tired, worried eyes.

"I mean," Crotty went on, "it's like the man who arranges my mortgage. He takes a fee for doing that.

Let's call it one percent. I suppose you'll be getting that? One hundred and thirty million dollars?"

The count was still trying to clear the green vision of money from his mind. The thought of money always made him vulnerable. "Of course not," he snapped. "It is nothing like that amount."

"How much, then?"

"I have nothing to say."

"Your clients."

"It is a sacred rule of my profession that the names of the clients are never revealed at any time in the course of the transaction unless they allow it to happen."

"Detective Owen has told you the likely consequences of your refusal to answer. Now I am going to tell you in a little more detail."

Crotty was out of his chair with amazing speed for such a big man. He walked around and stood behind the count. Then he grabbed the lambswool collar of de Chaillot's coat and lifted the count out of the seat and marched him to a map of Manhattan on the wall. Still holding the scruff of his neck, Crotty said very quietly: "Your clients are planning to blow this city up," he said. "It will probably mean the death of thousands, if not millions, of people right there."

He crashed the count's head hard against the map.

"I want to know the names of your clients," he said. He banged the head hard again.

"I'm going to find out," he said. "Even if I have to cut your balls off."

Had Commissioner Crotty not said this at that point, it is likely that the count, blubbering now and trying hard to hold onto his wig with one hand, would have started to talk. But the mention of castration reminded him of Evie Martin's knife and a similar threat.

"I'm saying nothing," he said. "I want my lawyer."

"Owen," Crotty yelled. The detective came in immediately.

"Take this decaying old fruit to any quiet, soundproof part of this building and don't come back without the name of his clients."

"We're fresh out of rubber hoses, Chief," said Owen. "And I don't want to fuse the lights with electric terminals. Let me take the count here back to his suite."

39

In two days' time, thought Evie Martin, she and George and the others would be safe. She and Mahle would be in a hideaway on a Wyoming reservation, and the others scattered, equally secure from the law, all over the nation.

She was lying in the teepee. Mahle was sleeping on the blankets next to her, breathing easily; but she could tell from the minute tremors on his eyelids that he was only just asleep, that the slightest unusual noise would instantly bring him awake and alert. It was a gift given only to warriors and hunters.

Evie thought of most men as soft and malleable and weak. But not this man. She could admire and look up to and even worship him because he had no weakness.

She had learned this very quickly. On that first night in the apartment when he had talked about the supertanker, she had been intrigued by him. But then, as he began detailing the operational terms and went to work with maps and charts and diagrams, she saw a man she could love.

She loved the enormity of his thinking. This was no two-bit bomber who set a second hand on a detonator and ran. This was real, precise thinking, billion-dollar thinking, with each step in the operation weighed against the odds by a cool, brilliant mind.

Christ, what a man, she thought. Leaves here as an

out-of-work astronaut and comes back able to sail a supertanker right into the mayor's backyard. And look what they had achieved. The banks and corporations, all those bastards who had taken the Indians' land and corrupted their men, look at them scrabbling about for the money.

And they would get the money. I bet Boyle is sweating, she thought, wetting his pants hunting for those billions. What a dream to buy Manhattan back with that money and rip down the concrete and build a real island community the way it used to be, governed by the laws of nature: each man and each animal and each plant would have a place in which to live and breathe. Oh, to live there and watch the rest of the world choke to death.

But they had done well. Even to get this far. All day long the networks had been pumping out the message that the Indian people were on their way back after so many years of the white man's atrocity and cruelty and corruption.

Christ, those networks must be hopping, flaming mad, she thought. Must be losing thousands, millions of dollars without commercials. And what was the worth to the Indian movement?

Throughout the day she had been feeling elated by the tension and excitement of what they had done. It had translated itself now into a powerful sexual feeling. I am, she said, a bitch in heat. And you, she mouthed, looking at the sleeping man next to her, are going to give me the screw of a lifetime in four minutes' time when I wake you.

She unfastened the leather blouse and took her big breasts in her hands and held them very gently, caressing the nipples between the fingers and thumbs. She thought about Mahle and the power in his body which she had to whip and pinch and claw to satisfy.

She eased the leather skirt up to her thighs and slid down her pants and opened her legs wide, letting her fingers explore.

She began breathing deeply, her head pushed back hard into the blankets, her body arched. Then she turned and saw that Mahle was awake, looking at her with a look of something akin to curiosity.

"Please, George," she moaned.

Mahle wore only shorts. He took his time removing

them, staring at her as he did so. Turning in one lithe, almost-lazy movement, he eased himself onto her. She pulled him into her and locked her legs hard around him. Her nails clawed deep into his back and buttocks as he began to pound into her, in a powerful, slow rhythm which speeded with the pain she inflicted, using her teeth now, too.

Then she ripped the leather thong from her blouse and lashed his back, bucking and riding under him. And as she began to shiver and then tremble and then shake with a deep, powerful, all-relieving orgasm, an alarm bell started to ring in the room outside. In seconds, Mahle was away from her and on his feet, drawing on his shorts. She was still writhing on the blanket of the teepee as he rushed to the control room.

Peter Eagle Heart was sitting at the computer, his finger pressed on the printout button, watching openmouthed as a stream of paper was fed from the machine into a neatly folded pile in a tray below.

"What's happening?" said Mahle.

"Look."

Mahle held the agitated printout in his hand and let it run through his fingers.

"Chess," he said. "The Capablanca opening. That City Hall machine has been quite well programed. Assuming it is Van Horn's work, I'd say he's a worthy enough opponent. Obsessed with the bishop, very unsubtle with the knights. But he's good."

"It means that they've locked on to us," Eagle Heart said. He was trying to appear calm. Mahle's acceptance helped.

"It's a good move," said Mahle. "Keep us busy, confused. That's probably why the mayor was being so impudent." He looked at the repeater screen.

"Now that is clever," he said. "City Hall is programed in this game to a perpetual check. They really are trying to clog our machine."

The two computers were now repeating only two moves; the game could end only in stalemate. Normally, under the rules of chess, this would have been allowed for eight moves only before the game was declared a draw.

"Van Horn can keep this going all night," said Mahle. "Clever. Except that we're programed to exclude negative-entry trivia before each command, either prefed or manual." He tapped out a number of coded signals to his computer.

"This could be entertaining," he said.

"What have you done?"

"That signal will instruct the City Hall budget computer to double every figure programed in its data bank and continue to infinity, which means that even the humblest garbage man in New York will shortly be getting checks for something like fifty times our ransom. I wonder if Van Horn knows that one."

Mahle turned and walked back into the apartment. As he did so, Pete Eagle Heart saw the weals and nail marks on his back and remembered the cigarette crushed into his palm.

At two minutes past 4:00 P.M. Ben made the decision to evacuate lower Manhattan. At exactly four o'clock he had watched the camera move from the digital clock and another five primers lock into position.

He pressed the buzzer on his desk. He was still staring at the television set when Mary came in.

"I want Jane Landesmann here," he said. "And I want Canaletto and the police commissioner. Then I'll want Altmeyer. Tell Van Horn I want this room debugged. We're not dealing with normal people. We knew that already, I suppose." He turned to the microphones. "We are dealing with deranged, psychopathic thugs. Mahle, I asked you for time. So you start playing games with those lives you have endangered. Okay, so now it's the end of the phony war. No more pleas from me. I warn you that I will seek you out, George Mahle, and destroy you myself if I have to. You can still take my advice and hightail it out of this city. Because we're coming after you."

Mary said: "Before you say anything else, can you read this?" She handed him a typewritten sheet.

"Mr. Mayor.

1. Captain Cusp is on his way in with a coordinated plan which he wants you to approve.

2. Commissioner Canaletto is checking the routes he is using for evacuation.

3. Mrs. Stonybridge says she will have a yes or no from several banks before long. She is hopeful.

4. Commissioner Crotty says that the police now have a definite lead but that the suspect won't talk.

5. The weathermen report that this snow is likely to continue for another two or three hours and that there will be no letup in the bad weather for another 12 hours, when there is a possibility of a thaw."

Ben said: "No P.S.?"

She kissed him briskly on the forehead and left the office.

The mayor of New York City looked at the clock on the television screen for a full, heavy, wearisome minute and then picked up the telephone.

"Will you get me the President at Camp David, please. And put the call through on the deputy mayor's extension."

40

Apart from emergency services, very little moved in the city that day. Manhattan was a labyrinth of unconnected paths from which few strayed, except children, animals, and a determined, dedicated few who plonked their way kneehigh through the banks of snow. Children were delighted to see their streets turned into empty, snowfilled playgrounds in which there were no cars except for those buried against the sidewalks, and few adults. Those with toboggans were out on the streets soon after dawn, and soon thereafter, almost every kid in the city had found some way—a plank, a stolen piece of sheet metal, or a garbage can lid—to be towed around the block and then tow his neighbor.

The city's half-million stray cats fared worst. Many of them had frozen during the night; those which survived found little to sustain them that day except winter birds which had died in the blizzard.

A number of energetic, civic-minded block leaders managed to persuade their bored, restless neighbors to shovel snow from the sidewalks so people could reach supermarkets—but few supermarkets were open. Their staffs were trapped at home or somewhere else.

Most people stayed indoors, living on canned and frozen food, watching television, missing the commercials, some learning about the American Indian. Indeed, most spent much of the day switching from station to station, searching for various unfamiliar programs. Many knew that something was wrong, that it wasn't just the snow.

If nothing else, New York was a city that worked. There were 16 television channels and 63 AM and FM radio stations to tell people that it did. But they were strangely subdued, spending most of the time repeating the Mayor's appeal to stay indoors, interspersed with weather forecasts and minor bits of news from other parts of the country.

New Yorkers had expected news of a great street-sweeping operation. Hourly they waited for the scraping business of the snowplows in their neighborhoods.

But they waited in vain. They heard nothing, only silence. For most of them, this was more ominous than anything else. New York was a city of noise. But now it was stilled. The most familiar sound that day, the thundering of helicopters, was mostly absorbed by the snow.

Those who had serviceable telephones and called City Hall to complain were told by a recording that the City Hall exchange was busy with emergency calls, that only essential services were being handled. Eventually even the youngsters of the city were subdued; except for a group of Harlem graffitists who, deprived of the subway, succeeded in tramping out a slogan which read "Flying Pigs" for the benefit of police helicopters.

Although the police were diverted by the disaster, crime in the city dropped to near zero.

41

"Mr. President."

"Hello, Ben, you sound kind of flat."

"Yes, sir, I'm afraid I am, at that."

"I hope you aren't letting that old battleaxe of a sister of mine get you down."

"Oh, no, indeed, sir. She's got all of City Hall jumping, me in particular."

"So what's the news?"

"I'm evacuating lower Manhattan. Starting as soon as we can."

"That's a big undertaking. Can you do it?"

"We can do it. But what I wanted to say, Mr. President, is that the operation here is in the hands of a very capable sort of Coast Guard captain named Cusp."

"Bob Cusp. You couldn't have a better man, Ben."

"What I was going to say is, I'd be grateful if you would give him every possible help from the federal end."

"Well, so far we've given him a nuclear sub, a whole pile of electronic hardware, and I've put the United States Navy at his disposal."

"Thanks, Mr. President."

"Any time, Ben. And Ben?"

"Yes, Mr. President?"

"He seems to think that you guys at City Hall are doing a pretty good job, too."

"You can start moving at six o'clock," said Jane Landesmann. "I'm sorry about the delay, but there were too many cars blocking the roads. I asked the drivers to keep a count, but I'm afraid they gave up after the first three thousand."

Ben winced and dared not look at Altmeyer who coughed nervously but said nothing.

"Mickey?"

Canaletto threw some papers on the table. "The operational plan," he said. "Based on an original civil defense plan, but one that didn't allow for snow. I'll get it typed up in a few weeks' time so you'll know what we did. Okay, so what happens is that you, Ben, will call the TV networks now and arrange for air time to tell the city what's happened—or as much of it as you choose to. I'll come on right after you and explain the details of the evacuation."

"And none of your silly damn jokes," Altmeyer said. "They've got to be made to realize how serious the situation is."

"If they see me being serious, they're bound to panic," said Canaletto. "I shall radiate confidence—and I shall be praying hard all the time."

"Get on with it," said Ben.

"The minute you start speaking, the first buses will be on their way down 42nd Street and then south onto First Avenue. By the time you've finished, they'll be taking up positions around Battery Park. By the time *I've* finished, there'll be a thousand cops around with bullhorns, floodlights, snowshoes, and emergency communications equipment, as well as ambulances for the sick and aged, a complete mobile maternity unit, an operating theater, a cardiac arrest unit, three breathing aids, and the police mobile mortuary."

"You think of everything," said Jane quietly.

"The police command unit will move with the medical auxiliaries, and a rear party will go over each street with bullhorns to make sure nobody's forgotten."

"Suppose they don't obey orders and decide to stay?" asked Altmeyer.

"Freedom of choice. Their first right. They can stay if they want to—nearer the fireworks display."

"What can they take with them?" asked Jane.

"Nightclothes and toothbrushes," said Canalleto. "The women can carry purses with the family cash. But that's all. The streets will be patrolled right through the evacuation period."

"They're not going to like that," said Ben.

"It's a question of time. There are a lot of people to move."

"Okay," said Ben. "Are you quite sure about six o'clock, Jane?"

"Positive. Unless this snow whips up into another blizzard."

"Jane, I'm very grateful to you. And I wish you luck, Mickey."

Ben picked up the telephone and asked for NBC and George Martinez, who was heading the networks emergency committee.

Martinez told him: "All the main network and city channels will be hooked up from five o'clock on for you and the other announcements, Mr. Mayor. But be sure to make the most of the radio services—I've got a feeling that we've lost a lot of our audience today with these Indian tapes. Too bad really; some of them were pretty good. I even know how to build a wigwam."

Once the helicopter carrying Ben and Canaletto had left, its lights flashing eerily on the snow-covered lawns, Mary Fyfield poured herself a cup of coffee and sat quietly in Ben's office. She finished the coffee, then walked round and switched on the television set and sat back in an armchair. It was the first time all day that she'd been still for more than two minutes. Throughout the day she had been answering Ben's telephone, handling angry city councillors, pouring bourbon for Mrs. Stonybridge, taking messages, typing lists for Canaletto, and keeping a maternal eye on the Mayor.

Of all the crazy things, she thought, here I am, Mary Fyfield, *Lady* Mary Fyfield, indeed, born in a stately home built 200 years before the American Revolution, a product of an exclusive, expensive girls' school, a woman much sought by the sons of the rich. And here I am, sitting in the Mayor's parlor in New York, sitting at the ringside of a potential disaster. And I am totally and irrevocably in love with that mayor.

Just what was it about him that had turned her so suddenly from an easygoing career girl (admittedly of no fixed career) into a singleminded, devoted servant? He was handsome, certainly; but, then, she had had handsome lovers. He was gentle in bed; but then she'd have loved him if he'd behaved like a wild stallion. No, she decided, it was his strength that she loved. A strength made up of honesty, compassion, determination, and a hundred other qualities she was still discovering in him.

The crazy chump, she thought; he wants to marry me. He loves me, and if there is one thing I know about Ben Boyle, he is going to go on loving me. So why not marry him? Of course, she would make a good mayor's wife. She and Ben could do for Gracie Mansion what the Kennedys had done for the White House. They could make the city something else.

But what then? She knew, and had known for a long time now, that Ben Boyle was destined for even higher things than the mayoralty of this city. This country badly needed a young, tough, honest president.

All right, so Mary Fyfield might make a good first lady of New York. But when it came to selecting a presidential candidate, her Englishness might do Ben a lot of damage. Americans were a peculiar people, she thought. To hear them talk, especially in this city, you'd think all of them had been born in some other country—in Connemara or Calabria or the Ukraine. Yet their First Lady had to be a native-born American.

No, she couldn't marry Ben. He was too important to the country, she decided, feeling vaguely smug, although, in truth, she was desperately unhappy.

She walked across the office and turned up the sound on the television set.

The face of a well-known movie star who had devoted much of his life to the Indian cause filled the screen. Even in this modern age, it was hard not to miss the sincerity in his voice as he detailed the abuses of the Indian people so long after the early settlers drove the Indians from the plains and cheated them out of their reservations. But even as he spoke a caption appeared under his face which read:

STAND BY FOR IMPORTANT ANNOUNCEMENT BY MAYOR BOYLE.

It flashed on and off and was replaced by a subtitle across the actor's chin:

MAYOR BOYLE WILL BE MAKING AN IMPORTANT ANNOUNCMENT IN TEN MINUTES TIME AT 5 P.M.

The actor was saying: "In a book called *The Road to Wounded Knee* a few years ago, a leading Indian spokesman wrote: 'If the government and the people do not heed the cry of the Indian before much more time passes, the activists will be driven underground for an all-out battle that could turn any area with a sizable Indian population into another Northern Ireland. The gears of our society are so meshed and so complex that even a small band of dedicated fanatics could throw the whole social order out of line. It might be wise for the government and white America to reflect that those who are without hope are also without fear."*

MAYOR BOYLE WILL BE MAKING AN IMPORTANT ANNOUNCEMENT IN SEVEN MINUTES TIME AT 5 P.M. PLEASE STAY TUNED FOR MAYOR BOYLE.

The actor finished with a short passage of speech over a film of the squalor and depression of the Navahos, of their decaying huts, their children with lifeless eyes, and their squaws, women with despair etched on their faces. "These were once the most fierce and independent people in this country which boasts so readily to the world of its own freedom," said the actor. "They have been decimated by the white man's diseases, by his greed for their land; they have been tainted by his corruption and slowly brought to ruin by the drink that he brought. They have seen their world shattered, the balance of nature destroyed, that balance which they so carefully and delicately kept because they knew, as we are only just finding out, that there is a meaning to all things on this earth.

* *The Road to Wounded Knee* by Robert Burnette and John Koster, copyright © 1974 by Robert Burnette. Reprinted by permission of Bantam Books, Inc.

MAYOR BOYLE WILL MAKE AN IMPORTANT ANNOUNCEMENT AT 5 P.M. STAY TUNED FOR MAYOR BOYLE.

"I pray, as all of us who love and respect the Indian people pray, that those words I spoke will not turn into deeds; that there will be no war in Indian country; that peace will prevail; and that all white men of goodwill will come quickly to understand the reason for that warning and will move their representatives into action to save the Indians of the United States."

The screen went to an even blue and the three chimes of the NBC station signal were played. A voice said, "NBC New York coming to you on Channel Four." The image was cut suddenly to a studio interior. David Chartham, the network's leading commentator, sat before a large map of New York. Chartham, who normally managed to keep at least a hint of humor in his affable face, even when breaking the most critical news to the nation, looked deadly serious.

"Good evening," he said. "In one minute Mayor Ben Boyle will be speaking to you from these studios. Before I introduce Mayor Boyle, I want to impress on everyone watching in New York that his message concerns you. It will be repeated several times during this evening. It is important that you make sure that your neighbor is just as aware of what the Mayor has to say as you are. I stress again the importance of listening to this announcement by the Mayor of New York. If you are children watching, I want you to run and get your parents to the television set. Go and do it now. Tell them it's very important. This broadcast will be repeated at six o'clock, at seven o'clock, and eight o'clock. So will the messages that follow. It will also be repeated on the city's AM and FM stations.

"Ladies and gentlemen, Mr. Ben Boyle, the Mayor of New York."

Mary leaned forward. The first TV shot of Ben showed him sitting in what seemed to be the very office she was in, flanked by the Stars and Stripes and the bright red flag of New York City. They had changed his white swearing-in shirt to a blue one with longer collar points. He was wearing a dark-blue tie.

Mary had seen him on TV on many occasions, but this

was the first time she had seen any sign of nervousness or apprehension on his face.

"Good evening," Ben said. "I'm afraid I'm going to have to talk to you about some bad news which affects all of us. It is something I have known about all day, but for a lot of reasons, I've had to keep it from you until now.

"Here it is. I took office last night in the middle of the worst blizzard this city has ever known. The storm brought this city to a complete standstill. That's one reason I appealed to you to stay indoors—until we could begin coping with the mess.

"But there was another reason for asking you to stay indoors. What I am going to say now may scare a lot of you. But please hear me out. Don't do anything in panic. Because a lot of things are happening at this moment outside in the streets that are intended to protect all of you.

"What has happened is this. A group of terrorists have succeeded in bringing a supertanker into New York harbor and mooring it off the west side of lower Manhattan. They are threatening to explode it sometime tomorrow evening. Now I repeat that. Tomorrow evening is the deadline they have given me."

Ben was bringing his fingers down on the desk in front of him and Mary heard the microphone ping with each tap. There was no nervousness now. "My darling's getting his dander up," she said and then remembered that the room was still bugged.

"Now, I'm not going to go into who these people are or their reasons for doing this lunatic thing, especially since they're doing it in the name of a cause which deserves to be heard.

"But I can tell you that the forces of law and order in this city are fully occupied in the search for these dangerous men and that the finest men in this country are being asked to help in the difficult and dangerous task of defusing this tanker.

"I want to say at once that I am so confident in their abilities that I'll lay very big odds against this explosion's ever occurring. But I'm not taking any chances with your lives. Therefore I have ordered a voluntary evacuation scheme to be put into effect immediately. This involves all those people whose lives are in any way in the slightest danger. This obviously will affect those of you on the southern end of the island.

"The reason I've delayed telling you this news until now—and I am grateful to all the media for their cooperation in this matter—is that we had to get the streets cleared in that part of the city. I was anxious that there should be no running away—that would have had disastrous results, especially in this weather.

"I just want to add that we—all of us—owe a great deal to the cooperation of the sanitation men of this city who voluntarily returned to work as soon as the extent of the blizzard was fully realized."

Ben coughed slightly, and Mary wondered whether there was some hidden meaning there for Frank Schenk.

"So as I say," he continued. "The street-clearing operation underway today has been done with the object of getting people away from the most vulnerable part of the city. In a minute or so, the commissioner for civil defense, Michael Canaletto, will be explaining the procedure.

"As the Mayor, I appeal to you to listen to him and do what he says. It's a highly complex operation, and it will take time. It will require a lot of patience on your part. It will also require a lot of courage, especially from those of you living near where the tanker is now.

"Sometimes it has struck me that it takes a lot of courage just to live in this city."

Ben smiled.

"But New Yorkers are tough. If they can put up with so many of our problems, I think it will take more than a bunch of cowardly hoodlums to scare them.

"Now, just one other thing. People living above 23rd Street are less likely to be affected, although I'll be asking all of you to go to civil defense shelters and wait for the all clear.

"So please stay where you are and don't, whatever you do, try to leave the city. There are only a few roads open, and these are required for the movement of people in danger and for use by the emergency services.

"Remember what I say—all of you. This explosion, should it happen, will take place tomorrow evening. By that time I am sure we will have moved everyone from the danger zone. Now listen to Commissioner Canaletto.

Listen carefully. Please do as he asks. It'll make it a lot easier for all of you and for us. Thank you."

The camera panned to the right and found Canaletto. Behind him was a blow-up of a map of southern Manhattan.

"Hi," he said and smiled. "My name's Canaletto. I've probably got the biggest job since Moses organized the Exodus. But I'll tell you that he was unlucky in his job because he didn't have the New York Transit Authority or the New York Bus Services, or a helluva lot of first-class cops and sanitation men to help him.

"Now then, if you people living down in the streets off Whitehall and Broad streets and Broadway south of Wall Street would care to look out your windows, you'll see enough buses to take Ben Boyle's relatives to a christening.

"Go on. Look. See, I'm right. Okay, so don't hang around—put on your warmest clothes and pack a pair of pajamas in a brown paper bag and just lock your house or apartment and get into the bus nearest your front door.

"Don't stand there arguing about it. And don't bring the rocking chair. There will be plenty of furniture where you're going."

Canaletto was radiating just the confidence that people needed. Ben had been fine, thought Mary. He'd made the people feel that they were all part of a fight against something evil; and Mickey was following up with the kind of language that they needed for this emergency.

"Okay, so much for the first of the multitude," said Canaletto. "Now I'm going to talk to the people next door. Wall Street, Pearl, Nassau—where all the money is. Just as soon as we've moved those people south of you, you'll see the floodlights and the cops, and you'll think you're in the movies. Get ready right now—and leave your jewels behind. Every street will be guarded against burglary. And God help anyone who tries it."

Canaletto paused and then repeated the last sentence.

"For the rest of the evening, as well, we will be coming to other blocks and neighborhoods. Please stay tuned.

"Now for all Spanish-speaking watchers, the news is that your particular time of movement is being given in the same way on Channels 41 and 47."

Mary turned the set off.

42

While Ben and Canaletto were making their way to the NBC Building, Detective Owen Owen was walking at an uncomfortable speed through the plaza of the World Trade Center, heavily handcuffed to an extremely reluctant Count de Chaillot. Owen was walking fast because dusk was dropping quickly on Manhattan, and he wanted de Chaillot to look at the view.

"I gather you turned down the chief's offer of a guided tour," he said. "Well, I'll show you a piece of New York instead. Come on, fatty, we've got a long way to go."

The elevator went to the 78th floor. Owen pulled the count out and said: "Hey, come and look out of this window." De Chaillot had little choice; he almost fell as Owen dragged him over the carpeting.

Owen stood at the window which looked out over the Hudson. Down below, her snow-covered decks reflecting the early lights of New Jersey, was the supertanker. Even from that height, which miniaturized everything, the ship was huge, formidable and blackly ominous.

"Take a look," said Owen, thrusting the unhappy count against the glass.

"Five hundred thousand tons of her. All the right mixtures of fuel inside her to blow up half this city, Count Chaillot. And it's your clients who are going to do it."

He felt the count push back from the window, shivering. Owen grinned with sardonic satisfaction.

"You don't like heights?"

"I'm terrified."

"Really. I like heights. It's my Indian blood. Indians are strange people. Not frightened by heights. That's how they built New York. Yet they can't take drink. Crazy, huh?"

"I want to go back to the elevator."

"Come on, Chaillot. Say, I had an idea. I thought that if I left you just looking at that tanker—knowing that when it went up you would be sucked through that heavy plate glass window—you might tell me the name of your client. Who *is* your client? Okay, come on."

They entered the local elevator. De Chaillot breathed a sigh of relief until he saw Owen touch the electronic button for the 110th floor.

"I thought, while we were here, that I'd give you a demonstration of how much I like heights. There's a brand new aerial on this building and the power isn't hooked up to it yet. Always wanted to climb it. Who's your client?"

Owen saw the terror in the Frenchman's face. Oh boy, he'll talk, he thought.

At the entrance to the roof of the center's south tower, the door was guarded by an armed marine.

"Sorry, no visitors," he said.

Owen produced his badge.

"What's going on?" the Marine asked. "The Coast Gaurd is putting up some equipment. All part of Operation Crazy Horse. Who's this guy?"

Owen held up the handcuffed hand of de Chaillot.

"Distinguished foreign visitor."

"Okay, sir."

On the west side of the tower's roof, Owen could see a gang of sailors wrestling with a long telescopic object. A tripod was clamped to the corner of the building.

From the ground, the aerial masts on top of the World Trade Center look, like the twin towers of the center themselves, to be slim and slender and so brittle that they could break easily in high winds.

Yet there on the roof, 1,350 feet above the river, they present a completely different picture. They are 200 feet high and built of light aluminium, designed in such a way that the wind resistance is controlled by delicately sculptured airfoils. Four steel cables anchored to each corner of the roof are the only supports.

A thin alloy ladder runs through the center of the aerial from roof level to the top.

Owen stood de Chaillot at the bottom of the ladder and jerked his head back so that he had to look up at the metal tower, which appeared to move at high speed against the dark clouds above it.

"Now, watch me climb up that ladder," he said.

The count almost fainted with relief.

"The only thing is that you're my prisoner and there'll be a hell of a row if I lose you. So we'll both go up. You go on that side and I'll go this."

"No, please—no!"

Owen grabbed the count by the shoulder and pushed him against the ladder. Then, still handcuffed, he started to climb, his face against de Chaillot's through the rungs.

When he had climbed two rungs above the count's shaking feet, he wrenched his wrist upward and lifted the screaming de Chaillot up to his own height.

And thus they climbed to the roof of New York; one man, his face set with a grim hardness, the other terrified and pitiful. A little higher, and the wind took the ill-fitting wig from de Chaillot's head and carried it high out over the Hudson.

At the top of the ladder, Owen gave one final yank and de Chaillot was clinging to the metal upright, his face close to Owen's, a look of animal pleading in his eyes.

Owen took a key from his pocket and unlocked the handcuffs. "I'm going to leave you to enjoy the view," he said, and started to climb down.

He had gone only two rungs when he heard the anguished howl from above.

"Evie Martin," the voice screamed.

Owen clambered quickly back up. "Evie Martin," he said. "Presumed dead in Wichita three years ago. Of course. Where is she?"

"I don't know. I swear I don't know."

Owen took out the handcuffs and used them to attach the count to the ladder. Then he hooked his strong wrists over the top of the aerial and heaved himself up until he stood on the very top of the highest point of New York.

He was unsupported, standing on a metal base three feet wide with light snow slapping against his face.

Casually he reached into his hip pocket and took out a two-way radio.

"Owen to Sprint One," he said.

"Sprint One."

"I want Commissioner Crotty, urgently, on the green channel."

"Ten-four, sir."

For a few moments, Owen stood in the gentle snow and looked at Manhattan. Below, toward the Battery, he could see the floodlights of the evacuation force and the long line of buses turning onto Broadway. Out on the Hudson, the *Jersey Lily* was floodlit now from all sides, and he could see, in the powerful lights, the outline of the attendant Coast Guard vessels.

"Crotty."

"Evie Martin, chief. Evelyn Foster Martin, age thirty-two. Presumed dead. Two jail sentences for explosives offenses. Last seen in explosion in Wichita, thought to have blown herself to pieces. Can you institute a check? She's our girl. If you remember, she inherited fifteen million dollars."

"Okay. Come back. Owen, that's a very clear signal. Where are you?"

"You'd never guess, chief, but I've got a damn good aerial."

He climbed down reluctantly. De Chaillot had fainted and was suspended by the handcuffs.

43

For the second time in twenty-four hours, Ben was riding the subway. This time the train was almost empty, a northbound local to Penn Station. A group of officials accompanied him; some, from the transit authority, were oversolicitous for his well-being, even to the point of dusting the plastic seats and apologizing for the graffiti.

It was at Michael Canaletto's insistence that he was going to the station to meet the first of the refugees. An NBC camera crew and reporter accompanied him and were checking out their equipment at the end of the car.

"The important thing is to let everyone know that the system is working," Canaletto had said. "If they can see you on the news bulletins, kissing a few babies, maybe, they won't mind standing in line for our buses."

Even as the doors of the train opened, Ben could smell food. The smell grew stronger as he marched through the exit gates, a smell of roasting chicken, of rosemary and marjoram and garlic, of meatballs and spaghetti sauce, an aroma which overpowered the usual subway smell of disinfectant and people.

Canaletto, who had preceded him by helicopter, stood proudly at the entrance to the station concourse.

"Welcome, Mr. Mayor," he said. "Our very first customer. Come on in the the pasta palace. It's all on the city."

Inside the concourse, behind a row of emergency ovens, stood a line of white-coated men, women and children, some almost hidden in the steam from the giant cauldrons in front of them. Fifteen long tables, each covered with a paper tablecloth, filled the rest of the concourse.

There were booths for inquiries, for lost children, for interpreters, for special medical care and for what was discreetly called "ladies' requirments."

The station's public address system was playing soft music.

"Well, I'm damned," said Ben.

"Like it?" Canaletto asked.

"How the hell did you do it?"

"I told my mama we had guests for dinner and she got organized. Most of these are my relatives. Wanna meet them?"

"Hell, not now. I'll say hello to your mama."

Canaletto looked at his watch.

"You've just got time. The first guests will be here in four minutes."

The hand-held floodlight of the camera team bathed Ben in a brilliant white glow as he walked down the line of kitchen helpers, stopping now and then to taste a sauce or to nibble at some pasta, with Canaletto close behind, beaming with pride.

At the end of the line, Canaletto ran ahead and brought out from the steam a small, dignified woman with curly gray hair. She smiled shyly at Ben and held out her hand.

"Since when do I shake hands with Mama Canaletto?" he said, hugging her warmly.

"Ah, but you are the mayor now, Ben Boyle," she said. "And look, we are on television."

"You're right," said Ben. He turned her to face the camera. A microphone emerged from the brightness of the lights.

"Here you are, ladies and gentlemen. The best cook in the city of New York. I've eaten at her table more times than I can remember. And she's cooking here at the first reception center.

"So if anyone is in any doubt about the quality of the service . . . well, what's on the menu, Mama?"

"Nobody will go hungry, that's for sure," she said. "We've made some minestrone and then there are some pancakes frittatine imbottite with a very nice stuffing, and there is tortellini and fettucine and lasagne verdi and there are chicken breasts. All very good."

"You bet," said Ben. "Thanks, Mama. Let me talk to your son here about the other centers. What's the food like at Grand Central, Commissioner?"

"It's a United Nations feeding job over there. Oxtail soup and locksen soup and hamburgers and paella and gefilte fish and a whole lot of Chinese food, too. Something for everyone."

"I don't know how you did it, Commissioner," said Ben. "But there you are, citizens," he turned to the camera. "As you can see, the city of New York is taking good care of you."

"Just one other thing, Mr. Mayor," said Canaletto. "When the folks have finished eating here there's a free, all-star spectacular to watch upstairs in Madison Square Garden. All of Broadway is giving its talents away tonight just to keep you amused while you wait for transport to the hotels and other reception centers we've got lined up for you."

As they walked toward the main door of the Penn Station concourse, Ben asked Canaletto: "Just how the hell *did* you do it?"

"One of the biggest boasts of this city is that we've got the best restaurants in the world. That means we have the best cooks in the world. It also means several thousand tons of preserved foods are in kitchens all over New York. They just opened a lot of cans. That's the truth of it, but don't tell a soul."

On the snow-covered roof of the station, Ben saw the landing lights of the police helicopter switch on; the rotors began to turn. Above the whine of the motor the pilot shouted: "They want you back at City Hall urgently, Mr. Mayor."

As they flew down the length of Eight Avenue, Ben could see a line of approaching buses and floodlights in the distance. A minute or so later, before the pilot banked steeply toward City Hall, he saw lines of people in the floodlights, policemen and firemen helping them over the thick banks of snow. Someone was being carried in a make-shift litter; another blanket-covered figure was being held high over the snow in a stretcher.

It was going to take a long, long time, thought Ben.

44

The change in Count de Chaillot after his ordeal at 1,300 feet was remarkable even to policemen who were used to watching suspects break down under interrogation. The arrogance was gone, as was the smugness and the condescension. Now he was anxious only to please. Detective Owen sat with him in the interrogation room and talked quietly but quickly. He glanced at his watch frequently.

"Okay, Chaillot, I believe you don't know where you met Evie Martin. But tell me, why were you so afraid to give us her name before?"

"She made a threat. A terrible threat."

"Like what?"

"She said she would . . . castrate me."

"That was Commissioner Crotty."

"No, but she, you see, she meant it."

"Okay, I'm going to take you through that car ride from Kennedy. You arrived there at 4:30 on a Tuesday evening. Right?"

"Right."

"You were blindfolded. You couldn't see anything?"

"Nothing."

"You could hear?"

"Yes. But only traffic and a few odd street noises."

"Let's try traffic first. What sort of traffic noises?"

"We were moving quickly and I would say that there

was a lot of traffic moving the other way. I could hear the swish of cars as they passed us."

"Then?"

"Then we were in a tunnel."

"Probably Queens Midtown."

"And then there was the noise of the city, you know, a lot of automobiles, sirens, people shouting for taxis. The car stopped and started a lot of times. I assumed we were in Manhattan."

"How long, would you say, from the tunnel to your final stop?"

"Maybe fifteen, twenty minutes."

"What other noises did you hear?"

"There was a very loud noise, what sounded like an explosion. It was quite near by. Then we turned, left, I think, and left again, and then the car stopped very quickly."

"And then?"

"I heard one door open and close. Then my door was open and I was pushed and pulled out very quickly. I was put in an elevator that smelled terrible and then the door opened and I was in the apartment having my blindfold removed."

"Okay, now describe this apartment again."

De Chaillot closed his eyes and went over the details of the Indian apartment.

"Did Evie Martin leave the room at all?"

"Only once. I think she went to telephone my news of the money."

"Did you see the room she went into?"

"Only briefly through the door."

"What sort of room was it?"

"Oh, it was quite different. It was bare and there were a lot of wires and typewriters."

"Typewriters? Could they have been computer terminals?"

"I wouldn't know."

"Big typewriters?"

"I only saw them briefly. Yes, I would say so."

"Okay, de Chaillot, one more thing. When you left you say it took ten minutes to get to your hotel?"

"No more than that."

"Which way did you turn when you left Evie Martin's?"

"The car was facing left. Then it turned left. I can't remember more than that."

"Do you remember any smells? I mean chestnuts roasting or pretzels? Food of some kind? You know, garlic or hamburgers or frankfurters? Or onions?"

"No. The elevator smelled so awful that my sense of smell was destroyed for several hours."

"What did the elevator smell of?"

"Urine, stale tobacco, marijuana, people."

"How long was the elevator ride?"

"It seemed very slow."

"Okay, wait there."

Outside, Evans was detailing two detectives.

"We're looking for a luxury pad in a flophouse. Somewhere, I would guess, in the West Forties or Fifties. Could be anywhere. But he said he heard an explosion. Find out if there have been any demolitions recently on that part of the island. Now this pad is decorated entirely with Indian furniture and paintings and craft things.

"You'll find half a dozen of these in the yellow pages—the American Indian Arts Center on Madison, Grey Owl in Jamaica, All Feathers—there's big money in tomahawks. Get to them and find out if any of them have delivered anything lately to an Evie Martin living somewhere in that part of Manhattan. Or Evie Martin anywhere. Take any available men. And you are red priority for the next helicopter that comes free."

When the detectives left, Owen picked up a wall telephone and asked for Crotty.

"Chief," he said. "I'm pretty certain that when we find Evie Martin we're going to find that master computer. I think we should talk to Van Horn. When we find it, he's going to have to handle it."

45

The long table in the City Hall planning room was filled with people when Ben came in from Penn Station. He pulled off his overcoat and muffler and took his seat at the head of the table. Some started to stand up, but he waved them down impatiently.

"Those terrorists have had the upper hand for too damned long," he said. "I'd like to think we are on the offensive in a big way."

He looked around the table.

The technician sat on his right. Van Horn was writing on a circuit diagram. He looked completely relaxed and confident; maybe he's too damned confident, thought Ben. Captain Cusp was showing a heavy growth of beard and looked more aggressive than ever. He was flanked by two Coast Guard officers whom Ben had not seen before.

Captain Bomboulas was as grave as ever; and Mr. Onodera, impeccably smart, looked fresh and alert. Jane Landesmann looked cool and pretty; Ben could see a new authority in her manner. Commissioner Crotty's rock-hard face was unchanged; and Owen, sitting beside him, looked edgy and anxious.

There were five newcomers at the table.

"Can I know who everybody is?" asked Ben.

Cusp spoke up briskly.

"Commander Button is our senior radio technician. Lieutenant Commander Masters is handling the other technical aspects in cooperation with Mr. Van Horn.

"These gentlemen," he said, indicating two other men in uniform at the end of the table, "are Captain Connolly of the Hudson River pilots and Captain Weiner of the New York harbor pilots."

"Welcome, gentlemen," said Ben.

Both pilots were in their sixties, retired ships' captains, Ben guessed. They looked as if they felt out of place in the committee room. They'd be so much happier on the bridge of that tanker, thought Ben. Or would they?

There was one more man at the table. He was dark and his hair was slicked back; he drummed his fingers on the table impatiently.

"And this gentleman?" said Ben.

The dark man turned slowly around.

"Me?"

"Right."

"I'm Goldberg from New Jersey."

Altmeyer interposed quickly. "Mr. Goldberg is the representative of Jersey City," he said. "I invited him to this meeting so that he can report to Mayor Rapallo."

"I hope that the deputy mayor has been keeping you fully informed, Mr. Goldberg," said Ben.

"Sure he has," said Goldberg. "What I want to know is why the hell you guys have insisted on doing all this yourselves. The Mayor of Jersey City has asked me to tell you that if that tanker goes up, Mr. Mayor, you'll be held personally responsible for the consequences."

It was an unpleasant moment which Ben would have delighted in exploiting. Instead, he smiled and said quietly, "Give my best wishes to Mayor Rapallo and tell him that he would be a most welcome and honored guest at my inauguration on Friday morning.

"And just to clear up the legal aspects of this, that ship sits on the New York side of the New York-Hudson County border—which makes it our baby."

Goldberg scowled but said nothing.

"Captain Cusp?" said Ben.

The little Coast Guard man stood up. "I think the police department may have the most important news, Mr.

Mayor. Their information may make a great difference to the operation we have planned."

"Commissioner?"

Crotty did not stand up. He waited thoughtfully for a moment before talking.

"Mr. Mayor, the lead we have is tenuous and may come to nothing. Very simply, we know who put up the money for this whole operation. We know her name and we know that the computer is almost certainly in the apartment where she lives. And we know that apartment is in Manhattan. We can only guess which part of Manhattan.

"Owen has instituted a number of inquiries which may narrow down the address. Inquiries are difficult in this kind of weather and with offices closed up. It will take time."

"But there's a chance?"

"A chance, yes."

"Okay, Commissioner. Captain Cusp?"

"Mr. Mayor, Mr. Van Horn is confident that if we can knock out one computer, there is a chance of getting on the ship."

"But when?"

"It's a risky business. Better finish the evacuation first. And we've assessed the laser heat system to activate the fire extinguishers. That's dangerous, too. The substances in that ship are too volatile."

"It's going to take a hell of a long time to evacuate."

"We'll be ready to move in any time after dawn. That is, if we know there isn't a human hand on a button somewhere. Mr. Van Horn thinks that the ship's computer can be overcome."

Ben turned to Van Horn.

"Can it?"

"By drastic means, yes. And by making certain assumptions. The first one is that these people have programmed a pretty careful fail-safe system into their computer. I mean, remember those two policemen. According to the original document, any attempt to board the ship meant an explosion.

"It didn't explode. I assume from that fact that when the computer gets a certain decibel count from a sound sensor, or a particular temperature reading from the body heat sensors, or a radar picture, which it can analyze, it makes up its own mind what action to take.

"In this case it decided to kill. On the other hand it could have taken a far more positive action to self-destruct itself and the tanker.

"I'd guess it would explode only in the event of a full-scale rush at the ship. In other words, if there were fifty or so people trying to board her with a lot of helicopters and ships near at hand."

"Go on," said Ben.

"We have to create a situation for which this computer is not programed. We've got to overload each of these systems to such an extent that it can't analyze because it's beyond its program. Then we can get aboard while it tries to work out what's happening."

"Make a lot of noise, you mean?"

"A hell of a lot of noise, a lot of heat through the laser system and a rock-solid radar echo that it simply can't understand. So instead of activating the detonators, it stops and checks and questions itself and its systems and doesn't just stop because it's programed to be exceptionally careful."

"You assume that these terrorists are exceptionally careful people."

"There're a lot of Indians living in that part of Manhattan, Mr. Mayor. And, from the experience I've had today, I can tell you that their representatives certainly know how to program a computer."

"Did you confuse them or did they confuse you?"

"It's just as well I kept a budget cover tape, Mr. Mayor, or I'd be looking for a job right now."

"Okay, so what now?" Ben asked.

"I'd like to cut the power in this city for two minutes at eight o'clock," said Van Horn.

"You'd like to cut the city's power?" Ben's voice was loaded with a weary exasperation.

"It's important for us to know whether this master computer is operating off mains or whether it has its own independent power supply."

"Okay, so what about the rest of the city? Hospitals, those poeple in kidney machines, iron lungs . . . you mentioned them yourself."

"They've been warned. The hospitals will go onto

emergency generators and individuals have hand-operated devices which will keep them going."

"So how will we know?"

"We watch TV, Mr. Mayor. If the camera moves, then they have their own power source."

"I take it City Hall has."

"Right, Mr. Mayor."

"What happens then?"

"Then we black the city out for two hours while we look for it from the air."

"For two hours?"

"During that time, Mr. Mayor, a number of army helicopters would range over the city with heat-seeking devices which will be able to pick out most of the generators working during that time. We have a list here from Con Ed."

"For two hours? You'd black out New York for two hours?"

"It might take longer," said Van Horn innocently.

"Jesus H. Christ," said Ben. "I've been mayor for less than a day. Half the population of Manhattan has had to be evacuated and now the lights are going out." Ben stopped.

"Okay," he said. "Do we have to do it all at once?"

"Oh no," said Van Horn. "District by district, according to the way the city is zoned."

"Thank God for that," said Ben.

"Can I proceed, Mr. Mayor?" asked Van Horn. "It's ten till eight and I'd like to confirm with Con Ed."

"Go ahead," said Ben. He waved Van Horn away perhaps a shade too irritably and regretted it immediately. He realized that he was getting tired, more tired than he could afford to be. This certainly was not a time for being short-tempered with his officials.

"Would any of you like a beer?" he asked. "Or some coffee? We might as well watch TV in comfort."

On the way to his office, the others walked quickly in a trail behind him through the corridors, Ben asked Captain Cusp: "Why the two pilots?"

"We have to be ready for every contingency, Mr. Mayor," said the man briskly. "We may have to pull that ship away from its moorings and take a chance that we can keep it on the same compass bearing until it reaches the widest part of the harbor. It'll be a hell of a job but these guys think it could be done."

"And they'd do it?"

"They've both volunteered."

"Well I'm damned," said Ben.

46

The snow continued to fall for most of the evening, sufficiently heavy to slow the complex evacuation and make movement by helicopter, especially at a few hundred feet through the cavernous black between the buildings, a scary process even for the most experienced pilot.

The fall added to the existing layers, which still lay, virgin and pristine, over much of Manhattan; but it was not strong enough to settle on those streets and avenues that had been opened.

It was one constant, cloying irritant for a city which knew now that it faced a bigger and far greater hazard.

Ben's announcement came at a time when New York was getting bored and frustrated by the isolating snow. Those who had been trapped in uptown bars and hotels were yawning and dispirited, tired of drinking, tired of long jokes about penguins and polar bears, tired of countless poker games and tired of each other's company. They looked to television for solace and found little in the monumental Indian polemic which had been thrust on the reluctant networks that morning.

Those who had been trapped at home fared better. For many it had been a satisfactory day of mending shelves and electric gadgets, of dusting and painting long-forgotten recesses, of playing with and discovering their children.

For others, there was time to make long and sensuous love. But with evening there was a restlessness, an anxiety to be out and moving; and still-falling snow added to this feeling of helpless claustrophobia.

This had been the mood of the city when Ben Boyle appeared on television and told New Yorkers of the threat of a holocaust. The mood changed with such rapidity that even the hard-headed people of New York were surprised with themselves. The stale sourness that had overcome them was swiftly overtaken by a feeling of purpose.

Within minutes men emerged on the sidewalks with improvised snow-scrapers and began to tackle the drifts with a ferocity born of long hours of boredom. They found old nuclear alert leaflets and started preparing their homes for the explosion. Windows were lined with Scotch tape; bathtubs were filled in the belief that water supplies would be cut. Family treasures were packed away carefully in safe places.

And with that natural sense of drama which is scarcely hidden in every New Yorker, they dressed for the part. Steel helmets, relics of two world wars, appeared among the street-scrapers. Even in the safer parts of northern Manhattan, there was a proliferation of "casualty clearing stations," where doctors and nurses gave free demonstrations of first aid.

And when the sidewalks were scraped clean and dusted with salt, the same parties of volunteers began to clear the streets themselves, a situation that would have been thought impossible a few hours earlier.

A few people panicked. Some piled their families into cars and drove hard along streets reserved for evacuation buses and found themselves shunted off into impassable roads by grim-faced, contemptuous policemen. Others ran for the subways but then discovered that they were traveling in a loop which brought them back to their own neighborhoods.

A few criminals moved through the snow-flecked night toward the disaster area in search of the rich pickings to be found in empty homes on the southern tip of the island. They found no mercy from the police, who earlier had shown courtesy and compassion to the old and the infirm and the children among the refugees. One young burglar was surprised climbing up a drainpipe; he was shot down after a short and perfunctory warning. Another ran from a cop only to gurgle his life away in a bank of snow, three bullets lodged in his lungs.

Those who were caught were thrown bodily, head first, into police wagons and taken to be booked.

But what really emerged that evening was a tremendous, overwhelming feeling of oneness and equality in adversity which opened up great avenues of kindness and warmth and friendship. Between the time Ben talked to the city and midnight, there were 60,000 calls to City Hall, to the police and other agencies, offering rooms for refugees, food, blankets, every kind of help, including money. And when they looked again later at the lists of callers, it was seen that they had come from all parts of New York, from the wealthier areas of Murray Hill and Fifth Avenue, as well as from Harlem and the poorer parts of Brooklyn and the Bronx.

47

The first blackout was short and quick and worried few people in a city which was braced for any eventuality. It happened at two minutes till eight and ended at two minutes past, when the power was restored phase by phase. There was mild panic in some elevators when they jammed, lightless, between floors; and some people, deprived suddenly of light, wondered whether the tanker had already exploded, and then relaxed in the knowledge that they were unhurt.

At City Hall the sound of the emergency generators bursting into power followed the shutdown immediately; the men and women in Ben's office watched the televison screen vanish to a jewel-like dot in the darkened room and then come back to life. The digital clock appeared on the screen exactly on time and switched as another primer fell.

"That proves one thing," said Van Horn who had been watching from the door. "It means you're going to have to make a very big decision shortly, Mr. Mayor."

The pretty blond telex operator in the Union Bank Building on Madison Avenue took the telex message from the "in" tray and set it up on her machine. She dialed a number.

DRESDNER BANK, FRANKFURT, her machine said. She pushed her "We are" key.

UNIBANK NEW YORK.

She began to type rapidly, not reading a word of what she was saying.

ATTN HERR DOKTOR WINKLER

THIS BANK ACTS AS COORDINATOR OF A SYNDICATE OF PRIME BANKS WHICH ARE ACTING AS GUARANTORS OF INTERNATIONAL LOAN OF WHICH YOU ARE APPARENTLY AWARE. OUR CONSORTIUM IS ANXIOUS FOR CONFIRMATION THAT FUNDS ARE AVAILABLE IN YOUR BANK TO MEET OUR REQUEST FOR A LOAN OF DOLLARS UNISTATES 130,000,000,000 FOR NEWLY CREATED UNITED NATIONS TRUST FUND. REPEAT THE SUM INVOLVED IS ONE HUNDRED AND THIRTY BILLION DOLLARS UNITED STATES. PLEASE CONFIRM THIS SUM AVAILABLE TOGETHER WITH INTEREST, TERMS OF INTEREST, ALL RELEVANT DETAILS.

GRATEFUL FOR YOUR KINDNESS IN GIVING UP PART OF YOUR HOLIDAY PERIOD BUT THIS SITUATION URGENT AS STRESSED BY TELEPHONE BY MRS STONYBRIDGE REGARDS BATEMAN UNIBANK NEW YORK.

The pretty girl waited for a moment. The telex spelled out:

MOM
WELL RECEIVED TKS
DRESDNERBANK FRANKFURT

She pressed a button which spelled out on the machine:

UNIBANK NEW YORK

She took the message from the six-inch spring clip that held it to the board on the lefthand side of the telex and put it in the "out" file, unaware that she had just set in motion machinery that would make New York City a perpetual pawn.

In a small shop on Madison Avenue, Detective Brian

French, one of Owen's best men, was trying hard to cope with the manager of the Shoshawnee Trading House Inc., a native of New Jersey called Kopekne, a little man who had never really understood why people paid so much money for real tomahawks and mocassins, especially when they were made so much more cheaply in Korea.

"Do you mail catalogs?" French asked.

"No. People, they just come and buy."

"Do you deliver?"

"Only big things."

"Like?"

"Oh, Indian carpets and furniture and things."

"Do you have a record of goods delivered?"

"I'm very bad on records. My wife comes in once a year and helps me with them."

"Can I see them?"

"Wait one moment, please."

He disappeared into the back of the shop. The policeman followed him into a room filled with packing cases, headdresses, beads strung from nails on the wall, and original Indian paintings which were obviously not originals.

The old man took a ledger from the wall.

"Here it says 'deliveries'," he said. He handed the ledger to French.

"Before I start on this, one question," he said. "A customer of yours called Martin. Evelyn Martin. Does the name mean anything?"

"Martin? No. Nothing."

The detective opened the ledger and took a pen from his inside pocket and started to work his way slowly down the list of names, dates, and addresses.

The blond girl in the Union Bank building lit a mentholated cigarette and turned on the transistor radio she had brought to the bank that night against the rules. After all, she'd been brought in on a banking holiday. The transistor was saying "A four-minute blackout hit the island of Manhattan and some parts of Queens and the Bronx tonight, plunging the whole area into darkness. A Con Ed spokesman said later that this was to be expected with the heavy demand made on the supplies and urged all customers to lessen their demands by cutting out unnecessary lights and power sources. . . . W.E.N.D. tristate weather calls for a low of minus four and a high of twenty-two tomorrow. It's freezing now in Central Park. . . . To recap the emergency, Mayor Boyle told New Yorkers tonight of a threat to explode a supertanker that is moored off the Battery by a, quote, bunch of cowardly hoodlums, unquote. Inquiries since reveal that the terrorists are a splinter group of the American Indian activist movements. Responsibility has been denied completely by the American Indian Movement and other Indian leaders. . . . This is W.E.N.D., New York, covering New York, New Jersey and Connecticut. . . . Mayor Boyle has said evacuation plans are in effect for lower Manhattan. Some citizens are already being moved through today's heavy snowfalls by a fleet of city buses and the subway. . . . More of the evacuation in a moment but in the meantime a message from the Dime Savings Bank. . . ."

The girl turned the dial on her transistor, settling on a hit pop song, and looked at her nails.

The telex machine in front of her started to clatter.

UNIBANK NEW YORK.

She automatically pressed the "We are" key and went on looking at her nails.

DRESDNERBANK FRANKFURT

She pressed the "Go ahead" key and waited.

The machine came to life. She guessed from the speed of the typing that they were using a tape transmission. Either that or the other girl was a much better typist than she was.

ATTN MR BATEMAN
FROM DR WINKLER

THIS TELEX IS SENT TO YOU WITH ENGAGEMENT AND RESPONSIBILITY FOR OURSELVES.

WE DRESDNERBANK OF FRANKFURT CONFIRM THAT WE ARE RWA TO IRREVOCABLE CONFIRMED SEVERAL

TIMES DIVISIBLE TRANSFERABLE OVERSEAS AND REVOLVING LETTER OF CREDIT IN FAVOUR OF THE UNITED NATIONS ORGANISATION CODE LIBYA/UGANDA/ZAIRE/ TRUSTEES FOR DOLLARS U.S. 130,000,000,000. (ONE HUNDRED AND THIRTY BILLION DOLLARS).

THIS SUM TO BE SUBJECT TO INTEREST AT THE RATE OF EIGHT PERCENT (8%) COMPOUNDED FOR TWENTY YEARS.

PRINCIPAL AND INTEREST REPAYABLE TWENTY YEARS AND ONE DAY FROM DATE OF LOAN.

The girl stretched her arms high over her head and exposed several inches of firm white belly to the talking telex machine. She yawned and looked at her nails again.

LOAN INSTRUMENT TO BE ONE NEGOTIABLE PROMISSORY NOTE WHICH WOULD FALL DUE AT END OF TERM.

UNCONDITIONAL GUARANTEES ARE TO BE MADE AVAILABLE BY PRIME BANKS.

She lifted her buttocks and eased the pants which were cutting her. She wished the bank would buy more comfortable chairs.

EMISSION 99.5 PERCENT. (NINETY NINE DECIMAL FIVE PERCENT.)

I should be out somewhere, she said to herself, not sitting here watching this damned machine.

FEE 1% (ONE PERCENT) ON THE CAPITAL SUM TO COVER ALL CHARGES.

She tapped her feet to the music and thought about being laid.

THIS OFFER REMAINS OPEN FOR THREE BANKING HOURS FROM NINE THIRTY A.M. UNTIL TWELVE THIRTY P.M. EUROPEAN STANDARD TIME TOMORROW JANUARY SECOND.

I hope they run me home, she thought.

ACCEPTANCE OF THE OFFER BY A KEY TESTED TELEX WITH RESPONSIBILITY FROM A U.S. PRIME BANK ACTING ON BEHALF OF THE OTHER GUARANTORS ADDRESSED TO DRESDNERBANK FRANKFURT FOR THE ATTENTION OF WINKLER.

She was thinking about being raped.

WE IRREVOCABLY CONFIRM AS A FIRM BANKING COMMITMENT WITH OUR BANKING OBLIGATION THAT THE FUNDS ARE AVAILABLE SUBJECT TO THE RECEIPT OF SATISFACTORY PRIME BANK IRREVOCABLE GUARANTEES.

Jesus, she thought, these guys do go on.

THIS BANKING COMMITMENT WILL BE CHARGED IMMEDIATELY RPT IMMEDIATELY AFTER FOLLOWING CONDITIONS HAVE BEEN MET. FIRSTLY WE REQUIRE KEY TESTED TELEXED RATIFICATION OF STATED GUARANTEES INDIVIDUALLY WITH BANKS AND CORPORATIONS CONCERNED. SECONDLY WE REQUIRE RATIFICATION OF STATED GUARANTEES INTO IRREVOCABLE LETTER OF CREDIT CONFIRMED ALSO BY KEY TESTED TELEX IN FAVOUR OF UNITED NATIONS TRUST CODE LIBYA/UGANDA/ZAIRE. THIS LC TO BE DELIVERED SIGNED BY PRINCIPALS TO THIS BANK WITHIN THREE BANKING DAYS OF OUR CHARGE.

WITH ENGAGEMENT AND RESPONSIBILITY ON OUR PART.

The girl lit another cigarette and looked vacantly at the machine.

WINKLER (DIRECTOR)
DRESDNER BANK FRANKFURT

She put a figure on the space bar and pushed another figure. She glanced quickly at the telex and typed:

TKS HONEY WELL RECEIVED.

She pressed 'We are'

UNIBANK NEW YORK

The machine clattered again.

DRESNERBANK FRANKFURT.

She ripped the telex from the machine and put it in the "out" tray. She turned up the transistor which was playing "City Morgue" and tapped her foot again to the music.

"So now we are cowardly hoodlums instead of red injuns on the warpath?" said George Mahle. "Mayor Boyle is overreaching himself."

"Pity we can't cut the deadline any more," said Evie Martin. She switched off the radio and looked up at three television monitors on the wall of the apartment. They were repeater screens which scanned the street outside the apartment and the entrance to the hotel.

"It's too calm out there," she said. "No one's hurrying; everybody is taking their time. We should have the bastards on the run by now."

"We have," said Mahle. "Evacuation, emergency feeding centers, it's a war posture. We do have a contingency for adding to the level of apprehension."

Evie looked down at him. "What have you got in mind, baby?"

"A little exercise in Indian warfare," said Mahle. "When the plains of this country belonged to our people, we used several methods to send messages. There were smoke signals, but they were really for nothing more than tribal identification. There were fast horsemen. And there were drums. A tribal drum had three uses. The first was religious and superstitious. Loud banging warded off evil spirits. The second use was a primitive, yet very effective, form of Morse code.

"The third use of the drum is the one the white man knows best. It was banged all night before a battle. It kept the white man awake and frightened. More than anything else, it kept the white man awake so that he was tired and dispirited and much more easily scared."

"So?"

"So we are going to sound the war drums."

Mahle stood up and walked into the computer room.

"Put system nine into effect immediately," he said. "But make sure that the sound sensors are compensated accordingly."

Exactly a minute after he had spoken, a message was passed from the computer on shore to the computer on board the *Jersey Lily*. The coded signal was deciphered in less than a millionth of a second, and the ship's computer selected the minute square of magnetic tape from which it would take its instruction. Automatically the machine activated one of its 800 operation channels and instructed a small charge of electricity to pass along a thin cable which ran from a small alternator in the engine room to the stern of the ship. The electricity leaped across a gap between two thin bare wires which were set in a mixture of cordite and amytol in the base of a six-inch distress flare. It was the first of George Mahle's war drums.

The sailors and Coast Guardsmen who were surrounding, the *Jersey Lily* saw it first—a giant cascade of minute. white sparks as the rocket soared, hissing and shrieking, to a height of 2,000 feet over the Hudson River before exploding with a deafening, hollow crash.

The younger sailors ducked involuntarily. Most of them felt a pang of fear. They had spent a lot of time looking at that super-tanker. They knew from experience and training just how lethal her cargo was. It was hard not to feel nerve endings exposed, almost impossible not to feel tension.

As the brilliant distress signal, suspended from a parachute, emerged through the snow, glowing like a great incandescent opal, turning the very snow blood red and ghostly, the men around the ship laughed nervously and went on with their vigil.

The refugees heard the crash of the midair explosion and there was momentary panic. Some women screamed; children ran to their parents. Some of the men caught their breath and waited for another bang. But like the sailors, they relaxed quickly when they saw the red glow and recognized it for what it was.

The sound of that explosion had been designed by the

makers to be heard from a range of 10 miles. The glow could be seen at an even greater distance.

But the snow absorbed much of the noise and the flare, each flake acting as a minute sound-baffler and reflector. Some windows in Manhattan rattled; the distant, red light could be seen from some of the taller buildings.

Ben Boyle heard the explosion and looked up from his desk. He pushed a button on his desk telephone and asked the operator for Captain Cusp. The captain's voice was strident on the radio link.

"Yes, Mr. Mayor?"

"What the hell's going on now, Captain?"

"The *Jersey Lily* is firing off distress signals," said Cusp. "Like the Fourth of July down here."

"Any danger?"

"No."

"Thanks, Captain. Keep in touch."

Ben found Mary and Mrs. Stonybridge sitting in the secretary's room. The old lady was in the same position she'd been in when he'd left her—feet on the table, cigar glowing, a bottle of bourbon, and a glass at her side. The bottle was almost empty.

"Just how the hell am I supposed to find a guy who was last seen tramping out over a grouse moor with four earls, a duke, and half a dozen baronets?" asked Mrs. Stonybridge.

"Who are you looking for?" asked Ben.

"The chairman of the National Westminster Bank," she said. "He's out on a New Year's shoot, and I want him to chip in for twelve billion bucks."

"Try Marrinish 215," said Mary.

"What's that?"

"It's a little pub called the Royal George," said Mary. "If it's raining hard—and it probably is—they'll be there."

Ben looked at Mary. "How the hell did you know that?"

She smiled enigmatically. "I just know."

Mrs. Stonybridge was already asking the operator for the number. "It's a personal call to Lord Fyfield," she was saying, "and its urgent."

"Lord Fyfield?" said Ben.

"Daddy," said Mary. "Can I speak to him after you, Mrs. Stonybridge?"

"Before you do that," said Ben. "I want to put out a statement. Tell the agencies that the terrorists are beginning to fire distress rockets from that tanker. I can only conclude that they are doing it because they themselves are in trouble."

48

Over on the Palisades it was sometimes possible to see yet another phenomenon that evening. When the snow occasionally eased, the lights of a hundred campfires could be seen burning brightly on the other side of the Hudson River. The old man, Peter Brown Bear, had been joined by others of his people. They stood around their campfires and talked quietly among themselves and looked through the snow at the lights of the city. Gentle-faced Iroquois stood side by side with Mohawks, Blackfeet, Creeks, and Hunkpapas, sharing food and passing whiskey among themselves.

Every minute more of them came to these heights. But these were not the noble horse soldiers of the plains, the mighty hunters, the Indians of legend and history. There were no feathers, no horses. They offered each other Camels and Chesterfields and filter-tipped Salems. They wore fur and felt hats and surplus army greatcoats and padded jackets like the old man's, made in places like Akron, Ohio. They wore boots and shoes made from oil byproducts in Albuquerque, these sons of the prairies, these descendants of Red Cloud and Sitting Bull.

Instead of the gracious, meaningful language of the great meetings of the tribes, they talked a drab, muttered English in the accents of the Bronx or the Middle West or California. They talked of dollars and cents and dimes for the telephone, of the new models from Detroit, of cash-flow problems in their businesses, of inflation and unemployment.

But in the center of this gathering, a medicine man was slowly and painstakingly kicking out a great circle in the trampled snow. When the circle was complete and the medicine man had taken an old cane-backed chair and sat facing across the river, no man in that growing multitude dared cross the line. Instead, they hushed as they stood among the crackling campfires and heard the first tones of his incantation to the Great Spirit to return the island of Manhattan to its rightful owners.

49

Mrs. Stonybridge was in fine form. Ben listened in amazement and admiration. In the space of six hours she had pressured and seduced and coaxed seven of the biggest banks in the world to act as guarantors. She had talked with sweetness to presidents and vice-presidents she did not know, throwing the name of her brother into the conversations with consummate skill. With her friends—and most of the men she talked to that evening were either friends or fearful admirers—she gossiped, inquiring about their families and their ulcers. Then she would spring a series of billion-dollar traps on them and refuse to listen to their excuses.

"Ah, Mr. Asiki," she was saying now, as Ben drank coffee and poured her another glass of bourbon. "You won't remember me, of course, but my name is Amy Stonybridge . . . you *do* remember? How sweet of you. Indeed, it was—in the Whitneys' pool. And how is Mrs. Asiki? What a lovely child she is. How's the weather in Tokyo? Really. No, my brother is very well, and has asked me to send his very special regards to you.

"Now I want to tell you why I'm calling. I know you're a busy man and you don't want me to take up your time . . . how nice of you to say that . . . but we have a problem here which I'm sure you'll be able to help with. I'm sitting next to the Mayor of New York City . . . ah, you've heard about the problem here. . . . I agree, but, then, the fact that it's a Japanese supertanker doesn't even enter into it and you can be absolutely sure that no blame attaches to you. What we're looking for are some guarantors for the ransom money. My bank is in for eleven billion dollars and we're looking to you for a similar amount . . . of course, you'll need to think about it, but remember that there's a government guarantee involved as well, signed by my brother. I'm quite certain we won't be needing to take this guarantee up, but it would be nice to have it in the bank, so to speak. No, Mr. Asiki, it's a guarantee, not cash . . . all right, you talk to your board and I'll call you back in what, say an hour? That's fine, Mr. Asiki. Now you will give my regards to Mrs. Asiki, such a sweet person. . . ."

Mrs. Stonybridge put down the telephone and fixed small brown eyes on the mayor. "The things I'm doing for you, Ben Boyle," she said. "The lies I'm telling. Now who was that? Dai Ichi Kangyo Bank of Tokyo. Must remember to cross them off as I go along.

"That girl, Mary, Lord Fyfield's daughter. Been talking to her. A really sweet girl. Loves you."

"I love her," said Ben.

"Her father sounds like a bit of a bully. Got on his high horse because I interrupted his grouse shooting. You do love her? Then marry her. Her old man was good for your ransom money. You look tired, Boyle. When did you last sleep? I don't need sleep. Just close my eyes for five minutes and I'm awake again, as lively as a flea on a fox."

As she took a quick swig of the bourbon, Ben asked her: "Are we going to get these guarantees?"

"I hope to God you do," she said. "It's still touch and go. The French banks are still acting as though they want to see New York blown up. Probably do."

There was a knock on the door. Van Horn looked in apologetically.

"Excuse me, Mr. Mayor," he said. "But we're ready to go ahead with the next blackout."

"Okay, go ahead," said Ben. "I've already given my consent."

"It isn't quite as simple as that," said Van Horn. "If I can just explain. The police are now quite sure that this computer is hidden somewhere in the West Forties or Fifties. They've narrowed it down from the clues given to them by this man, de Chaillot."

"That's good," said Ben.

"It's good, in that we may not have to black out the whole city. But the problem is that when we've blacked out this next particular part, the only way that we're going to find this emergency generator is by using heat-direction finders suspended by helicopter. We have six army helicopters waiting at the Port Authority heliport right now."

"So where's the snag?"

"Well, it's this. Those helicopters are also fitted with a laser beam attachment down which they can transmit a strong magnetic field which will destroy the data process and memory bank of any computer. In other words, we can knock out the master computer if we can find the power source."

"That's good."

"Except, Mr. Mayor, there are a lot of alternative sources of power in that part of the city.

"It will be difficult enough for the helicopters to navigate by radar. They won't really have time to analyze the heat sources from our maps."

"What are you saying, Charles?"

"I'm saying, Mr. Mayor, that we're going to have to damage a lot of electronic machinery and a whole lot of computers in the process. There will be a lot of angry people around tomorrow."

"They'll be a damned sight more angry if half the city is blown up," said Ben. "Go ahead."

Van Horn was about to close the door when Mrs. Stonybridge asked: "What was that name you mentioned, young man? De Chaillot?"

"Yes, ma'am."

"Edouard de Chaillot?"

"I think so, ma'am."

"Okay, young man, thank you."

When Van Horn had closed the door, Mrs. Stonybridge said: "Why doesn't anyone tell me anything? What're you doing with Chaillot?"

"He is our prime suspect. The police have been grilling him all day."

"If only I'd known. I'd have gotten the truth out of him in five minutes. Do you know what that little bastard once did? He proposed to me one morning and sodomized my nephew in the afternoon."

The crews of the Super-S-340 twin-rotor helicopters had been highly trained for one of the most dangerous forms of modern warfare. They were frontline flyers whose job it was to be first over the enemy lines, flying low, weaving and dodging, seeking out enemy missile emplacements. They carried no armament; the weapon they did carry would not kill so much as an insect.

It sat behind the pilot and the navigator, this weapon, heavily encased in lead shielding. It contained a powerful alternator which built up a million watts of power and fed it into an electromagnet which, in turn, released a silent, yet devastating, force field along a laser beam.

Another vital piece of equipment, the heat-seeking target analyzer, sat in front of the navigator. In these helicopters they were set to search for the temperature of the cylinder head of a gasoline or diesel-driven generator.

The effect of the powerful electromagnetic field was simple. It demagnetized and rendered impotent the tapes and wires and discs that gave missiles their guidance.

The crews were being briefed in the drab, lime-washed pilots' room of the West 30th Street heliport. A major stood before a map of Manhattan and pointed to the district immediately south of Central Park. "At exactly 0930 this part of the city is going to be blacked out. Between Fifth Avenue, here, and Sixth Avenue, here, from 34th Street, here, to Central Park. We're going to make a series of lasar sweeps over the blacked-out area.

"This means operating by radar. It also means a lot of hazards like eighty-story buildings which will be throwing off ghost reflections and confusing your equipment. So take your time. Keep your landing lights on at all times, and pray that the forecasters are right about the snow stopping."

"What are we looking for?" asked one of the pilots.

"A generator. There are about 200 of them in these fifty blocks. The one we're after is powering a computer that could blow that damn tanker up."

"Why don't we hit the tanker?"

"Because they figure we'd blow it up if we got within half a mile of it."

"Jesus."

"Now there are certain specific nontargets. Don't go for any buildings which you see floodlit from the street. These are known computers—medical records, banks—that sort of thing. But hit anything else and then go back and hit it again. You might destroy a few kids' train sets and kill off a few TV cowboys, but it's that computer we want."

The crews, who had been eating New Year's lunch in Omaha a few hours earlier, dispersed.

"Christ Almighty," said one navigator. "I don't mind the desert or the mountains. Hell, I'm at home there. But this place. Oh, brother."

"Have you ever ridden in a New York cab?" said his pilot. "Now *that's* dangerous."

50

Detective French had spent a long, impatient hour scouring the ledgers and complicated paperwork in the Shoshawnee Trading House and was beginning to feel he was at a dead end. Then he saw it. An entry dated four weeks before which said: "Cpt $1,200."

The bored owner had been sitting beside him, sighing frequently.

"What's this?"

"Oh yes, that was a carpet. A lovely handwoven Blackfoot carpet, eighteen by thirty, hand-dyed. It was in the window for a long time."

"Who bought it?"

"Doesn't it say?"

"No."

"She paid cash."

"Who?"

"The girl. Big girl with a dark face."

"What else?"

"That was it. She was Indian, I guess. She looked like an Indian—you know, pigtails and leather gear with tassles."

"Okay, so where did the carpet go?"

"Let me think."

"You must have a record of delivery."

"I'm thinking."

"Think hard."

"Joey Dorman, he'd know."

"Who's Joey Dorman?"

"She came into the shop and bought this carpet. Joey does my deliveries. He was here and loaded the carpet for her. That's right. She drove back with him."

"To where?"

"I don't know."

"Doesn't Joey Dorman bill you?"

"Sure, maybe once every three months. We don't deliver a lot."

"Where do I find Joey Dorman?"

"Search me. He's not what you'd call an established delivery service, with a fleet of vans and trucks. He's just a small trucker."

"He must have a telephone."

"Oh, sure." The manager looked at a penciled list of names and numbers on the wall. Here you go—Oxford-three-two-one-three-six."

French was already dialing the number.

"Mrs. Dorman? This is Detective French of the New York Police Department. I'd like to talk to your husband. No, Mrs. Dorman, it's about a delivery he made. Well, where can I find him?"

French made a note on a pad.

"Thanks, Mrs. Dorman. I want you to take his number when he does call and let me know it. My number is five-seven-seven-seven thousand, and the name is French. But make sure that you get your husband to call me as soon as he calls in. It's very important." He put the telephone down. "Dorman was trapped over on Central Park West last night and he hasn't left the number he's at. Hand me those yellow pages," French said.

The six helicopters took off in turn and joined a fast series of circuits over the blackness of the Hudson, their crews listening to a steady countdown through their earphones. Three minutes before the blackout was due, they formed an even line parallel with the north-to-south avenues and moved east over the city.

These were not the normal, friendly, ubiquitous police helicopters that roamed over the rivers and city; they were roaring, crusading giants, their engines straining, their rotors clutching angrily at the air as they rushed headlong over the city.

The six lined up again over blacked-out Sixth Avenue and moved into the area where the search centered. The snow had thinned sufficiently for their navigators to see the buildings ahead of them in the fierce glare of their landing lights.

On the instrument panel of each helicopter was a radar screen and a series of colored lights that glowed amber for a suspicious target, red for a positive one, and bright blue for a final identification. The navigator pressed a button at that point and the silent beam shot downward.

The first casualty was the King Carol Record shop in Times Square, the victim of a premature shot from a waiting helicopter which had received a blue signal from a road-repair generator in the street. In less than a second a quarter of a million cassettes and stereo cartridges were freed of music.

On drove the probing, dodging helicopters in a cacophony of near-miss and screaming swerve, low between the buildings, recording hit after hit.

A bank computer went next; its computer registered 10,000 demagnetized checks on an empty printout. Adding insult to this grave injury, the helicopter turned and poised and stabbed down again with its laser and destroyed the bank's complete record of transactions for the previous 20 years.

It was hard to distinguish, in that snow-blind sky, between the buildings that were floodlit and those that were simply lit up in the landing lights of the machines. One helicopter dipped low and picked up a clean blue signal from the Public Library and wiped clean the data bank which listed a million books and which erased for all time a priceless collection of music tapes.

Another beam, intended for an emergency generator powering one of the bigger hotels on 59th Street, hit a snow-stranded taxi which, before the blizzard, had been carrying four computer tapes from the Inland Revenue Service Satellite in Harlem to headquarters in Wall Street.

But there was no sign of the mayhem except in the two television stations just off Sixth Avenue where, despite floodlights and flashing warning lights, a helicopter swerved dramatically and destroyed 50 master tapes of

"I Love Lucy," a complete new drama series which had cost several million dollars, and the row of tapes made on behalf of the League for Real Justice for the Indian.

The helicopter crews were not to know it yet, but the whole exercise had been rendered pointless from the beginning, when the radar on the *Jersey Lily* had pinpointed the helicopters over the Hudson and George Mahle had prudently switched the distant computer to its preprogramed state and had turned off the generator in the Hotel Marlborough.

"Mrs. Stonybridge is either fast asleep or drunk out of her mind," said Mary. "I tried to wake her, but she takes no notice." Ben, who had started to doze himself, pulled himself up from the soft mayoral chair and followed Mary along the corridor. Amy Stonybridge was indeed in a deep, profound sleep, her eyes lightly shut and her mouth slightly open.

"A whole bottle of whiskey," said Mary. "And two mouthfuls of liverwurst sandwich."

"She's all right," said Ben. "We ought to put her to bed. It's the least we can do."

"And where are you going to sleep?" Mary asked.

"Sleep? Who's sleeping?"

"You are, Ben Boyle. Everything's in hand. Leave it to Captain Cusp and his pirates for an hour or so and get some sleep. You'll need it tomorrow."

Ben was already leaning over the supine form of Mrs. Stonybridge. He picked her up. She was like featherdown in his arms. He carried her to his suite and laid her gently on the bed.

"I'll leave her to you," he said to Mary.

"I'll leave her alone," said Mary. "She wouldn't look right without those flying boots on. She hasn't stopped talking all day, poor dear. Let her sleep."

"Come and have a drink," said Ben. "I could sink an ice-cold Budweiser with a minimum of effort."

They went into his office. He poured Mary a scotch and soda and cracked open a can of beer for himself.

He sat back in an easy chair, drank from the can, and looked at Mary.

"You never told me your old man was a banker," he said.

"We're all a bit ashamed of it," said Mary. "The snob side of my family regards banking as trade."

"Like plumbing?"

"Were you a good plumber, Ben?"

"I am a good plumber. The best goddamned plumber in Queens." He said it with sincerity and then looked slightly ashamed.

"My father's a good banker," said Mary. "The best goddamned banker in Britain."

"So what are we saying?"

"I don't know."

She lifted her glass.

"Confusion to our enemies," she said.

"The trouble is, they don't seem to be easily confused. Van Horn couldn't do it."

"Poor Charles," she said. "He really thinks he can persuade their computer to commit hara kari. This man Mahle seems a worthy opponent."

"That's been Van Horn's message all day." Ben eyed the red-and-white beer can in his hand. "I only wonder whether I wouldn't have been better off to call in the federal experts at the beginning."

"Ben, Charles Van Horn spent time this morning calling up half the computer experts in this country."

"And?"

"And they approved of his ideas."

"They did?"

"He asked me, too."

"Why?"

"Because I know people."

"And what does that mean?"

"It means, Ben, that you have a lot of faith in Van Horn and you'd far rather a New Yorker, a man with a brilliant academic and practical record, an employee of your city, sorted this problem out. Because the last thing in the world that you would want is for this building to be overrun with FBI and CIA and federal technicians."

"I felt like that this morning. Now I'm not so sure."

Mary stood up and walked across to him. He reached up and took her hand and kissed it.

"You're tired, Ben," she said. "You're tired and you're worried and I don't think you need to worry in the slightest with the people you have working out there. Captain Cusp is using all the federal resources he needs. And so is Van Horn. But it's a New York happening, Ben. It's your city doing it."

"I guess so," said Ben and kissed her hand again. "What I want to know, Mary Fyfield, is where you get your energy. You've been up all night and racing about City Hall all day and now you look fit for ten sets of tennis."

"I'm normally a lazy slob," she said. "Perhaps it's love."

Ben felt the waves of tiredness begin to wash over him. His eyes were heavy with fatigue and he felt his muscles begin to melt as Mary stood behind him, stroking his neck.

"Love," he said, "is sending me to sleep."

"Sleep for an hour, Ben," she said. "Old Altmeyer is watching the shop."

"Old fuss guts," he said dreamily, and fell asleep just as the door opened and Van Horn walked in.

Mary put her fingers to her mouth. "Don't wake him," she said. "He's bushed."

Van Horn gaped for a moment and then whispered: "Just as well. I was only going to report another disaster."

Ben opened his eyes and sat up.

"Tell me," he said.

"The laser attack seems to have damaged a lot of vital electronic equipment all over midtown," said Van Horn. "We don't know whether we've knocked their computer out. But we have succeeded in destroying some of the Indian videotapes."

"That'll make a lot of people happy," said Ben. "What about the television time bomb?"

"Still functioning," said Van Horn.

"Eighteen hours," said Ben. "Pour yourself a drink, Charles. It's going to be a restless night for all of us."

He was glad to see that Van Horn, alone among his fellow-beseiged, drank orange juice.

"I'm beginning to get funny views about all this," said Ben. "About computers that can blow half this city to hell, about companies which put eight men on a half-million-ton ship, about educated activists. Things like this make me feel vulnerable, much more vulnerable than I should need to feel."

"You can't blame computers. They just do as they're told."

"But look what they can do. Look at these two machines, holding the city for ransom between them. Chattering away like a pair of housewives without a chance of anyone butting in. Thinking in millionths of seconds, killing people by calculation."

Ben stood up and shook himself.

"I'm just a simple tradesman," he said. "I've worked with my hands all my life. I wouldn't know the difference between a binary code and a flowchart. But I've seen a hell of a lot of good men forced into early graves because some damned computer has given them a workload they couldn't cope with. They've been computer-trained, computer-hired, computer-fired, and computer-retired. The computer decided when they were sick, when they were redundant, when they were lazy, and it gave them good marks when they worked hard. Except that it remembered the good marks and expected good marks all the time. The computer knows every damn thing about us, all of us in this country. Our pay, our taxes, our unpaid bills, the color of our eyes, our blood type, our sexual habits and our credit-worthiness. A damn machine can decide whether I'm good for a five-hundred-dollar loan. Not the bank manager, not him. He just talks to the computer."

"Speaking of banks," Van Horn said quietly. "We seem to have wiped out the entire memory system of the Gotham City Trust Bank tonight. Every tape is empty."

"It strikes me," said Mary, "that the litigation which follows this adventure is going to keep the law courts busy until doomsday."

"Wiped out every tape?" said Ben. "Best news I've heard today. "Do you know what that means? It means that there'll be work for several hundred kids who've left the schools of this city and can't find jobs. Kids with good minds."

"It would be good to think you were right, Mr. Mayor," said Van Horn. "But you're not. Those paper jobs don't exist any more. A handful of programers will do it all for them."

"Okay, Charles, you can't win. But I would like to see the maximum input of humanity into our City Hall computers."

"How do we do that?"

"Well, we have direct control of 200,000 civil servants

in this city. And a big say in the affairs of another 200,000 teachers and hospital workers and people like that. I'd just like to know that the computer knows that sanitary inspector X has an ulcer which gives him hell, that sewerman Y has a nagging bitch of a wife and that's why he's always falling down on the job. . . ."

Mary laughed. "Pretty picture," she said.

"Now you're talking about invasion of privacy," said Van Horn. "We try not to do that."

"Well, I'd rather know that the computer knows that it's time I had a dental check up or took a vacation than that I was two bucks overdrawn at Chase Manhattan," said Ben.

"Come on and get some sleep," said Mary. "I must say, though, I don't like the idea of these supertankers plowing their way over the seven seas with some wretched machine on the bridge. Give me a steely-eyed captain with twenty-ten vision any time."

There was a whining sound coming from outside on the lawn and then the whistle of helicopter rotor blades. The noise kept up until the helicopter roared away at what seemed a dangerous speed.

"Who the hell was that?" asked Ben.

Mary went across to the door and said: "I don't believe it. I just don't believe it."

She went out and came back almost immediately, carrying a note. Her face was a mixture of disbelief and amused incredulity.

"Look at this," she said, handing the note to Ben.

It was written in the spidery manner of the old.

"Dear Ben Boyle," it said. "Thanks for the bed and bourbon. Had a good sleep. Woke to remember that I've got an all-girl poker game in Westchester tonight. Anyway, you need the bed. Take that nice Fyfield girl with you. It'll set you up for tomorrow. I've got all the cash you need except for about 22 billion bucks because the French are playing silly bastards as usual. Anyway, I might win it at poker. See you in the morning. Have a good night. Love, Amy Stonybridge.

P.S. Is that man Altmeyer married? His eyes are so bad that he can't see how old I am."

"Christ," said Ben. "All that booze and she's flying a

helicopter. Suppose she goes over and tries to beat up that supertanker?"

"Oh, she'd win," said Mary. "Superwoman meets super-tanker."

She turned to see Van Horn sitting pensively, orange juice held lightly in his hand. "A penny for them, Charles?"

"Oh, I was just thinking about how we could humanize the City Hall computer."

"Put flowers on it," she said. "Why don't you get some sleep?"

"I'm not sleepy. We're trying to find some way to sabotage the microwave signals between the master and the slave computer. When this snow eases, we're going out to the radio ship and start experimenting."

"Sounds fascinating," said Mary lightly.

"It's a question of calculation, based on getting onto their frequency at exactly the right moment and. . . ."

Mary showed him out.

She turned to Ben who was still clutching the note from Amy Stonybridge.

"You read what she said," said Mary. "It's like a royal command. Come on, Mr. Mayor."

Through all that night, there on the cliffs that overlooked the island, the medicine man worked steadily, mumbling words in guttural low tones, while others stood at the edge of the circle stamped in snow and chanted and shook ornately carved rattles into the night.

As the trailers and automobiles struggled through the snow to join this gathering on the Palisades, their occupants grew quiet at the sound of the ceremony. There were several hundred Indians now; and they were being increased in number throughout the night by more of the nation's tribes. Chickasaws stood close to Wyandottes and Kiawas talked quietly to White Mountain Apaches.

There was a large circle around the medicine man now, as they watched him perform the elaborate ritual which preceded the final supplication, which would take place at dawn.

They watched him walk with long, grave steps over the trampled snow and fall on his knees in the very center of the circle. Then he threw down an old multicolored blanket, heavily frayed at the edges, and placed on it the accessories of primitive prayer.

First he scattered a bag of sand on the blanket, then feathers, hoops, small boxes of herbs, cornsheaves, and plants. A large, plastic container filled with water was handed to him by a chanting assistant. Slowly, with imprecations mouthed soundlessly, he mixed seven different colors of paint. On his knees in the snow, the old man painted his lean face with long streaks of each color. Then he sat back, cross-legged, his eyes reaching into the blackness of the night, and prayed in a shrill monotone while the other men chanted and shook their rattles into the night.

In the distance the lights of Manhattan could be seen much more clearly now. It was even possible to see the giant arc lamps illuminating the *Jersey Lily*.

The even green line across the cathode-ray screen in front of Pete Eagle Heart was glowing brightly; it gave a sickly pallor to his face as he lit his thirtieth cigarette of the night. He looked at the clock over the main computer and saw that it was nearly one-o'clock in the morning.

The others were sleeping at the far end of the computer room. Mahle was with Evie Martin.

In the past few hours, Pete Eagle Heart had begun to feel strong tremors of misgiving about Mahle, Evie, and the others he had joined so willingly 18 months before.

He had found death an ugly and shattering experience. Certainly it had been right to kill Willy Joe on the deck of the ship, but there had been something terribly cruel about the way Mahle had staged it. It was an unnecessary little drama; to use a human being to test the electromatting had been clinical, cold, and vicious. Wasn't that ship filled with instruments? A simple galvanometer would have told them all they wanted to know. Nor did he like the killing of the policemen. There was no justification for that. It was the same heartless Mahle who was so determined to show his strength. But was it strength? Was it a bravado born of fanaticism which would not, could not stop?

He turned down thirty billion dollars, thought Eagle Heart. Thirty billion.

More than the Indians of America had ever spent in their history. Thirty billion for real schools instead of the cruelty-ridden travesties of schools he had been forced to attend. Real Indian hospitals instead of the poor wards of the white man's charity. Thirty billion dollars would provide work and a real life for his people, give them the land they needed, the air, a freedom for which they cried out.

But Mahle had to go for the jackpot. And Boyle had said that it was not going to be. They had gone too far, he thought. They would not get the money because they had asked too much. Nor would their terms be accepted by the government, because they had asked too much.

That meant that they would explode the ship. Or Mahle would.

That coldness and arrogance, the whip marks—even on the ship he had once seen Mahle's back cut and bruised from self-flagellation—and the cigarette in the palm?

Pete Eagle Heart realized at that moment in the morning that George Mahle was mad. In the same moment he saw the bright green line in front of him begin to break up and form a jagged pattern which meant intruders.

Mahle was in the room almost as soon as the alarm bell rang. He peered over Eagle Heart's shoulder and pressed a key on the computer terminal.

The screen flashed on and words formed.

SONAR INDICATIONS. TWO MINIATURE CRAFT APPROACHING HULL 030 DEGS RANGE APPROXIMATELY 100 FEET. DEPTH 40 FEET.

"What now?" said Mahle.

The computer continued.

ANALYSIS INDICATES FIBERGLASS BUILT "J" CRAFT POWERED BY COMPRESSED AIR. TWO-MAN CREWS.

"There is nothing they can do from underwater," said Mahle. "Except open the vents and flood the tanks. That won't help them."

INTRUDER DESCENDING TO RIVER BOTTOM.

"They're just being inquisitive," said Mahle. "If they move any closer, increase the volume of the sonar. It may deafen them—and let them know that they are observed."

On the muddy bottom of the Hudson the crews of the two transparent submarines closed the forward hatches, unscrewed a number of wing nuts, then slowly backed away, leaving two conical sections lying 100 feet from the hull of the *Jersey Lily*.

It was three hours before Detective French talked at last to Joey Dorman. The deliveryman had not been in any hotel on Central Park West. On the contrary, he had been visiting a woman friend in the Bronx and had taken advantage of the blizzard to stay. He was not the only one in the city to do that on New Year's Eve.

"Now listen," he was saying over the telephone. "I don't wantcha to say a word to my old lady where I've been, see? I mean, you know how it is, sir. Anyway, what can I do for you?"

French told him.

"Oh yeah, that carpet. Yeah, a big girl, big, the sort you wouldn't mind getting your leg over, you know. Where? Oh yeah, it was to a hotel. Well, you might call it a hotel. I wouldn't. It's a flophouse. Yeah, that's right, I was really surprised at a girl like that living in a joint like that."

"What was the name of the hotel?"

"Wait a minute. It was off Broadway, I remember. You know, one of those streets off Times Square where the hookers grow. The hotel, the Hotel Marlborough. Jesus Christ, you've never seen a more rundown rat-pit in your whole damned life. The Hotel Marlborough, at 45th and Broadway. What a stink—you've never smelled anything like that elevator."

"Did you go up in the elevator?"

"No way. I loaded the carpet in and she gave me five skins and shut the door."

"Did she speak to you at all?"

"Only when I sort of propositioned her in the truck."

"What did she say?"

"She said 'fuck off white man,' or something like that."

"Okay, now listen to me. I'm coming over with a picture of this woman, and I want you to make a positive identification for me. Don't leave where you are or I'll have every cop in the city looking for you."

"I ain't going no place, sir."

French put the phone down and dialed Owen's extension.

"We're almost there," he said. "One more move and I think we've nailed Evie Martin."

Throughout the night the big, soft-sprung buses of the city roared and coughed their way along Eighth Avenue and the other exits from southern Manhattan, their drivers happy not to have to watch the clicking coin machines and even happier that there were no traffic lights.

The reception centers were crowded now, but there was no sign of any breakdown in the orderly system dreamed up so quickly that morning by a new commissioner.

The refugees came as so many had come to this city before them, in overcoats and with paper bags. Greedier ones had tried to load suitcases filled with precious belongings into the buses. But they had been turned back with scant sympathy by the drivers and the police.

Sometime before dawn most of the southern tip of the island was deserted. Broadway, the Indian track that bent and twisted its way through a maze of streets and avenues was still and subdued, except, that is, where it passed City Hall.

51

Ben Boyle lay in a sleep that was as deep as any he had known. Mary was reluctant to wake him. She shook his shoulder, but he went on sleeping; she pinched the soft flesh behind his arms, but he grunted and went on sleeping. She bit him gently on the back of the neck, but he slept on. Finally she began tweaking his hair; he turned suddenly and instinctively pulled her down to him.

"What time is it?" he said.

"Three o'clock and all's well," she told him. "You've got a Ben Boyle war committee at three-thirty. Commissioner Canaletto will be here at four-thirty, and I've decided to marry you. Have some coffee."

"Is Cusp here?" he said.

"Not yet," she said. "I thought I'd get you awake first."

"Then come here," he said.

"Once in City Hall is quite enough," she said. "Quite a collector's item for some. You've got work to do. Go and have a shower before my glands start working."

Mary walked over to the shower and he heard it begin to run. He sat up in the bed and drank the strong coffee she had brought him. He felt his mind slowly arrange itself into a semblance of order. Not a very good semblance; that he knew. But he was aware of a 500,000-ton ship off the Battery and of a man called Mahle who was going to blow that ship up. He was aware, quite suddenly, that he was the Mayor of New York.

He stood under the shower for several minutes, letting it run hot and then cold and then hot again, in the belief, fostered in childhood, that this was good for getting the blood circulating.

Then, just as he was getting out, the curtains were pulled aside and Mary, wearing a transparent plastic bathing cap, was standing beside him.

"Captain Cusp called and said that his helicopter was overheating and he'd be fifteen minutes late." She started to soap his chest.

"How old are you, Ben Boyle?" she asked him.

She pushed him directly under the spray and held his head firmly under the jet and watched the water spill over his face and bring his hair down over his forehead.

"You know damned well how old I am," he said and swallowed water and started choking.

"Then why are you so deaf?" she shouted.

"Because you're holding my damned ears," he said.

"You didn't hear what I said, then?"

"You said Cusp was going to be late."

She put her hands very hard over his ears and said: "I said that I was going to marry you."

"Where did you get that silly looking hat?" he asked.

"I stole it from the hotel," she said. "Did you hear what I said?"

Ben took the soap from the tray and soaped his hands carefully and then placed them on her breasts. She allowed him to soap them gently and then pressed her body against his and kissed him very hard.

She pushed him away from her and held him at arm's length and looked at him, smiling and letting the running water hide the tears on her cheeks.

"I love you, Ben Boyle," she said. "You cloth-eared old creep."

She pushed him out of the shower and, as he dressed, he could hear her singing, "It's my kind of town, Chicago is . . ."

DRESDNERBANK FRANKFURT

UNIBANK NEW YORK

ATTN HERR DOKTOR WINKLER
CODE LIBYA/UGANDA/ZAIRE

UNDERSTAND FROM MRS STONYBRIDGE THAT FOLLOWING BANKS HAVE AGREED OR ARE LIKELY TO AGREE GUARANTEES TO LOAN IN AMOUNTS OF ELEVEN POINT NINE BILLIONS UNITED STATES DOLLARS EACH.

BANK OF AMERICA, CITICORP, CHASE MANHATTAN, BANQUE NATIONALE DE PARIS, DAI-ICHI KANGYO (TOKYO), BARCLAYS BANK (LONDON), NATIONAL WESTMINSTER BANK, (LONDON), FUJI BANK (TOKYO), DEUTSCHE BANK (FRANKFURT), SUMINTOMO BANK (OSAKA), AND CREDIT LYONNAIS (PARIS). TOTAL ASSETS OF THIS CONSORTIUM EXCEED UNITED STATES DOLLARS 354,777,000,000. MRS STONYBRIDGE ACTING AS HEAD OF CONSORTUIM WISHES YOU TO KNOW THAT THESE GUARANTOR BANKS BACKED BY GOVERNMENT GUARANTEE SIGNED BY PRESIDENT OF THE UNITED STATES OF AMERICA ARE SATISFACTORY BEFORE PROCEEDING FURTHER.

REGARDS BATEMAN UNIBANK

MOM
TKS NEW YORK WELL RECEIVED
DRESDNERBANK FRANKFURT
UNIBANK NEW YORK

By six o'clock that morning, Amy Stonybridge, now wearing a long maroon velvet dress, heavily studded around the neck with jewelry, still sporting her flying boots, was back on the telephone in City Hall. She pecked at a corned beef on rye and called the president of the Banque Nationale in Paris.

"Now look here, Jacques Cavioch, I know damn well where you've been. You've been hiding from me in the arms of the foreign minister's wife, and it's no use denying it because the president told me and you'd never guess where *he* was. Naughty boy. How is your charming wife . . . what do you mean, don't talk so loud?

"Listen here, you know what I'm after. I'm after twelve billion dollars, and I want you in the consortium. Don't sound so surprised, dear boy, you've known about this for the past twelve hours and my spies told me that you ran out of the bank screaming and frothing when you heard about it.

"How *is* your wife? And Madame Pastis? And that lovely Lola girl who came over with you last time? What do you mean, don't talk so loud. Darling, I can talk real loud. All right, then, let's talk about the money, my dear. Oh my God, not you too. No, I don't need the twelve billion in cash. I want a guarantee from you. Oh, they're all in. Barclay's, Credit Lyonnais, Citicorp . . . well, they couldn't afford not be be, could they? I mean it's all very well for you to sit there flashing your assets. No, of course it's secure. The U.S. government is underwriting the whole deal with my brother's signature on it. My bank? Of course, we're in; what do you think I'm doing here at this time of the morning?

"Anyway, dear, think of the prestige you'd be missing. You wouldn't be able to show your face in the Bourse if you didn't come into Amy's syndicate. How long? Two hours at the outside. I know you don't like giving in to terrorists. But this is New York, my dear. I mean, you couldn't let New York blow up, could you? You could? But you'd like the prestige of saving it. I thought so. Now you just get back into that board meeting and give a nice solid vote for auntie. Any time it looks like they're blowing up Paris, you know you can count on me."

"It seems to me we've got two choices," said Owen. "We charge in bull-headed and hit them fast with gas and smoke and all guns flying in the hope that they can't get near the computer in time to detonate—"

"They probably have to press a simple code word on the computer," said Van Horn. "That would be enough. Or it might even be a speech-activated code word spoken into a microphone."

Commissioner Crotty sat forward and put his elbows on the desk and joined his fingertips.

"Forget that," he said. "It's taken long enough to find these people, and now that we've got them, we don't want to precipitate anything like an explosion. So what's the second choice, Owen?"

The meeting was taking place in the actions room at headquarters. At the far end of the room there were a number of television monitors with one large dominating screen.

Owen said: "We'll have a Sprint set-up in operation outside the hotel in about ten minutes. The whole place will be under complete surveillance. I'd like to spend an hour studying that place from top to bottom. Trouble is, the hotel is so damned old that we won't be able to get the builder's plans, and, going on what the count said, they may have turned the whole of one floor into something like a fortress."

"The elevator worries me," said Crotty. "It looks like the only way in."

"So I guess we should infiltrate," said Owen. "That flophouse is filled with some of the saddest dropouts, worst junkies, really sinister creeps in New York. We'll send in a few more from the Central Park Detail."

"Wouldn't it be easier to hit them with the laser system?" said Crotty. "It worked on pretty well everything else in that part of town."

"That could only work if they were taken by surprise," said Van Horn. "Now that they know we're playing around with force fields, it will give them time to either hide their tapes in lead-lined boxes, or, worse still, to activate the detonators."

One by one the television monitors on the wall began to light up.

"Here's the target area," said Owen.

The monitor showed the hotel. The picture was fuzzy at first but it was brought into fine focus and the picture was held.

A second monitor was concentrating on the doorway of the hotel. It was deserted. The camera was able to pick out, in fine detail, the scraps of paper, the empty cigarette packages which littered the lobby, the elevator doors and the "No Visitors Aloud" sign.

Two more cameras scanned the street. The operator of one was able to zoom into the foyer of the gay movie house next to the hotel and focus steadily on an advertising poster which showed two young men in a passionate embrace.

"Where are the cameras?" asked a voice from behind them. It was Ben, newly arrived from City Hall. They stood up and he said, "For Christ's sake, sit down and show me the movies. What's this?"

"This is where the Indians are," said Crotty. "Our cameras are hidden, two of them in a doctor's office opposite the building and the other two in a broken-down truck a little way down the street. We chose the doctor's place because he specializes in high-society clap cases and has a door in the next street for film stars and executives."

Owen pushed a number of buttons on a small director's console in front of him. He spoke into a microphone.

"Okay, stand by for a take," he said. "Camera one, I want a close look at that hotel, every door and window and the roof, and take it slow and easy. Camera two, I want the same with that lobby. Camera three, if you don't get off that damn picture, people will start to wonder."

The camera which was focussed on the gay picture pulled back immediately into the street, panned slightly to the right, and came into equally fine focus on a sign warning about the perils of syphilis.

"Better," said Owen. "Three and four, when I come to you I want the street in both directions, bums, anybody or anything like good store doorways or other vantage points. Are you ready VTR?"

"Ready when you are," said a voice from a loudspeaker in the corner.

"Okay," said Owen. "We'll start with camera one and then the others as the pictures come up. Put a clock up please."

A clock was superimposed on the main monitor. It began to tick its way in seconds toward a red line, at which point the taping would start.

"What are you doing?" said Ben.

"We're putting the whole scenario on videotape," said Owen. "It means that we can make a longer assessment and get our building experts and others to see whether there are any flaws in their armor."

The hand of the clock reached the red line, and Owen said "Okay one. Start at the street level and work your way up slowly. No, slower, please."

The camera moved very slowly, pausing at each window, sometimes returning at Owen's request. The lens was so strong, with its built-in light sources, that they were able in that room to see men and women sleeping, a girl with long, straggly hair getting out of bed and scratching the scabs on her punctured arm, and a young man reading *Playboy* and fondling himself under a blanket.

As the camera reached the top floor of the building, Owen said, "Hold it there please, one." They were looking at the blacked-out windows of the computer room. "Pan right along that floor," said Owen. The camera obeyed and slid, still very slowly, from left to right.

"A little higher."

It moved up and started the same operation of panning along the windows.

"Stop there."

It stopped.

"Now zoom in as close as you can."

The camera was in fine close-up now. They could see the outline of each brick and the crumbling mortar.

"Left a little. There was something under the eaves."

The camera moved.

"Hold it right there."

There, under the eaves, was a camera Mahle had set up for very much the same purpose.

"Shit," said Owen. "That's going to make infiltration a damn sight more difficult."

52

The blond girl in the Union Bank was asleep when her telex began to chatter. She waked and with only one eye open reached out and pressed the "We Are" key and looked at the words which appeared fuzzily in front of her.

UNIBANK NEW YORK
DRESDNER BANK FRANKFURT
ATTN MR BATEMAN
CODE LIBYA/UGANDA/ZAIRE

THANK YOU FOR YOUR PREVIOUS TELEX. I CONFIRM THAT THE DRESDNER BANK IS RWA TO NEGOTIATE THIS LOAN DURING THE TIMES STATED AND THAT THE GUARANTOR BANKS NOMINATED BY YOU ARE ENTIRELY SATISFACTORY.

I AM PLEASED TO BE ABLE TO INFORM YOU THAT THIS BANK IN CONJUNCTION WITH THE UNION BANK OF SWITZERLAND WHICH IS ACTUAL FUNDING BANK HAVE AGREED TO WAIVE NORMAL COMMISSION OF ONE PERCENT AND TO ACCEPT POINT TWO RPT DECIMAL TWO PERCENT OF THE TOTAL IN UNITED STATES BONDS OR SOME SUCH ACCEPTABLE EQUITIES. THIS BOARD HAS MADE THIS DECISION ON THE BASIS OF WHAT WE NOW REALISE IS THE BASIS FOR URGENCY.

EMISSION RATE OF NINETY NINE POINT FIVE PER-

CENT MUST REMAIN ON INSISTENCE OF PRINCIPALS IN MIDDLE EAST.

WE WILL BE IN POSITION TO PROCEED ON RECEIPT OF KEY TESTED TELEXED GUARANTEES FROM YOUR CONSORTIUM.

WITH BEST WISHES AND CONCERN FOR YOUR WELL-BEING.

SIGNED WINKLER (DIRECTOR)
DRESDNERBANK FRANKFURT

The girl glanced at the message, then reached out and typed with one finger:

TKS WELL RCD
UNIBANK NEW YORK

Evie Martin was sleeping. It was a restless, disturbed sleep. She turned her big dark body frequently, slamming her arms down on the blankets and groaning.

Mahle watched her, but the sight of the langorous spectacle did not move or arouse him. He was concentrating on the day ahead. It was going well, he thought. The laser attack had failed. So far, there was no indication that the police were anywhere near finding them.

He switched on the surveillance cameras and looked at the street. It had been cleared of snow. That was good. It meant that their exit would be made that much easier.

There was a delivery truck 30 yards up from the hotel. Its hood was up and emergency lights were flashing. Nothing else moved except a stray cat and the undulating plastic figure of a go-go girl in the window of a clip-joint at the end of the street.

How could they be found, anyway?

Evie had brought in out-of-town builders to convert the top floor of the hotel into this apartment. No one at City Hall was going to ask questions about conversions, especially in buildings already condemned.

Only she, he, and the others knew the location.

Except that the laser helicopters seemed to know exactly where to hit them. Had that been guesswork, or did they know more?

He put it down to guesswork. Now for the rest of the day, it would be a question of precise timing. By noon he would have received a message from a computer terminal in New Jersey that would indicate the money was forthcoming.

The Ugandan ambassador to the United Nations had been expensive to corrupt; it had meant a cash down payment of $100,000. A further million dollars would be paid from, or rather extracted from, the trust which he had managed to set up with Libyan and Congolese colleagues.

There was a muted jangling of alarm bells in Mahle's brain.

The Frenchman who had fixed the money. She had brought him here. How secure was he? From what Evie had said, he had left the apartment scared out of his skin. She was quite sure he would never talk.

He walked over and shook Evie awake. "How sure are you of the Count de Chaillot?" he said.

"Absolutely," she said. "Christ, he stands to make fifteen million bucks from this deal."

"Where is he?"

"At the Plaza. Waiting."

"Phone him."

She stood up and walked softy across the room to the telephone. She dialed the hotel and asked for the count's suite.

A voice answered sleepily.

"Hello."

"Count de Chaillot?"

"Speaking."

"Evie Martin. Remember what I said to you?"

"I remember."

"Well, keep your mouth shut. I mean it."

She put the telephone down.

"He's okay," she said to Mahle.

"Go back to sleep," he said. "And you can start packing when you wake up. We'll be out of here by two P.M."

The detective who had spent much of the night rehearsing his imitation of the count's voice turned to the man standing next to him with a tape recorder.

"Not much point in tracing that call," he said. "We've nailed her anyway."

53

The infiltration of the Hotel Marlborough took place as smoothly and quickly as Owen had hoped. As first light dawned on the city, four of the hotel's residents, all of them clearly heroin addicts in search of the fix which the snow had deprived them of, emerged on the street, shivering and desperate. The cameras tracked them to Broadway, where they were picked up by plainclothes policemen and hustled into a police van.

Inside the van their clothes were removed. They watched with stupefaction as four detectives put them on. The detectives then studied the junkies carefully and began to make up their faces and put on wigs.

After a few minutes the detectives climbed out of the van and made their way to the hotel. They entered the lobby under the close scrutiny of their own cameras and the ones operated by George Mahle.

Variations of the same procedure were followed for an hour, until Owen had 12 men in the building. Now he waited for a break; it came when a tall black man came out of the hotel and walked up toward Sixth Avenue.

Thirty minutes later a tall black man came back down the street clutching a supermarket shopping bag. He stumbled several times and seemed to have difficulty in finding the hotel. Finally he took a pair of glasses from his pocket and looked up at the name. Then he went in quickly.

In the actions room, even Crotty managed a smile. The "black man" was Charles Van Horn.

Ben said: "Hey, look at Charles. Maybe we should keep him that way. It would make City Hall look pretty good with the Racial Discrimination Board."

On the Palisades the medicine man had cried and moaned and roared his supplication to the Great Spirit throughout the night and his voice seemed to have gathered strength with the dawn. Now, as a bright, watery sun bathed the island in incandescent brilliance, he stopped his chanting and held up his hands to the sun.

The drums stopped beating and the rattles were stilled and the throng around the medicine man joined the old man in reaching for the brightest light in the sky. There was a long, even silence which was broken only by the sound of children playing. A solitary woman started the sound in a shrill, high-pitched voice which wavered at first in the clear air of the morning and then found an even note and stayed on it. It was a sound like no other human sound, a long wailing sound that was half cry, half exultation.

Another woman joined the cry, and another. In the time it took the medicine man to stamp and scuffle in a weird dance over his sand paintings of the island opposite, 2,000 women had taken up the long, interminable cry which could be heard now, carried on the veering wind, in Harlem and even on Fifth Avenue.

The men joined in now. The sound grew in volume and power and became more and more penetrating and more and more unearthly.

This was the sound the soldiers of Custer's cavalry had heard, the sound that had defied the plainsmen and the encroaching wagon trains; the sound cried out against the slaughter of buffalo and bison, against the pillage of land by greedy men, against the senseless and meaningless killing of defenseless women and children by men who had known hunger themselves and whose pasts, in the garrets of Europe, had taught them ruthlessness and the will to survive in this measureless, rich continent of America.

It was the sound of an angry nation and it was heard all

day, all over that silent city, as it had not been heard since the year 1641, when Dutch soldiers plundered and raped two Indian villages in Manhattan, killing every inhabitant, man, woman, and child.

54

At exactly noon that day the combined police and Coast Guard operation against the terrorists was started by Captain Robert Cusp with the word "go" spoken into a microphone on the U.S.S. *Whaleback*. Simultaneously a series of precisely timed plans were put into effect. A series of powerful directional loudspeakers began to direct every conceivable sound in the register toward the ship. Some speakers aired martial music, some played acid rock, some played Beethoven and Wagner; other speakers radiated powerful waves of subsonic and ultrasonic noises. A stream of F-71 fighters came hurling down the Hudson River at supersonic speeds and the double explosions of the broken sound barrier crashed against the *Jersey Lily*. There was no letup.

At the same time, 12 helicopters flew around the ship, dropping great streams of radar-reflecting strips of black metallic paper; powerful Coast Guard radar-jamming transmitters added to the confusion of the machinery on the ship.

Twenty laser beams were directed at the heat-seeking sensors on the ship.

Beneath the ship, the two conical ends of the midget submarines began to utter equally baffling sounds.

The operation lasted for exactly 30 minutes. During this time, Captain Cusp was lowered from a height of 300 feet onto the deck of the *Jersey Lily*, where he stood, wearing ear protectors, and defiantly threw 10 of the sensors nearest him overboard.

At the same time, on 45th Street, Owen's men charged the apartment on the top floor of the Hotel Marlborough.

George Mahle was beginning to feed the punch cards into the computer when it happened. A skylight burst open above him and a cylinder of C.S. gas was thrown in, followed by one at the far end of the control room. Instantly two policemen in gas masks and bullet-proof jackets leaped down from the skylight.

Coughing and retching, Mahle left the computer and ran to the apartment, slamming the door locked behind him.

The other five Indians drew guns from their desk drawers and began to fire at the police.

Four were killed outright. Pete Eagle Heart was shot in the lung.

Inside the apartment George Mahle found Evie standing, her face defiant, against the tepee. The long curved knife was in her hand. He said, quietly, "Forget it. They're all around us."

He kissed her with a tenderness that surprised her and then took off his shirt. He pulled up the hand which held the knife and he put the blade against his chest.

He looked at her and she saw warmth in his eyes.

"There," he said. "Just there. Upward, through the rib cage and into the heart."

There was a crashing against the door.

"Please," he said. And he leaned forward as she plunged the knife into him.

When the police finally managed to break the door open, they found her standing over the dead body of George Mahle. She was not crying or showing any other sign of emotion; she came with them very easily, almost docilely.

Van Horn, his face still blackened, was in the elevator with Owen when the computer exploded and burst into flames. A few minutes later, Pete Eagle Heart, lying on a stretcher in the hotel lobby, told Van Horn: "Only the money can stop the explosion. Get the money. And tell them not to cut channel one on the ship computer. We made it foolproof."

At a given signal from Captain Connolly on the desk of the supertanker, eight large oceangoing tugs raced in unison from the fleets of ships on the New Jersey and Manhattan sides of the Hudson and took up positions, four on each side, a few yards from the massive ship.

"How long before you can start?" Cusp asked the Hudson pilot.

"As long as it takes to cut through the moorings, Captain. "We've two cutting crews at either end with the biggest oxyacetylene outfits in the port of New York. The problem is that the anchor chains will have to part at exactly the same time. That's where the tugs will come into their own."

"You're sure they know what they're doing?"

"Quite sure." Captain Connolly, like Cusp, was not a man who liked being doubted, especially by Coast Guard men, for whom he had a mild seaman's contempt. "I've been up all night with the tug captains and mates, working with models down in the office. They know that there are certain bearings they have to work by and these have been synchronized in numbers. We'll bring her down with the tide to the first real bend, which is midway between Battery Coast Guard station and Ellis Island. Then the starboard tugs ease her against the tide and the port tugs control her position. That's how we'll get her out. Crabwise, right down to the Narrows."

"How long is it going to take?"

"We'll be off and away from this ship long before she blows, that's for sure."

Cusp turned and watched Captain Bomboulas and Van Horn inspect the hatchway to the main bridge area. Van Horn, his hair ruffled by the slight wind, was testing the metal door with a variety of instruments. Then the captain checked his heavy rubber gloves and grabbed onto the metal handle and slid it open very slowly while Van Horn peered inside. He motioned for the Greek captain to hold the door still. Then he slid his hand inside and felt against the wall.

He looked carefully at the inside of the hatch and then eased the whole of it back, made another check of the hinges and paintwork behind the hatch, and beckoned Bomboulas forward. There was a short passageway and then a heavy wooden door. Bomboulas pulled the handle and opened it quickly.

Immediately he reeled back, clutching his mouth with one hand pushing Van Horn violently onto the deck. He ran to the side of the ship and began to vomit.

Van Horn recovered his breath and smelled the heavy fumes which were pouring out the hatch by now. He called over to Cusp.

"Listen, Captain, we're going to need breathing apparatus. They've flooded the whole bridge with exhaust fumes."

Cusp spoke rapidly into the two-way command radio.

"They'll be right with you, son," he said. "How's Bomboulas?"

The Greek captain, ashen, turned from the ship's rail.

"You realize what they've done," he said and turned once again to vomit. He retched and took a deep breath. "They've disconnected the inert gas pipes. That means that we're going to be unable to quench the vapor in those tanks."

"What about foam?"

"They will probably have cut those pipes, as well. How long before the breathing apparatus arrives?"

"You're in no fit state to go walking about, let alone in breathing apparatus, Captain," said Cusp.

"It's my company's ship, don't forget. And I know the geography."

"Okay, have it your own way. This looks like the breathing apparatus now." He pointed to a helicopter circling the ship.

While the helicopter bringing the tubes of compressed air and breathing tubes began to lower its cargo from the heights imposed on it by Van Horn, cutting work had begun on the heavy anchor chains at either end of the *Jersey Lily*. The chains weighed half a ton each and were a foot in diameter.

Two crews worked on each chain from two small boats lashed on either side. They could work only as fast as the continual rocking and jerking of the boats allowed them to. Even with the thermal lances, which speeded up the whole process of oxy-acetylene cutting, it was a process that seemed impossible to finish in days, let alone a few minutes.

The operation was watched by two young Coast Guard officers at either end of the ship who talked continually over their walkie-talkies, estimating the distance yet to be sliced through, knowing that they would soon be talking in fractions of inches and that one mistake could lead easily to their being blown sky high along with the ship.

On deck, high above them, Connolly listened to their conversation. He paced impatiently up and down the metal deck, anxious to see what was happening in the river below but hampered by the very size of this ponderous monster which he was expected to con without a wheel or a quartermaster through New York Harbor and into the open sea. But oddly, such was the challenge of what was to come, he did not stop to consider that he was in grave danger.

"Can't you get me on that damn bridge?" he shouted to Cusp. Cusp handed him a breathing mask and a cylinder of compressed air. "Follow the Greek," he said. "But be careful. You're conducting this opera." A few minutes later, the white-haired pilot and Van Horn followed the Greek into the hatchway.

Watching them from the deck, Cusp crossed his fingers.

55

The task that had been set the Hudson River pilot would have been considered impossible at any other time. It was, as Connolly had told his tug captains during their briefing, like trying to move a 140-story apartment block crabwise down Fifth Avenue on rollers without breaking a window.

But this ship was bigger than that and rode high out of the water, exposed now to every caprice of wind and tide. Her weight was such that the tugs, the only method of steering her, would be operating in nightmare conditions. One minute they would be using the full flank power of their powerful engines against the towering steel hull, the next, they would be nursing that same hull as gently as though it were an eggshell.

Allowing for 10 degrees of latitude on each side of the ship's moored position, just 20 degrees of the compass to work within. It was an impossible margin.

She had to be moved, coaxed, persuaded down seven miles of the harbor while the technicans on board tried to defuse her.

No, it was goddamn impossible, Connolly thought. There were bends to be taken, difficult enough to negotiate in a 6,000-ton freighter.

A 20-degree margin. There were channels in which the depth, which was the most critical factor in this operation, often changed with every tide, with every inrush of silt and mud from the melting snows upstate.

There were currents that ripped and weaved their way around the Battery where the East River joined the Hudson, currents strong enough to swing this elephantine brute of a ship 50 degrees off her course with a frightening ease.

No, he had told the tug men, it was too damn ridiculous. It was out of the question. They should wrap it up and go home. It was only the fact that he was well insured and his kids had grown up and he was a mad Irishman that had made him give it a try anyway.

The tug captains nodded agreement, except that nothing in the world would have stopped them from joining in.

These eight grizzled, somber men in reefer jackets and duffel coats had already jointly signed a salvage contract with Lloyds of London and the Eftyvoulos Line which would mean the sharing of $10 million among them if the ship could be brought safely through the Narrows and into the open sea. The fact that they would be risking their lives in doing so meant little to them; risk was very much part of their daily routine. Like Captain Connolly, they saw this as a navigational impossibility which only they could pull off.

Inside the bridge of the *Jersey Lily*, Van Horn, heavily encased in the rubber breathing suit, peered through his glasses and the thick glass of the helmet at the computer which dared him to stop it from working. The ship's clock stood immediately behind it. He looked around hopefully for the camera and the priming mechanism.

No way, he thought. That would be hidden, almost impossible to find.

He walked around the control area, sucking hard at the compressed air, which smelled of rubber and metal, searching for something that might help him. A printout, maybe, or a code book, or even a scrap of paper that would give him a chance to feed the right series of digits into this machine and reverse its program.

No way. Okay, then, he said aloud into the mouthpiece, let's fix the compass.

He walked across the spacious bridge, remembering the directions of Captain Bomboulas, and saw the door marked "Gyro Room." He examined it carefully and opened it with the care of a cat burglar.

The gyrocompass mechanism was housed in a long, blue-and-white, metal cabinet. Even through the heavy rubber helmet, Van Horn could hear the whine of the electric motor, although he could not detect the almost noiseless hum of the gyroscope itself, turning steadily and with unbelievable accuracy on jeweled bearings deep inside this box.

He had spent an hour that morning with engineers from Sperry-Rand looking at just such a complex assembly. They had discussed ways of tampering with the mechanism and had proposed an equal number of ways of jamming the compass, in order that the ship could move freely.

The head of the New York City technical services took a long screwdriver on his hip. He knelt down in front of the cabinet. For an instant he allowed the images of his wife and children to pass through his mind and then began to unscrew a metal plate.

This was a job the engineers had said might take six hours to complete. He glanced at his watch. He had three hours; the computer was still whirling and turning on the bridge outside.

56

DRESDNERBANK FRANKFURT
UNIBANK NEW YORK

ATTN MRS STONYBRIDGE OR MR BATEMAN
CODE LIBYA/UGANDA/ZAIRE

URGENT. KEY TESTED TELEXED GUARANTEES NOW RECEIVED IN SUMS OF ELEVEN DECIMAL NINE BILLIONS DOLLARS UNITED STATES FROM FOLLOWING BANKS COLON BANK OF AMERICA, CITICORP, CHASE MANHATTAN, DAI-ICHI KANGYO, BARCLAYS, NATIONAL WESTMINSTER, FUJI BANK, DEUTSCHE BANK, SUMITOMO BANK. NO INDICATION GUARANTEE FROM BANQUE NATIONALE DE PARIS OR CREDIT LYONNAIS.

ARRANGEMENTS HAVE BEEN MADE WITH UGANDAN AMBASSADOR AT UNITED NATIONS TO RECEIVE AND ACKNOWLEDGE TOTAL SUM.

OUR CLIENTS REGRET, HOWEVER, THAT NO PAYMENT CAN BE MADE INTO THE UNITED NATIONS FUND UNTIL WE AND THE UNION BANK OF SWITZERLAND ARE IN POSSESSION OF THE FULL GUARANTEES. WE AND UNION BANK WILL REMAIN OPEN THROUGHUOT EVENING AWAITING CONFIRMATION OF GUARANTEES FROM FRENCH BANKS.

WINKLER (DIRECTOR)
DRESDNERBANK FRANKFURT
UNIBANK NEW YORK.

"Now the French government is going to let this city blow up," said Mrs. Stonybridge.

She poured a stiff bourbon into her glass and drank it in one gulp. "Bastards," she said. "Copulating French bastards." She picked up the telephone and said, "Darling, I want my brother, the President, and I want him immediately. I don't care where he is. I hate to think what's going to happen if I don't get him."

In the main pump room of the *Jersey Lily*, Captain Savvas Bomboulas, who had been born into a poverty-ridden family in Salonika and had become the senior flag captain and a director of the Eftyvoulos Line, surveyed a labyrinth of pipes, tubes, dials, and other machinery.

He singled out one particularly big, asbestos-covered engine exhaust tube which ran the length of the room and climbed the wall before disappearing into a tunnel. Bomboulas climbed the rungs which extended from the tube and crawled along the top of it. Then, crouching low because of the cylinders of compressed air on his back, he made his way into the tunnel.

"Is that my brother?" His voice on the line sounded tired, obviously not anxious to talk to her.

"Hi, Amy."

"Jack Stonybridge, you're going to have to call up President de Crecy and tell him that if he doesn't let his banks guarantee this New York ransom, you'll cut off diplomatic relations, stop importing wine into the United States, and insist on the repayments of all our loans to them immediately or go to war. Did you hear what I said?"

"You want me to declare war on France?"

"Total goddamn war. Typical of them. Promise the money and then go back on the deal. Anyway, you just tell him from me that I've always thought he was a conniving little you-know-what. I gave his mother a silver dollar when he was born. I wish it had lodged in his throat. What the hell is happening that they can't put up twenty-four billion? And you can tell him from me, as well, that if there is so much as another minute's delay, I'll call my randy little friend from *Humanité*—

he's a communist, but he's a darling—and give him the dirt on the whole French Cabinet.

"And what's more, Jack, what's all this I hear about you and the Argentine ambassador's wife? I mean if it's true, I think it's quite disgraceful. A man of your age. Is it true? Doesn't matter. Let's get New York sorted out."

"Amy."

"Nasty little creep. Never could stand French politicians, especially that one. Or their bankers. I mean the whole damned world is in on this deal. We still figure we can get that tanker moved in time, the whole of this city evacuated, and there are the goddamn French screwing the whole deal. How's Nancy's ulcer? You just get on that hot line to Paris and tell him that I'm on the warpath."

"Amy."

"Don't you 'Amy' me, little brother, or I'll buy the *National Enquirer* and expose you."

"Jesus Christ, Amy."

"*Now* it's sacrilege. If the poor, starving English can do it, the bloated French can. Hell, Jack, I've seen restaurants on the Champs d'Elysee take more money than this in an afternoon. We've got guarantees from the Japanese and from our own banks—breaking all the laws, by the way—I hope you'll stick up for us, and what about those devious, venal, frog-eating French?"

"Amy?"

"Don't bother me, I'm busy."

"Amy. I've just spoken to de Crecy and explained the whole setup. He's recommending that the money should be forthcoming immediately. His decision has the backing of the French cabinet. You should have the message through by now from the two banks. Now, big sister, did you hear that? And Nancy's ulcer is better than it was. It's snowing in Washington. Will you stop bugging me, because I've got a lot of other problems, too."

"Do I understand you to say that the French have agreed to the guarantees?"

"Yes."

"About goddamn time, too."

Mrs. Stonybridge looked over at Mary. "Well, we've

straightened out the French. I've always said that what this country needs is a strong woman at the helm. Now we've got her."

"One minute to free the stern," said the voice through Captain Connolly's radio.

"Tugs move in and hold her position one," he said immediately.

"Two minutes to free the bows."

"Take your positions."

The eight tugs crept in with maddening slowness and held their positions, a foot between them and the hull.

"Stern free," said the voice.

"Now!" said Connolly.

The eight tugs moved in as one, pinning the tanker in position.

"Hold her right there."

Connolly watched the gyrocompass on the upper bridge deck where he stood. He checked and double-checked the magnetic compass which he might have to rely on if Van Horn succeeded.

"Thirty seconds to free the bows."

"Stand by."

He could see nothing of the tugs, nothing of the men who were cutting the ship adrift. He stood there alone on that plateau overlooking Manhattan and uttered a brief prayer to his patron, St. Patrick, and another to St. Christoper, and a final one to St. Elmo, the patron saint of sailors.

"The bows are free. All yours, Captain."

There was no sign or hint of movement, but the *Jersey Lily* began to drift very slowly on the outgoing tide; on the bridge, a white-haired captain, staring intently at the compass, gave a series of orders at a speed which left him breathless and exhilarated.

"One and two slow ahead. Five and six give way. Good, hold it there. Five and six half power head. Hold it, one and two. Three, four, seven, and eight, give me some sternward power. Good. Now cut your revolutions and take it very steady. And one and two give me a brace against five and six. Good. Hold it."

The rapid litany continued. He was relying on the captain of tug number eight to insure that the ship was moving in the right channels. Captain Cusp was giving him his lateral bearings from the deck.

The great tanker was moving ponderously but surely now toward the first obstacle. It was a slight turn which would have been accomplished easily had the ship been moving ahead under her own power instead of astern under the power of eight engines controlled by eight men at the command of one man who could not even see the source of his ship's movements.

They were approaching that part of the river where the Battery's southernmost point was due east of the ship and the towers of Ellis Island were exactly to the west. Captain Cusp's voice came through now.

"Coming on to bearing."

The *Jersey Lily* still appeared to be hardly moving.

"On bearing now."

The pilot glanced around quickly and spoke into his radio. "Five, six, seven, and eight—dead slow ahead together. One, two, three, and four, brace yourselves. Good. One, two, three, and four, hold it for ten seconds from now. Good. All tugs slow ahead."

He looked up from the compass, again for a matter of seconds, and saw that Manhattan was getting smaller and that, if nothing else, he had probably saved the World Trade Center, which he had never much liked as a building, anyway.

Thus they crept down the Hudson and into the Upper Bay. The biggest ship in the world was on her way back to the sea, manned by four men, each of whom was trying desperately to save her from destruction.

Michael Canaletto came bursting into Ben's office, a beam of achievement stretching wide across his face.

"Mr. Mayor," he said. "I have the honor to report that this city is now empty of all people, except a few potential suicides and cops, from 23rd Street on down. And I'm also here to tell you that we are now evacuating City Hall and that the central heating has been turned up at Gracie Mansion for you."

"You must be kidding," said Ben. "We're still waiting for the ransom. And I've just heard that they've managed to move the ship."

Canaletto became suddenly serious.

"She could still go at any time, then?"

"Right. With four men on her and a whole fleet surrounding her."

Canaletto crossed himself and looked at the ornate ceiling. "God help them," he said.

Ben stood up suddenly.

"To hell with it," he said. "I can't sit while it's all happening down there." He walked quickly to the door.

"Mary," he shouted. "Get me a helicopter ready outside. And where's Mrs. Stonybridge?"

He found the old lady sitting at a telex machine in the city's communications room. She was typing furiously, her cigar stuck at an absurd angle in her mouth.

She stopped and pressed a key.

"Okay, Ben Boyle," she said. "Now you should see the answer."

There was a long pause as they watched the machine together. It was the first time, Ben reflected, that she had been awake and silent since she had stormed into his life.

The machine started to clatter.

CITHALL NEW YORK
UNIBANK NEW YORK
ATTN MRS STONYBRIDGE

FOLLOWING MESSAGE RECEIVED FROM DRESDNER BANK FRANKFURT TEN MINUTES AGO RELAYED TO YOU NOW AT YOUR REQUEST:

WE CONFIRM THAT FOLLOWING ACCEPTANCE BY OUR CLIENTS OF UNCONDITIONAL GUARANTEES FROM ELEVEN PRIME BANKS WITH FURTHER GUARANTEE FROM GOVERNMENT OF UNITED STATES THAT, UPON YOUR TELEXED ACCEPTANCE, THE SUM OF ONE HUNDRED AND THIRTY BILLION DOLLARS UNITED STATES WILL BE PAID INTO THE SPECIAL UNITED NATIONS ACCOUNT TO BE ADMINISTERED SOLELY BY THE REPRESENTATIVES OF LIBYA, UGANDA, AND ZAIRE IN TRUST. PLEASE INDICATE YOUR ACCEPTANCE IMMEDIATELY.

WINKLER (DIRECTOR) DRESDNERBANK.

The machine signed itself off.

She turned to Ben: "There's your ransom, darling. You can't say I didn't try."

"The trouble is," said Ben, "that the ship is moving away from Manhattan but it can still explode at any minute. And if we accept this money we'll never get it back."

"Can't say," she said. "There'll be a hell of a stink at the UN, but technically it will belong to them and the Indians, and New York will be heavily in debt for a long time."

"Jesus," said Ben.

"It's your decision, Mr. Mayor."

"We'll take the money," he said. "Mrs. Stonybridge, do you mind if I have a pull at that bottle?"

Mary was standing outside his office when he got back.

"Commissioner Canaletto tells me you're going to fly over the ship," she said. "Ben, why take a chance like this?"

"I'm not taking any chance," he said. "Cusp is, and Van Horn and the others. I can't really sit around here any longer."

He kissed her lightly on the cheek.

"I love you, Mary," he said. "Now you get down into the shelter with the others. I'll see you."

When he got into the helicopter he found Canaletto sitting in the back seat.

"What the hell are you doing here?" he asked.

"Just coming for the ride," said Canaletto, grinning broadly.

In the gyro room of the *Jersey Lily*, Charles Van Horn, lying on his side, his head almost touching the electric motor which powered the compass, took a deep breath of foul-smelling compressed air and closed the vital circuit inside the long cabinet. He waited for a few seconds and decided, finally, that the ship was not blowing up.

He hauled himself up and made his way through a haze of gray fumes to the elevator which ran from the engine room of the ship to the navigation bridge deck. There he found Connolly snapping orders into his microphone.

"One and two, you're going too fast. Go astern, for Christ's sake. Five and six, go full ahead for five seconds.

Now!" Connolly watched the compass move inexorably toward the danger mark.

"Holy Christ, move five and six!"

The compass was moving fast now and he watched, helpless, as it crossed the five degree line. He stood waiting for the blast.

He heard Van Horn cough behind him.

"The gyro is disengaged, you'll be pleased to know, Captain."

"Say that again."

"It's okay now, you can steer any course you like."

The captain grabbed the technician and kissed him on both cheeks. Then he picked up his radio and said quietly, "Okay. Relax. Get ready to turn her around off the Liberty Island bell."

In room 4006 at the United Nations, His Excellency the Ambassador for the Republic of Uganda, the Right Honorable Sir Kwame Umboto, Knight of the Bath and holder of the Order of Idi Amin, lay dead drunk on a carpet as the telex machine clattered out the message that one hundred and thirty billion dollars was available on his receipt of the message.

The ambassador had been given specific instructions on how to handle this message. He was to accept the fund, make one telephone call, and speak two code words to the voice that answered.

Those two words to other members of Mahle's organization in New Jersey would put into operation the simple signal which would deactivate the computer on the *Jersey Lily* and insure the immediate release of Captain Armstrong from the attic where he wes being held.

The bell on the telex rang several times.

The ambassador lay on the carpet and snored.

The helicopter made several circuits of the tanker below. In the lights of the Coast Guard vessels that escorted the *Jersey Lily* down channel, Ben could take in the whole scene.

The massive ship was turning now, the tugs easing her bows around slowly until she appeared to tower over the Statue of Liberty.

The clock on the helicopter's instrument panel read 1645. An hour and a quarter to the deadline.

Ben spoke into his microphone.

"This is the mayor of New York. I want to speak to Captain Cusp on the *Jersey Lily,*" he said.

"One moment, Mr. Mayor," said the controller. "You are through to Captain Cusp on air to ship frequency. Go ahead."

"Captain," said Ben. "What's happening down there?"

Cusp's voice, broken by static, shouted: "As you can see, Mr. Mayor, we are turning the ship around but it's going to take a hell of a time because we don't want to ground her, and we're very close to doing that."

"Sure, but is she defused?"

"No sir. Mr. Van Horn says that the computer is still operating on the one remaining channel, and there is nothing he can do to stop it except take the risk of pulling all the plugs. He says that the chances are that she will go up if he does."

"What about the fire-prevention equipment?"

"Captain Bomboulas is below. He says that the whole thing is a mass of spaghetti where they have disconnected the pipes. He's doing his best to fix them, but it's a hell of a job. I've sent for engineers, but I'm afraid it will take too long."

Ben stared ahead at the windshield of the helicopter. He heard the words come from his mouth.

"Maybe you need a good plumber," he said.

Cusp's voice crackled back.

"Just what we *do* need, Mr. Mayor."

Ben said quietly, "Okay, Captain. There's one on the way down."

He turned to the pilot.

"Can you get me onto that ship?"

"Are you sure you know what you're doing?" said the pilot.

"I'm the mayor of this city. Get me down there."

"Anything you say, Mr. Mayor."

Suspended by the helicopter's winch, 200 feet over the tanker, spinning slowly with the lights of Brooklyn flashing in the near distance and the whole of Manhattan stretching out in the next moment, with the fleet of ships spread out in the blackness around him, the Mayor of New York said aloud to himself and the world at large: "Of all the crazy, stupid, screwball things to do. The mayor of this city? Christ, I should be in the funny farm."

The elaborate fire-extinguishing systems that served the *Jersey Lily* were housed in the very stern of the ship. It was here that Ben, now clad in the heavy, rubber breathing gear, found Captain Bomboulas.

There were 18 large pipes leading from the inert gas conversion unit which separated the molecules of carbon and other waste from the engine exhausts.

They needed a plumber, thought Ben. Jesus Christ, what sort of joke was that? These pipes were each a foot in diameter, made of steel and far too heavy for one man to lift.

Bomboulas was struggling with one of them, trying hard to force it back into the extraction hole of the converter. He could see the agony in the man's eyes as he held it up and tried to force it back into its socket.

Ben joined him and helped to take the strain. Together they rammed the huge pipe into place. There was a universal coupling which secured the pipe. Ben quickly slid it along and began to screw it into position, forcing it around and feeling the heat of the gas beginning to burn his hands but continuing to push the joint around and around until the pipe was safely home.

As they grabbed at the next steel pipe, Ben noticed two other figures working in the smoke-filled room. The two engineers asked for by Cusp were now busy at the same task. It took them nearly half an hour to complete the joints.

Inside the rubber suit Ben was drenched with sweat. Bomboulas made a follow-me gesture to Ben and led him back to a staircase which brought them both onto the deck.

Ben peeled off his headpiece and shook hands with Bomboulas.

"Guess we did a good job there," he said.

"I'm not sure," said the Greek quietly. "Those tanks are about the size of the average cathedral. And they're particularly volatile at the stage these people left them in. It might work—but I'm doubtful."

"You don't mean we've been wasting our time?"

"Not at all. Nothing which might save this ship could be called a waste of time. The engine is pumping the gases into the tanks. That is good. Now I shall go to the control room and increase the engine revolutions to maximum in order that the maximum amount of gas is used."

"What about foam?" asked Ben.

"Not a chance," said Bomboulas before he pulled the breathing headset back over his wiry hair. "They've slashed through the wiring circuits. It would take days to put the system together again." He adjusted his air supply and went back into the bridge structure.

As he did so, another hatchway opened and Ben saw the tall figure of Van Horn burst out on to the metal of the deck and rip off his helmet. Sweat had congealed his long hair into a dark mass and he was deathly pale. He stood gasping in the cold harbor air.

He did not take in the dark figure of the Mayor at first.

"Charlie," said Ben, "what's happening?"

"You shouldn't be here, Mr. Mayor," said Van Horn. "I'm afraid the ship is going up. I've neutralized nine of that computer's ten channels. But I dare not shut the machine off entirely."

As they talked, Ben could feel the ship begin to vibrate under his feet; and the soft, distant whine from the engine room became a distinct roar.

"Captain Bomboulas is doing what he can," said Ben. There was a new sound, this time a powerful clamor of rushing air.

"What the hell?" said Ben.

"Forced air ventilation, thank God," said Van Horn. "He's clearing out the gas up there."

At that moment they were approached by an angry Captain Cusp.

"Will somebody tell me what the hell is going on?" he demanded. "I'm supposed to be running this operation. And what on earth are you doing here?"

"I'll tell you what I'm doing, Captain. I'm plumbing. We've just fixed the pipes in this ship so we can flood the tanks with gas. There are two of your men down below tightening up my joints."

Van Horn cut in.

"I'm afraid she stills stands a good chance of blowing up at the stated time, Captain."

Cusp looked at Ben.

"What about the money, Mr. Mayor?"

"When I left, the ransom was about to be paid. They should have the message by now. Will we know that, Charlie?"

"I can only guess that the computer will automatically switch itself and the fail-safe device off," said Van Horn.

"But we won't know for sure," said Cusp.

"Not for certain, no."

Cusp held up his hand radio.

"This is control," he said. "I want Captain Weiner of the harbor pilots on board immediately, and I want the pilot boat to make sure that it picks up the mayor and Mr. Van Horn and Captain Connolly. The port companionway is now safe for use."

He turned to Ben and Van Horn.

"I'm going to take a chance," he said. "I could moor this ship in the very middle of the Bay where it would do the least damage except to naval and other maritime services. Or I could get her out into the open sea under her own power. If she blows up, the pollution will be just as they said in the letter. Crippling."

"So?" asked Ben.

"So I'm going to go hell bent for leather through the Narrows and into the Atlantic," said Cusp. "Then I'm going to aim her east and get the hell out of it by helicopter. The navy can use her for target practice."

"I'm staying with you, Captain," said Ben. "I wouldn't miss this for all the Stonybridge gold."

UNIBANK NEW YORK
DRESDNERBANK FRANKFURT
URGENT. FOR THE ATTENTION OF MRS STONYBRIDGE. WE ARE GETTING NO ACKNOWLEDGMENT OF THE FIRM OFFER MADE TO UNITED NATIONS FUND ON NEW YORK TELEX 21341/AB UGANDAMIN. UNTIL THEN NO TRANSACTION CAN TAKE PLACE. CAN YOU CONTACT AMBASSADOR AND ENSURE ACCEPTANCE?

WINKLER

"Full ahead," said Captain Weiner, who had taken the

ship over from Connolly. "Get those tugs to give us the maximum push and then get out of the way. And Captain Cusp, can you get your ships to dowse those damn lights. I want to see the fairway."

The voice of Captain Bomboulas came over the speaker on the navigational bridge deck.

"She's set to full revolutions, pilot. About four minutes to five knots."

"Thank you, Captain."

Even in the tension of that moment, thought Ben, who was standing behind the pilot, they observe the courtesy of the seas. Nice people, sailors.

The *Jersey Lily* trembled as she began to gather speed. With her crew of three captains, an electronics expert, and a plumber who had been the Mayor of New York for less than two days, she began to churn the waters of the bay. Still increasing her steerageway, she made her way through the darkness toward the safety of the open sea.

Detective Owen burst into Room 4006 at the United Nations. The ambassador was sleeping deeply on the carpet. The message was sitting on the telex machine and the bell was ringing furiously.

To hell with protocol, Owen thought. He picked up a decanter of water and poured it over the ambassador and then reached down and slapped the chubby black face hard until the man came awake. He looked up at Owen and grinned.

"What's up, man?" he said.

"Listen, you drunken crud," said Owen. "There's a message on your machine. Answer it."

"Oh my God," said the black man. He pulled himself up from the floor and started to reel. He stood over the telex machine and had to grip it hard to stay standing.

"Must make a telephone call," he said. He lurched across the room to his desk and fell, knocking the Ugandan flag to the floor and smashing a picture of his country's president on the wall behind him.

He managed to sit at his desk and read the phone number on the pad in front of him.

He dialed slowly. The telephone was answered immediately.

The ambassador said "Red Cloud." There was a click at the other end.

The black man smiled at Owen.

"Now I shall answer the telex."

It was Owen's turn to smile.

"Oh no, you don't, baby," he said.

The city of New York had Detective Owen Owen, the son of a Sioux Indian, whose pay was $180 a week, to thank for saving it a debt of $130 billion.

57

The *Jersey Lily* was making good speed now. Ben could see the outline of the Verrazano Bridge, graceful and elegant, ahead of them in the bright moonlight. He was suddenly aware of Bomboulas beside him on deck. The Greek spoke hesitantly.

"Mr. Mayor, please?"

"Go ahead," said Ben.

"We have only ten, maybe fifteen minutes before this ship explodes. You should not be here."

"We'll be off before she goes," said Ben. "Anyway, I trust Van Horn's fixed that computer."

"Mr. Mayor, as the senior flag officer of this line and the representative of the owners, I am assuming command of this ship. I want you off immediately. That is an order."

"And Van Horn and Cusp and the pilot," said Ben. "And those engineers. No way, Captain. I'll stay with the team."

"I want you *off,*" Bomboulas repeated, his voice now loud. "I'll take this ship into the open sea. It is my responsibility. I have asked Captain Cusp to call up the helicopters for all of you. You are not to disobey."

Ben made a face. Then he smiled.

"You know, in a funny sort of way I was beginning to enjoy the boat ride—sort of feel we've conquered the monster. But, oxay. Van Horn goes first—he's got a wife and kids. I just hope to Christ there's time for Cusp and the pilot to obey you."

Their conversation was blasted by the sound of helicopter engines flying low above the moving ship.

"They'll obey," shouted Bomboulas. "The law of the sea applies to the Coast Guard and to pilots, as well."

Ben watched as the big figure of Van Horn ran along the deck to catch the harness which had been winched down for their escape.

He turned and offered his hand to the Greek.

"Sorry for my rudeness, Captain," he said. "And thanks."

Bomboulas still clasped his hand. "You might remember for me, please, to tell my company that I, too, disagreed with their economy policy."

In the bedroom of a small suburban house in Brooklyn, 15-year-old George Moyes had just finished assembling a radio construction kit he'd received for Christmas.

He plugged the set into a wall socket and turned the dial around to the citizens' radio wavelengths on which he knew he could operate without a license.

He pressed a button marked "transmit" and pushed down a key. Then he began tapping out his name in slow, painstaking Morse.

As he came to the letter "M," another hand pressed a computer terminal key in New Jersey, two miles away. An Indian confederate of George Mahle's was issuing an instruction to the ship's computer to render the *Jersey Lily* safe.

Twelve digits were needed.

The digits were transmitted. But the millionth of a second that it took to relay the group of figures to the ship were confused with the dot in the letter "M" transmitted by the boy in Brooklyn.

The time was 500,000 milliseconds to six o'clock.

The computer on the ship accepted both signals and scanned them with total thoroughness in a matter of another millisecond. Having analyzed them, processed them, and filed them in its data bank, it rejected them.

At exactly 1800 hours, when all the zeros on the ship's digital clock came into line, the computer instructed the final primer to fall into position. The magnesium flares along the length of the *Jersey Lily* ignited her cargo at the very moment that the ship passed under the Verrazano Bridge.

Ben was 300 feet up, swinging perilously close, when the explosion came. He felt the helicopter above him leap furiously upward, caught in the sudden heat. In one instant, then, he was sure he would be roasted. He whirled, helpless, thrown about like a child's yoyo as the helicopter plummented and slid within only a few feet of the sea. Then the ship began splitting evenly into two parts.

The blast of the further explosion lifted the helicopter again with such force that Ben felt the agony of limbs almost torn from his body by the harness.

Moments later, the pilot won the fight against the fury of the explosion. Ben was winched very slowly into the cabin.

As they turned toward Manhattan, he had time to see, very briefly, what had happened. The bridge had buckled and fallen on the blazing tanker. As Van Horn had predicted, the liquefied natural gas, escaped from its refrigerated compartments, had set the sea on fire. Fires were already raging in Brooklyn and along the Jersey shoreline.

"We're going direct to City Hall, Mr. Mayor," the pilot said.

They flew on toward Manhattan. As they landed, the whole of the city was lit by the orange glow from the inferno at sea.

Altmeyer was already beside Ben's desk. He tapped an impatient civil servant finger on a sheaf of papers which lay there.

"These are all for your urgent attention, Mr. Mayor," he said.

"Can't they wait?"

"Certainly not," snapped Altmeyer. "We're already lost two administrative days to those Indians. These matters must be dealt with *now*."

Ben sighed.

"Mr. First Deputy Mayor," he said. "I've just come from being treated like a goddamn rag doll in the air.

I'm going to be a mass of bruises; I've hardly got a bone to call my own."

Altmeyer snorted.

"Anyway," said Ben wearily, "what the hell are we going to do about Brooklyn? There's a full-scale emergency there."

"Commissioner Canaletto, Commissioner Crotty, and the fire department are quite capable of handling that. In the meantime, there's a meeting of the finance committee scheduled for nine-thirty tomorrow, and these budget figures have to be reviewed in advance. There's also the question of the cars scattered all over this city—do you realize how many insurance claims we'll be facing? And Frank Schenk wants to talk to you. Says it's urgent. And what his urgent means is that there'll be no garbage collection tomorrow if you don't get hold of him now."

Ben gazed at the deputy. Oh, you poor cold fish, he thought.

"And another thing, Mr. Mayor," Altmeyer went on. "We haven't the slightest idea just how much damage young Van Horn has done to the City Hall computer with his cowboys and Indians game. It could run into millions."

"Okay, okay, Altmeyer," Ben said. "Having saved the city, I guess we'd better get down to making it all worthwhile."

He picked up the papers and started to read. Within minutes Mary came quietly into the room. She walked behind the desk and put her arms around Ben.

"What exactly did you say in the shower?" he asked.

"You're much too busy for that sort of discussion," she said. "I'll tell you later."

She kissed the top of his head lightly and then gently closed the door behind her as she left his office.

His world is the world.

AMBASSADOR

A novel of romance, terror, and nonstop excitement

STEPHEN LONGSTREET

Ira Ellsworth Redmond is the Ambassador. His new home is the palatial American Embassy in Rome, scene of glittering parties where money, power, and seductive women are the currency of exchange, and where three fanatical terrorists make life—and death—the currency of fear for Redmond, his beautiful mistress, and the rest of their hostages in a blazing drama of dagger-edged diplomacy and nerve-shattering tension.

Amid the splendor of Rome and the rarified world of international diplomacy, this relentlessly powerful blockbuster of scandalous passion and high-level intrigue unfolds—the explosive new novel by the man *Time* magazine has called "The most readable of American writers."

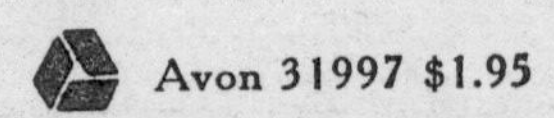

BASS 1-78